Applause for *The Edge of the World*

"Growing up is serious business—unless you do so with Phil Callaway. Then it is also a rollicking adventure—in spite of the fact that life may throw you some intriguing curve balls."

Janette Oke, bestselling author of *Love Comes Softly*

"Reading Phil Callaway's writing is one of life's pure pleasures."

Ellen Vaughn, co-author with Charles Colson of *The Body*

"Callaway's gift of humor and storytelling abilities combine to make *The Edge of the World* a runaway hit! I've been a big fan of Phil's writing for many years now, and this, his first novel, is clearly one of his best works. From page one, you'll be hooked!"

Martha Bolton, author of over 50 books,
former staff writer for Bob Hope

"I read Phil's books not just for the laughter and great stories, but for perspective and balance. If you need a fresh shot of joy and hope, this book's for you."

Lee Strobel, author of *The Case for Faith*
and *The Case For Christ*

"A spellbinding memoir of childhood—both funny and forgiving—that points us past its memorable characters to the miracle of God's grace."

Sigmund Brouwer, author of *Crown of Thorns*

"My library is filled primarily with non-fiction works. But every once in a while a novel comes along that compels me to give up precious shelf space. This is such a book. It is splendid, with many a twist. Callaway ricochets flawlessly between excellent character development and an ever-thickening plot in this classic read. Read it and weep. Read it and laugh out loud. Then buy 17 more copies for all your wild and crazy friends."

Joel A. Freeman, Ph.D., author and filmmaker,
Chaplain, Washington Wizards

"Very few authors make me laugh out loud. Phil Callaway makes me roar."

Ken Davis, comedian, motivational speaker, and author

"Callaway brings his deft touch to the world of fiction in this mesmerizing coming-of-age story about growing up _____ close to grace. Highly recommended!"

Every Man's Battle,
Focus on the Family

"It is no accident that the _____ novel is a town called Grace. Through the joys and _____ ses of family life a young hero grows up in Grace—in more ways than one. _____ nor and honesty we have come to expect from this gifted writer we find ourselves growing a little too."

Karen Stiller, *Faith Today*

"Phil Callaway has dusted off and polished up some fond memories of childhood, while treating us to a rip-roaring good yarn, filled with humor, truth, and grace."

Pat Williams, Senior Vice President, Orlando Magic

"I'm pleased to play a cameo role in this story, but better yet, I'm moved by the redemptive theme and the way Callaway handles his characters with equal doses of humor and affection."

Chuck Girard, pioneer Christian musician

Further applause for Phil's writing...

"Need a shot of sunlight on a cloudy day? This book's for you. Need a whisper of God's love in a noisy life? You'll hear it as you turn these pages. Need a touch of calm in the midst of chaos? Phil Callaway has provided it here. This book is for all who desire to love God and love life and get confused doing both."

Max Lucado, author and minister

"Our lives are parables through which God chooses to speak. Phil Callaway's new book reveals this, out of his own life, and makes the business of listening to your life more than just bearable, but truly joyful. God speaks through the small and ordinary in extraordinary ways. Phil has listened and heard—and thankfully decided to share it with us."

Michael Card, author, teacher and singer/songwriter

"For many years I have enjoyed reading Phil Callaway's articles in *Servant* Magazine. His transparent communication penetrates the heart and gives a lift, a laugh and a lesson.

Steve Green, author and recording artist

"Reading Phil Callaway is like playing in Holy Sand. You're having so much fun, you don't realize how much has gone into your shoes and is now sticking to your life."

Chris Fabry, author and host of Moody Broadcasting Network's *Open Line*

"Everything Phil Callaway writes is full of life because he's discovered a fabulous secret: The joy of Christ doesn't go away, even when life is a mess."

Luis Palau, International evangelist and the author of *It's a God Thing*

"This book is nourishment for the soul...a pleasant journey and meat for the soul."

John Fischer, author and musician

The Edge of the World

Phil Callaway

HARVEST HOUSE PUBLISHERS

EUGENE, OREGON

Cover by Left Coast Design, Portland, Oregon

Cover photo © Peter Griffith/Masterfile

This is a work of fiction. Names, characters, places, and incidents are products of the author's imagination or are used fictitiously. Any resemblance to actual persons, living or dead, or to events or locales, is entirely coincidental.

THE EDGE OF THE WORLD
Previously published as *Growing Up on the Edge of the World*

Copyright © 2004 by Phil Callaway
Published by Harvest House Publishers
Eugene, Oregon 97402
www.harvesthousepublishers.com

Library of Congress Cataloging-in-Publication Data

Callaway, Phil, 1961–
   The edge of the world / Phil Callaway.
     p. cm.
   ISBN-13: 978-0-7369-1662-2
   ISBN-10: 0-7369-1662-8 (pbk.)
   1. Teenage boys—Fiction. 2. Montana—Fiction. I. Title.
   PS3603.A446E34 2005
   813'.6—dc22   2005003036

Printed in the United States of America

05 06 07 08 09 10 11 12 13 / BP-MS / 10 9 8 7 6 5 4 3 2 1

For friends I grew up with.
In hopes they'll return to Grace.

Preface

On the day I finished this manuscript, my eighteen-year-old son and I were on a flight together somewhere over Idaho, listening to the captain apologize repeatedly for delays he had not caused and thank us yet again for choosing this airline (which was losing financial altitude fast). We had just finished an unusually fine breakfast there in Economy, a four-egg omelet ripe with red peppers and bursting with purple onions, when I excused myself to lurch my way back to a starboard restroom a small amber symbol assured me was vacant. My heartburn had returned, and it felt as though a small moose was sitting aboard my chest doing the Macarena.

I do not know to this day why I had the disc in my shirt pocket, or why I brought it on the trip at all. But earlier in the day, just moments before we embarked, a lethal virus had assaulted my computer, melting the book, stealing our meager financial records, and destroying a host of untapped e-mails. The backup minidisc in my pocket was all I had left of the priceless manuscript, and I wasn't about to let it out of my sight.

Already the publisher had promised me it would be a huge success, using words like "Oprah" and "Number One" and "Ample Merchandising Opportunities." Already John Grisham and Tom Clancy had endorsed it with adjectives like "beguiling," "delicious," and "national treasure." To prove the company's commitment, the publisher had written me a generous check with more zeros than I'd seen before on a slip of paper that short.

I was thinking of those zeros as I caressed the disc in that tiny room. My son and I were spending a healthy portion of the sum on a weekend of golf in Palm Springs—a silly thing to do perhaps, but why not? The rest would go to missions. Besides, the boy was in the aftermath of a turbulent relationship, and over an omelet I'd had a chance to counsel him that when adversity arrives, we must remind ourselves that God is good, that this will not last forever, that sometimes life hands us a chance to start again, a chance to improve things a little.

It was one of the primary themes of the book, which, I think it important to note, is a work of fiction. You see, I grew up in a small northern town, a relatively cold place where if people are not warm to each other in wintertime, we suffer all year long. Since I still spend much of the year here, it would be rather unneigh-borly of me to tell stories of my childhood just as they happened. People here are nice, but they are not dumb. They read about a neighbor of mine named Ben Reeves whom I have described as "a stout but lively man, with dark leathery skin like a well-polished boot, vertical wrinkles scratched upon his flat forehead, and eyebrows so thick they tend to pull the curtains on his face," and Fred Steeves knows who you're talking about, as do a hundred others, including his mother who once taught you Sunday school and has been buying your books to give to friends.

Prophets looking for honor in their hometown always end up a little long on disappointment, and if they choose to write about that town, honor may be the least of their concerns. Instead they will find things like anonymous letters in their postbox, oranges in their exhaust pipe, and shaving cream on their rhubarb pie.

It was tempting to write about the town in which I grew up, for it is a marvelous place, rich in hilarity and populated by people who stepped right out of humor novels. But for now I had better stick to fiction.

It really is a shame though. There was Mrs. Von Brouwer (Edna was her first name I believe—though I was never allowed to use it), the Dutch Reformed owner of our ice cream shop, who once grew so impatient with my indecision as to which flavor I desired, that she scooped me all three, thereby inventing Neapolitan ice cream, a flavor I prefer to this very day. I also think of my grandfather loudly correcting our minister during a sermon on the second coming of Christ. The minister insisted that it could happen at any time, but my grandfather said no, the Bible said Christ would come "like a thief *in the night*," so we were safe during the day. And then there was the time I took part in an impromptu wedding ceremony at the ripe old age of five—as the groom. It is a difficult thing to reach twenty-one and have to confess to your fiancée that you were already married early in life but that you have grown distant and don't know where your wife lives, what she looked like when she entered high school, or what her name was…was it Mary or Beth?

Pulling the disk from my pocket, I gave thanks again that I'd been able to salvage the story and that I was sticking to fiction. But when I stood to my feet and pushed a certain international symbol, the sucking sound that ensued was enough to frighten the most sturdy of heart, and my natural response was to clap my hands tightly over my ears.

In so doing I dropped the disc. And watched in horror as twenty-four chapters, the climax, the denouement, and the epilogue disappeared together down a four-inch hole to Nowhere, Idaho. Only a pale yellow Post-it note escaped, fluttering dramatically to the floor.

Stooping, I cradled it in my hands as if it were the lone survivor from some horrible nautical tragedy into which I could breathe life. The note said, "Book…Growing Up…Backup." I shook my head in the mirror and watched the tears race each other down my cheeks.

Gathering my emotions, I asked a flight attendant for help. He shook his head. I reminded him in desperation that those things can be pried open. He said they couldn't, but that I could fill out a complaint form if I had suggestions. I staggered slowly back to row 17, seat B, a defeated man badly in need of a drink. The flight attendant complied and brought me another tomato juice on the rocks—with double pepper.

By the time he did so, that manuscript was the best thing I'd written in my entire life. By the time I took a sip, it was part Hemingway, part Shakespeare, and borderline Plato. By the time I reached the ice cubes, that manuscript was no longer a manuscript, it was a work of literary genius, destined to change the western world, parts of Australia, and possibly New Guinea. I began to feel sorry not just for myself but for all the people who would miss out on its influence. People who would never know how badly they needed something they didn't even know they could not get.

When I finally told my son about the tragedy, he smiled and said with wisdom rarely found in a teenager, "Adversity won't last forever, Dad…you must remind yourself that God is good…that sometimes life hands you a chance to start again…a chance to improve things a little."

I asked him if he would like to wear some tomato juice, maybe some ice cubes too. He grinned rather widely. That grin got me thinking once again of the wonder and mischief of childhood. And so I shall write this story for a second time. Perhaps this time I will get it right.

The man who lives in a small community
lives in a much larger world...The reason is obvious.
In a large community we can choose our companions.
In a small community our companions are chosen for us.

—G. K. Chesterton

One

Home

I f ever you reach the lowest point along Highway 13, just south of Spruce Lake, where the road takes the only bend you'll see for miles and patchwork wheatfields surround you, rich with black soil that once lured settlers from the east, you will find my hometown.

You can't miss it, they always say.

But most people do.

To the west, windswept hills that are mere wrinkles to some folk begin to climb toward the mountains like children eager to assert their independence. To the east, red-tailed hawks circle high above places with odd names like Hector's Hollow and Three Tree Gap into a broad-brimmed sky that refuses to quit. If you should feel the need to stop for the night or order a plate of fries (lightly sprinkled with vinegar) at the Garlic Grill, you may see a handsome couple walking haltingly, their faces toward the setting sun, their hands gently entwined, their countenances brightened by unintentional smiles. Stop and they'll point you in the right direction. Breathe deeply and you'll catch a hint of canola mixed with fresh-mown hay, and if the wind is stirring from the south, a little manure—something the locals don't notice so much anymore.

The gravel on Third Avenue will take you right past our white-stained house, half-buried in dust, the one with the wide backyard that slopes gently toward a lazy stream. The single-story home is built of timber harvested from a sawmill a hundred miles westward, smeared with drab plaster—in some places gray, in others white—and topped with a dual-pitched mansard roof with patterns in the shingles. The roof was a mistake, according to my father. Apparently the one filling the order had just been fired, and his last act of defiance was to ship a freight-car load of the wrong shingles 2000 miles west, shingles that were worth a bundle. "Now, if we just had a house to put under them," I once heard Dad sigh. As it is, our house is primarily constructed of half-inch plywood. The windows are trimmed in it, the sparse furniture made of it, and I often extract lengthy slivers on account of it.

Most of our yard stops growing grass by early June, its blades innocent victims to the bare feet of a dozen neighbor children and a thousand imaginary football games where Johny Unitas and Deacon Jones convert outstanding plays disguised as mere mortals like us. "Better to raise children than grass," my mother says from time to time from her perch on the sofa, and Dad peeks out from behind the newspaper as if to question her logic, as if he's not so sure. Perhaps he'd like to sit in the grass one night and locate certain planets without having to dust off his pants before bedtime.

Sometimes at night, when the sun glides behind the mountains, Dad tells me stories, and if I had to pick a favorite I would have him tell me of my birth.

From the moment I drew my first breath in room 117 of Grace Municipal Hospital, all I really wanted was adventure. And a midnight snack, of course. Others yearned for comfort, for the blankets to be wrapped tight, for soft music playing, and for ample reassurances for the journey ahead. Not me. I arrived one minute before the clock smacked twelve, on February 29 of a leap year,

1964, the year China tried out its first atomic bomb and the U.S. Surgeon General first warned of the dangers of tobacco. My father was far from home that night—picking up engine parts for some-one—but insisted he had wakened with a start in a strange hotel room precisely at midnight, certain there was one more Ander-son in the world and pretty sure it was a boy.

Baptists are not usually privy to such visions, so you can imag-ine his surprise when the truth was confirmed by a long-distance phone call.

"I think we'll call him Barry," he told the nurse, and then, throwing back the covers, he rose on his bare feet to celebrate the miracle with a long swig of ginger ale, a quick gargle, and an enthu-siastic holler.

Somehow the handle was lost in the translation, and my mother named me Terry. ("Isn't that sweet," she told the nurse. "He wants him named after my younger sister.") And naming me was almost the last thing she ever did. Nearly forgotten, I whim-pered nearby as a doctor and four nurses hovered over her like ministering angels, feverish to prolong her life, desperate for a heartbeat. Our destinies hinge on moments like these, on things we cannot know and certainly cannot control. I later learned that the doctor was furious with both my parents for what I could not know, and he muttered his displeasure even as he tried to save her life. When at last the nurses were patting one another's angel wings, one of them noticed me smiling at the ceiling and cooing softly and said, "Oh shoot, we forgot to weigh him." So she did: cleaned me off and laid me on some cold Imperial measuring scale, though I had to be reminded of these things later.

The very next Wednesday in the *Grace Chronicle* I was the lone star of Birth Announcements on the inside back page:

Born to John and Ruth Anderson, a boy! Terry Paul.
Weighing seven pounds, one inch.

The last word was an error, of course, a typo typical of the newspaper. I have kept the clipping to this day.

Tonight, Dad is rubbing the growing pains out of my skinny legs as he tells me the story.

"Why was the doctor angry?" I ask.

"What do you mean? Who told you that?"

"Tony."

"Well son, it doesn't much matter. What matters is—" Then he grows silent and changes the subject. "I'd have been home," he says regretfully, "but for the snowstorm. It was clean tuckered out by the time it got here, so it only left a foot or two. But it had blown in from Alaska, where it dumped 346 inches on the Thompson Pass. Can you believe it? The record still stands. Look it up if you'd like."

I wouldn't know where to look it up or how or why. Dad never tells lies. Not even little ones. He is rubbing my legs harder now, staring out the window into the darkness. "Still, the blizzard hit like a freight train without a whistle. I was only sixty miles north of here when it landed, and I wanted nothing more than to get home. But when I started for the car in my boots, I went snow-blind. Couldn't see a thing. Had to turn back."

"You only had boots on?" I'm not trying to be funny.

He laughs pretty hard at that one, rocking back and forth a little, easing up on my legs. Then he is gazing out the window again. "I knelt in that hotel room in my pajamas, Terry, my bare feet still on, and I just knew I needed to pray for your mother." His eyes are moist, probably red. "Yes sir, I fell asleep right there on my knees. Never did sleep in that bed at all." Here a smile steals across his face. "And I dreamed of throwing the football one summer afternoon with my youngest son."

"That's me," I say.

"That's you."

"But it's winter now."

"It is."

"We can ice skate."

"We can and we will."

He is stroking my black hair now, tugging at a stubborn knot. "Well, it's time for your prayers, Son. Goodnight."

I wonder if other twelve-year-olds get their foreheads kissed, or if they wipe the kisses off like I do.

How I love my father. He is the closest thing to a hero a Christian boy is allowed, for we are not encouraged to admire the folks of earth. "God is the only perfect one," says our pastor. But Dad comes a close second. The only thing he cannot do is sing. What comes out sounds like a cat being squeezed too hard. Upon trying out for the Father's Day Men's Chorale, he was informed they were looking for someone to help take the offering. It seems to be his only fault, for Dad is the most honest man I have ever met, a mechanic who never cheated a soul, who can often be found guilty of nursing a soft spot for those with old cars that misfire or with bank accounts that do the same. The vehicles we drive never run quite right, but the irony was lost on me until years later. "That Anderson fixes everyone's problems but his own," someone said. And someone was right. Our front yard is littered with crankshafts and bumpers and alternators and at least one old wreck at any given time.

We drive older cars partly because we have no money and partly because Dad tried to buy a newer one once (with the help of a check my grandpa sent) and the experience spooked him. For weeks he'd had his eye on a two-tone 1965 Pontiac Bonneville with a neglected odometer. We prayed about it every night, and finally the arrangements were made and the price agreed upon. According to my brother, the salesman (a greasy-haired little fellow from another state) motioned my father into his office and set a contract before him as if it were hot soup that would cool off if he didn't hurry up and grab a spoon.

Dad looked it over carefully, pen hovering, poised to strike, when the anxious salesman lowered his voice and whispered, "My boss will be sending you an evaluation form in about a week. Questions about my service and stuff. You bring it by my place, and I'll getcha a free tank of gas."

My father was still squinting at the fine print, not paying much attention.

"You don't need to fill out the evaluation when it comes," the salesman explained with a wink. Dad looked up. "I'll do the work for you—I'll just mark 'outstanding' in every category. No one needs to know."

Normally my father believes that anger is an expensive luxury, "just one letter short of danger," I've heard him say, but this day it was a luxury he could afford. First he gave the salesman a good working over about truth and integrity and how more money just makes you more of what you already are and in his case he must have been a thief and a sneak from day one and maybe that was okay in Kansas or wherever he was from but out here it wouldn't cut it, not in a thousand years. "A man who stoops to make a buck isn't worth his weight in coat hangers," said Dad, standing to his feet and dropping the pen on the desk with a thud. "You know the price of everything and the value of nothing! There's a bus leaving in ten minutes. Be under it." Then he ripped up the contract, tossed it in the air, and slammed the poor befuddled man's door so hard you could almost hear his ribs rattle.

And so it is that we drive old cars.

Dad says it doesn't much matter in the grand scheme of things. God can supply us with a new one any day, or do something even more miraculous—He can keep the old one running. Right now we drive a DeSoto Diplomat with a 318 engine, a long lame boat that rides low and limps around corners like a wrestler after a badly mismatched fight.

We were riding somewhere in the Diplomat, Dad and I—to pick up some groceries at Solynka's, I think—and I sat on the passenger side unable to see much, save the tops of the trees whipping by my window. I was only eight or nine at the time, but I can draw on the image to this day: my father at the wheel, his oily mechanic's hands dwarfing it, his optimistic smile brightening my world whenever he glances my way.

"Dad, what's wrong with Mom?"

"We're not really sure, Son."

He is quiet long enough for me to decide I'd better come up with a replacement question: "Why don't we have much money?" which went over equally well. There was silence as more trees sped by. The question was a valid one, I thought.

Finally I asked, "Why'd they call it Grace?" I am speaking of where we live, of course. I'd always found it a funny name for a town. Perhaps you do too. Some stop here expecting a miracle, like Lourdes, but all they get is a town of 1200 where nothing is more ordinary than the commonplace.

"Well, Son," he begins, which means we'll be a while, "Pennsylvania has towns like Panic and Fearnot. Ohio has Dull and Knockemstiff. There's a place called Grace in North Dakota, but its roots aren't nearly as tangled as our own. This is an unusual town, Son. You watch carefully, and you'll discover that wonders never cease."

"Tell me about it, Dad. About Grace. The name, I mean."

I stretch my hands behind my neck and suck air through my freshly-brushed teeth. A kid my age has nothing but time, an immense stretch of it ending nowhere fast, so I sit still, knowing the story will be worth hearing if my hero does the telling.

The facts, I later learned, were gleaned from *A Brief History of Grace* by Ryan Franklin III (Franklin Press, 1921, 98 pages), which you can still pick up in the library here; you won't have to stand in line. Franklin's great-grandfather, the pioneer and sharpshooter, set out with twenty-eight relatives for the long trek from upstate New York back in the spring of 1829. But within one month, family feuds had whittled their number down to two. Worst of all, Franklin and his wife had lost their daughter to smallpox. "Only one thing kept their little caravan moving west," claims Dad as he eases the big DeSoto into a slow left turn, his arm out the window on account of a faulty blinker. "It was the promise of land and the dream he had for his dear wife Maggie that one day she would have a place to pick flowers within sight of the Rocky Mountains and a never-ending kaleidoscope of pristine sunsets to view from her back porch."

Dad doesn't need a thousand words to paint a picture.

"Toward the end of their journey, as Ryan and Maggie nudged the horse-drawn wagon over a steep rise, the landscape changed abruptly, and they sat in silent awe, gazing widemouthed at the tallest mountains they'd ever seen, mountains that poked holes through clouds hovering 11,000 feet above moose the size of elephants. They sat like this for a full two minutes before noticing that they had parked on the edge of an ancient Indian burial site without a permit and that a dozen Cherokees were a hundred yards to the south, some of them bearing flowers to lay on the graves, the others bearing down fast upon the poor settlers. With nowhere to go and no time to grab a rifle, Ryan held his poor wife with one arm and turned the other toward the sky. He prayed for mercy and fended off thoughts of being scalped or of spending their first winter in captivity—he learning to hunt with the tribe and Maggie whacking buffalo hides into blankets and discovering the fine art of cooking bear and wolf.

"'Dear God,' Ryan entreated, 'get us out of here, and I will build a monument to Your name.' The two of them clung to each other, Maggie sobbing softly, not daring to glance up, and Ryan calling out in prayer. When at last they lifted their heads, the Indians had vanished without a trace. They were clean gone, as if they'd never arrived—except for some little wreaths of daisies left on the graves."

"Wow," is all I can think of saying, so I do. But though we've been parked in front of the grocery store a minute or two already, Dad is not finished.

"They made camp that night, September 9, 1829, along the banks of Hi-Ho Creek, and Ryan wrote:

> Dear Jernal,
>
> Have come far enouf. Have needed enouf miracles. Two days hence mite call it kwits. Am tyred out but thanked up. Beans tonight. Sure would like stoo. Good nite for now.
>
> R.

"And that's where our little town began, a lazy five days west of the Cherokee ancient burial ground, Son. I've lived here thirteen years now. And it's a fine place. Flat as a pancake, I know. But we can see the mountains, so there's always hope."

The DeSoto is still running, though Dad has pulled the keys from the ignition. Finally she dies with a shudder. He laughs and shakes his head. "Too bad we weren't born rich instead of so good-looking."

"But what about Grace? Where'd she come in?"

"Oh, I almost forgot. Franklin, our intrepid adventurer, was going to call the town Lo-Lo, a mispronounced French word honoring Captain Meriwether Lewis, the explorer. Or it may have been a Chinook Indian word meaning to pack or carry. I'm not sure. But as he began carving an L into the sign, he remembered that promise to God and thought, *Why would I name this here town after a miserable and depressed man with a drinking problem when I can name it after my dear little girl Grace, who lived life with a twinkle and made me a happy man?* So he used the sign with its lone 'L' for firewood and addressed his journal once again. 'I shall call it Grace,' he wrote with much more deliberate and determined strokes. 'Grace stands for "God Rescued And Chased Endians".'"

Dad turns to me with a grin. "He wasn't much of a speller, our Ryan."

I grin too, though I have missed something.

Come to think of it, I missed out on a lot of things in those days. But in time I did get this: Those who long for adventure should be careful what they wish for.

I suppose it's helped to remember the advice my father gave me as we came out of Solynka's that warm summer day, a loaf of bread and two cans of beans between us.

"Terry Paul," he said, "Sit down, buckle up, and hang on."

Two

Rapture

On August 4, 1976, the Rapture of the Church took place. I was sleeping at the time. But before I tell you about it, allow me a little more background.

Franklin's Creek, named by the first settler upon its banks, ripples through our back yard, slicing the town of Grace in half lazily but efficiently almost down the middle. Though I'm sure no one set out to do so, with one or two exceptions, our side of the town is populated by churchgoing folk and the other side... well, it accommodates those who sleep in come Sunday. When asked to conduct a funeral for Robert Moore, owner of the town's only tavern, our former pastor, Mr. Francis Frank, responded with a succinct note: "Let the dead bury their dead." He was a terse man, was our pastor, but his words pretty much sum up the sentiments here. We are taught to remain untainted by the world, in it but not of it, and such commands seem easiest to obey long-distance.

From my backyard I can gaze across Franklin's Creek at The World, being careful not to stare too long at people who drink things we would not on Saturday night and engage in activities such as cutting their grass and throwing the football Sunday afternoon. "Pagans," my brother Tony calls them, and he should know, him being sixteen and all.

Tony is four years my elder and a smarter cookie than I will ever be. Lean, but showing signs that muscles are a distinct possibility, he has translucent eyes that are trustworthy yet dancing with mischief. A network of tiny freckles spans his tanned face as if some modern artist had flicked brown paint from his fingertips and created a masterpiece. Tony is everything I want to be and am not: redheaded, popular with the girls, quick with the tongue, funny, and athletic. This morning Dad has him stuffing fiberglass insulation into the walls of a tiny addition we are building, a place for the two of us to sleep. It has a west window—a view of the Rockies—and soon the thick insulation will help Tony play his music a little louder, though he hasn't mentioned this to Dad. The extra room will be nice. As it is, I'm on the bottom bunk of a two-bunk room that crams three boys into a hundred square feet. In the winter, when the windows won't open, my dad refuses to go in there after about ten o'clock. Holds his nose and blows kisses from the hall. I guess he is needed elsewhere.

"What kind of cheese you cutting in there, boys?" he laughs. "Gouda?"

I'm not sure Mom and Dad were praying for more children after Tony came along. He is a high-strung child who filled their quiver to two, alongside my older brother Ben, who looks not at all like me, and who smokes like a chimney when no one is looking (I sometimes finish the leftovers). My big sister Elizabeth is exactly one year older than me and will enter puberty shortly. My father talks about surrounding the front yard with razor wire to keep the boys away, but I think he's kidding.

I am the youngest. The caboose, my brothers call me. A mistake, my third grade teacher once said. I sometimes wonder if they'd miss me at all if I packed my bags and hopped a boat bound for my grandparent's homeland of Scotland. But I'm quite sure they would. I may be the caboose, but they seem to like knowing I'm back here.

It is early August. This morning, after an hour of insulation work, Tony feels he has done his share, so he saunters into the backyard, where I am examining ants with a magnifying glass. He coughs. Once from the insulation, twice to get my attention. "Hey," he says, as if my response is incidental, "how'd you like to be rich enough to buy an ice cream?" I lower the magnifying glass, trapping a few dozen ants in the act, and blink with suspicion. He's made promises like this before.

"I'll give you a quarter to stuff those walls. Promise. It's easy work, but I've got other stuff to do."

If there's one thing a poverty-stricken child cannot resist, it is the promise of change in his pocket.

And he is right. The work is easy, but it's painful too. An hour later, I am standing in the bathroom stripped to my undies, scratching anything that itches, which is pretty much everything. I squint into the wood-framed mirror as if practicing for the movies. "I'd like to strangle my brother," I say out loud, acting it out, choking someone. The trouble with scratching is that it pushes the tiny shards of glass deeper, and by lunchtime I am lying on the sofa, feeling like a biblical character named Job and wondering if he had an older brother. "You should have used gloves," Tony tells me, sounding very much like Job's friends. I watch as he tries to hide his sadistic smile. "Long pants would have been good," he adds.

"Where's my quarter?" I am scratching my forearm.

—◆—

Sometimes at night when our prayers have been said and the lights are all out, Tony tells us spooky stories like *The Legend of*

the Molten Minstrel, the tale of a folksinger by the name of Jeremiah Williams, who came to town for a concert one Halloween
night. According to Tony, the show was held at the community hall
and was crammed full of pagans from the other side of the creek.
Some of them had been drinking, and all of them were humming
along to the familiar ballads when suddenly at the stroke of
midnight a lady in the front row began to scream, "His feet! His
feet!" Jumping to her own, she fled the room and was never seen
or heard from again.

Concertgoers craned their necks for the reason and were horrified to see long, skinny claws protruding from Mr. Williams'
trouser cuffs. Chicken feet. And then—*poof!*—he was gone, guitar
and all, without a trace. Except for the strong smell of sulphur,
which lingers there to this day.

I've learned to cover my head when Tony starts telling stories
in the dark, but it's okay tonight because my oldest brother, Ben,
is hosting an imaginary talk show from Atlanta, Georgia, wherever that is. The show is called *Evenings with Ben* and it comes
on the air with loud theme music courtesy of Tony, who is reclin-
ing five feet north on the other bottom bunk. He plays the imaginary tuba with his lips and badly needs lessons. Sometimes I
summon the nerve to call in. Tonight's topic is end-time theology, and Tony is a special guest on the show as an expert by the
name of Reverend John J. Johnson, who has come to talk about
The Rapture of the Church. Pastor Johnson is trying out a
Southern accent tonight, and when I call in with a knock-knock
joke, he is not amused and reminds me that we are in the last days
here and this is hardly a time for fooling around and that if I don't
smarten up, there is not only eternal judgment, no sir, there is more
insulation work to do.

"Just one knock-knock joke, please, Sir?" I insist, interrupting the Reverend John J.

"All right then," says my oldest brother, the radio host, clearing his Southern voice and trying to sound patient, confident, and mature.

I pull the covers up to my neck. "You start."

"Okay," says Ben. "Knock, knock."

"Who's there?" I ask, amazed he's fallen for it.

He pauses, unable to think of anything. "That is the dumbest thing I've heard in my life."

"Gotcha!"

His accent is missing now. He rolls over and glares down at me in the semidarkness. "You're so juvenile," he says, but I don't care about him using big words because I am laughing so hard that I fall purposely out of bed and hit the floor with a bump for emphasis, reducing the show to dead air. Tony, the tuba player, snickers a little and pinches me until I jump back between the covers.

"I've got one," says Ben, forgetting he is hosting a top-rated show. "Knock, knock."

"Who's there?" I ask.

"Lucy."

"Lucy who?"

"Lucy lastic makes your pants fall down."

We can't remember hearing anything quite so funny in our lives, and when Ben starts his wheezy little laugh that isn't quite right because of all the cigarettes, it's dominoes from there.

"Settle down now," Dad hollers from the living room, rumpling his newspaper.

Though Ben is the eldest, he is an inch shorter than Tony. I'm never quite sure what he will do next, and he often sneaks out at night, returning late and smelling like a wet tobacco plant.

During the day I try to think up questions to stump my brothers while they are live on the radio. Questions like, "Do fish ever get thirsty?" and "If a pig eats bacon is it a cannibal?" or "Would you rather have your middle toenail pulled off with tweezers or a paper cut on your eyeball?" But tonight I am exhausted from all the insulating, and I lay my scratchy arms behind my head and listen for a change.

At twelve years of age I've heard about The Rapture only once or twice before, though I'm sure our new pastor has talked about it often. One Sunday evening we went to a church across town that some consider liberal to watch a film called *A Thief in the Night*. It was the first horror movie I'd seen in my life, the tale of a beautiful blond girl named Patty whom I imagined myself marrying someday and making very happy until I learned that she is already married in the film. In fact, her husband becomes a Christian, which for some reason disappointed me. Life is great for the two of them, though, until one morning when Patty awakens to the discovery that her husband's razor is buzzing loudly in the sink, the alarm clock is ringing by her bed, and he has climbed right out of his pajamas and completely disappeared.

Shocked, she listens as the radio informs her that millions of others have vanished as well, that cars and jet airplanes have crashed around the world, leaving chaos and bewilderment in the streets. One dramatic event follows another, and soon Patty realizes that this is no alien abduction, it is worse: She is living in the End Times spoken of in biblical prophecy.

"So if they leave their pj's behind, is everyone in The Rapture naked?" I ask, genuinely wondering. Tony snickers at first and Ben joins him. Tony clears his throat and goes back to being Pastor John J. "Ah think so, Son," he drawls. "The clothes will simply naught stay with y'all when you's travelin' at that rate a speed and on that tap a trajectory."

Somehow I fall asleep listening to them talk about the end of the world, the Mark of the Beast, the Great Tribulation, and how the liberal pastor's license plate is 665, one number short of being obvious. As sleep begins to overtake me, I lie there wondering what it would be like to be left behind. Mother says I don't need to worry. That kids who've asked Jesus into their heart will be the first to go, and I did that three or four times during the horror movie. Why then do I have a growing sense of uneasiness that began last Sunday morning when I dropped a nickel in the offering plate with my thumb and index finger while smoothly removing a quarter with the other three?

I pull the pillow over my head to shut out the thoughts, but they continue to swirl: Is it wise for a kid to put a pillow over his head? What if you can't breathe and you slowly suffocate in your sleep? I bet it's happened. But there's no way I'm calling the show to ask my brother Tony.

—⁊⁊—

Sunday morning comes early here in August. By six A.M. the light creeps through our single-pane bedroom window, gray at first, then silver, then salmon pink. The ceiling sponges it up for a while, but finally the hues start to bounce around, smacking me between the eyeballs, beckoning me to come out and play. I ignore the call by pulling the pillow over my head and drifting off again, but by seven-thirty the voice is irresistible and the ceiling looks as if handfuls of brightly colored confetti have been tossed against it until they stick. I rub my eyes and sit up.

The bed beside me is vacant, the covers rumpled.

The top bunk is empty too.

Strange. Especially for a Sunday.

Usually Dad has to pour cold water on my brothers' heads to help them get to Sunday school by 9:30. I rub the sleep from my eyes, sit up, and throw my legs over the edge. I can smell pancakes. Pajamas are scattered on the floor, two sets of them, rumpled as if my brothers jumped out of them suddenly.

No one is in the living room either, though the radio is tuned to loud static. I wonder what happened to *The Hour of Decision*. My sister, Liz, is gone. And worse still, my parents' bedroom is empty. Odd. Mother rarely leaves the house. I can't remember the last time she did.

I am standing in the kitchen now, feeling small and alone and very frightened. The table is set with six plates, and two of them hold half-eaten and soggy pancakes. A fork is on the floor. Water is running in the sink—something my parents never allow—and beside the fork lies a dishrag exactly where it landed. A strange feeling grabs hold of me, like an older brother has caught up to me from behind and is squeezing my stomach until the stuffing is gone.

On the green chalkboard beside the phone are these words:

It's happeni—

The "i" ends in an upward swirl as if the writer had been lifted by stage wires into the sky.

I rush to the window and look outside. Our car is in the driveway, sound asleep, and across Franklin's Creek Mr. Jennings is cutting his grass. Figures. He'd be the last to go. I stagger to the kitchen table and lean against it. My tiny legs won't hold my weight, and I sink to the floor.

Out our kitchen window, clouds of smoke billow toward the sky, and I am crying more tears than I thought possible.

The Rapture has happened, and I've been left behind.

This is no movie. This is no dream. The Great Tribulation has arrived, and the horror has begun. I throw myself onto the couch and begin to sob.

—ɯ—

I am lying quite still on our lime green sofa nursing a heart attack and planning for the end of the world—where I will live (in the hills), what I will eat (deer meat and raccoon), and whom I will marry (Peggy Jennings, the pretty little pagan girl from across the creek, although her older brother Matthew will be a nightmare at family reunions)—when the door is flung open and the troupe traipses in, looking weary but highly excited. The tightness in my stomach vanishes in the twinkling of an eye.

"I can't believe he'd do that," are the first words I hear my father say as he leads the entire family—minus me—back into the house. Mom is leaning hard against his shoulder, exhausted. It is about eight o'clock.

"Do what?" Tony is probing for information.

Mom and Dad exchange uncertain glances, perhaps wondering if the younger ones can handle such information.

"You all right, Son?" my mother asks me, slumping awkwardly onto the sofa and rumpling my hair.

"Ya. I'm fine."

"We decided to let you sleep, you had the pillow on your—"

"I'm fine," I say a little testily.

"You don't look so well."

I wonder if the tears have left too much evidence on my face. "What happened?"

"Hey, who left this on?" Dad shuts off the tap and then the radio and sits down across from me. "Well," he begins slowly, "it seems that Bernie Vanderhoof burned down his very own service station."

"What?" asks Liz. "Why?"

"To get the insurance money, I guess. I always wondered about that man. Used to water down the gasoline with who knows what. The police have him now. Strange, the things men do for money."

"You shoulda seen the place go up!" stammers Ben, sprawling on the couch beside me, as if he needs a cigarette. "It was great! Didn't you hear the gas tanks explode? Stuff was shootin' a mile high. Looked like the end of the world. I can't believe you slept through it."

But I did. I slept through the biggest fire—and one of the biggest scandals—ever to hit our little town. And as I slept with that pillow over my head, Tony made sure he was the last to leave the house. Tiptoeing around with uncanny foresight, he carefully arranged pajamas, tuned the radio, dropped a dishrag and a fork. He turned on a faucet here, a stove there, and scratched ten big letters on a chalkboard—letters that scared me half to death: "It's happeni—"

It takes me a while to get over it, but as I sit in church that morning listening to Pastor Davis' sermon entitled "Who Is My Neighbor?" a big grin starts to crawl right across my face and I realize that I'm not so dumb after all.

Later that night, while my brothers are at youth group singing choruses like "It only takes a spark to get a fire going…" (which probably makes them think of Bernie Vanderhoof), I tiptoe into our bedroom and open Tony's bureau drawer. On a freshly starched pair of jeans I leave a note thanking him for the shiny quarter I find in his wallet. It says,

Thanks for the mon—

Then I pull on a glove, rub lots of fiberglass insulation on the inside of three pair of his underwear, and quietly leave the room.

Three

Mother

To this day I don't know what I bought with that quarter, which surprises me because there were so few of them hanging around.

It's funny how people will brag about growing up in abject poverty but only years later when the shock of it has begun to wear off. They'll boast of how little they had back then and how lean were their Christmases. They'll tell you that remembering a single birthday present is a struggle for their cognitive faculties, save for that little ragtag doll they named Sally ("Whatever happened to her?") or a rubber band gun their father made out of clothespins someone threw away. "Those were the happiest years of my life," they'll tell you, eating their prime rib. "Kids nowadays just don't know how good they have it."

And maybe they are right.

Nostalgia ages well. The times have never been quite so good as they used to be.

I heard folks talk this way when I was a child, and I thought to myself, "Let me get this straight. You were happier poor? So why don't you give your money to me right now? Checks. Cash. Whatever. It's the least I can do. Take it off your hands. I'll be happy just to see you happy again." But I never summoned the courage.

I hope you won't think less of me if I confess that the good old days went by largely unappreciated by me. A struggling mechanic like my father doesn't go in for show, but show is what a child my age longs for. I wanted to be on the lead Clydesdale. I wanted so many things I could not have. Like licorice sticks and motorbikes and snowmobiles on which I could hit the tops of snowbanks at full speed, bouncing off them like they were whitecaps. I wanted to buy candy—bags full of it—and eat until I was sick enough to stay home from school and snack on soda crackers and Old South orange juice and watch our new colored television from a crushed velvet sofa, which we did not have. Of course I knew we weren't allowed to eat in the living room, nor did the church and school allow us a TV on account of Psalm 101:3, "I will set no wicked thing before mine eyes." And so I lowered my hopes, coveting instead a pair of flared pants with no previous owner and my very own bicycle with the seat still intact, objects which were no more available to me than a snowmobile as it turned out.

As September steers toward October, our pantry is as bare as a plucked goose. "Poverty is hereditary," jokes my father. "You get it from your kids." But he is quick to add that it has nothing to do with us, that each of us is God's special gift, and that he wouldn't trade a one of us in on a lifetime of peace.

Why must some of us pray that there will be a delightful meal in our immediate future while others deliberate over which size cabin they should build for their summer retreat? I once asked my father this, and he said, "Success is not measured by how many doors you have to lock at night. We are not a poor family, Son. We just don't have much money." It took years before I thought I knew what he meant.

At night I find myself praying earnestly for a million dollars. I tell God I'll tithe a full fifteen percent if He'll burden me with it. That I'll be a missionary in Africa too. Or Pakistan.

Have I told you why we are so poor? I suppose I should.

A good portion of Dad's meager salary pays for the doctor and the medication, which don't come cheap. Dr. Mason does house calls each Thursday, his face scrunched into a permanent scowl, his fat jowls an obvious burden to the rest of his face. I don't blame him. It's tough to be cheerful, looking as he does. He murmurs around Mom's bedside, launching big words and dispensing measured doses of hope.

My earliest memories of my mother are of a high-energy fireball of a woman who scurried about, always cheerful, always active, always busy straightening things. She would zip my parka for school so fast that I'd strain my neck to keep it from getting nicked. When I arrived home she was there, concocting something marvelous in the kitchen, slamming eggs against the side of the pan with one hand or chopping onions, laughing at the tears that came with the act. My mother was the only woman I will ever allow to clean spots from my face by spitting on her hand, and she had an innate sense of who needed what and why and when.

I've yet to see anyone more adept at dropping a cheap pound of hamburger into a searing skillet, surrounding it by diced onions and cayenne pepper, and making you think you'd just stepped into the finest restaurant in Europe. Summers we spent outdoors, pulling weeds and picking beans—sometimes eating both. We enjoyed fresh garden vegetables well into October: sliced tomatoes, shelled peas, cabbage salad. Our kitchen floor was a sticky mess but well worth the pickled dills, both carrots and cucumbers. After a meal, Mother was in no hurry, and she made sure we weren't either. As if the food were not enough, the conversations around that table were the dessert since there was often none of an edible variety. Without saying much, Mother seemed to know how to keep them going. She would smile and nod as we told her about our day, laugh umpteen times at the same joke, and bear with unlearned visitors as they rambled foolishly on about the rising price of gasoline, the latest conspiracy in Washington, or the certainty that the end times were but a heartbeat away and Henry Kissinger was the Antichrist.

Besides Christmas, the one consolation of those long winters was that skillet. It drew people like a beacon in the night. High school students eagerly crowded our table, as did visiting ministers and drifters the pastor sent our way.

Several plaques hung from our walls, though some came crashing down, victims of the indoor hockey we played using a rolled-up sock for a puck. The plaques were Bible verses, all of them, and she had chosen the one in the dining room, nailing it up there herself: "For He satisfieth the longing soul, and filleth the hungry soul with goodness."

Times change.

By my ninth birthday the energy had been replaced by a constant fatigue and forgetfulness. Conversations shortened, and the skillet became a danger to the now clumsy hands that had once washed my needy face. Her moods would swing wildly; she became irritable, and one terrible day the police wrestled away her driver's license. Surely this would pass, we told ourselves. Wishful thinking this. But sometimes wishes are all a boy has.

Mother spends most of her days in bed now, a ragged cloth draped across her forehead, the covers pulled high, the dark green blind pulled low. I feel such pity for her that I would do anything at all to have her sit upright like Lazarus and walk out of that tomb. Instead she stays put, rising from her bed only to tuck us into ours.

In the early morning she shuffles down the hallway in ragged slippers, adjusts the thermostat upward and burps softly. "Excuse me," she always says, even when she knows we are probably asleep. Her walk is like that of a sailor who's been at sea too long, and though I can never remember the name of the disease, I've heard it whispered in conversations I was not supposed to hear. Whenever she eats with us, which is rare, I clamor to set the table, allotting her the finest of each utensil, the newest plate, the cleanest glass. Twice in the past year, an ambulance hauled her to the hospital for suctioning procedures she found dreadful, so Dad mixes her food in a blender, the one luxury we can afford. We try not to stare as she slowly gums the goop like Pablum and awkwardly swallows a cocktail of pills Dad metes out, praying they will do the trick.

Every night I pray too, but whenever I pass her room and see her lying there I am reminded that God doesn't seem to do much with my prayers except stockpile them for some divine purpose. I don't understand it. You'd think it wouldn't be too much to ask the Creator to help a kid out.

Liz is our primary chef now, and the trouble with eating my sister's food is that five or six days later after the shock has worn off, you're hungry again. I should be kinder, but it's not easy for her, filling Mom's shoes. Elizabeth, or Liz, as I call her, is our resident sheepherder too. Part girl, part border collie, she likes things done quickly, her way.

On the evening of my twelfth birthday, when the whole world was opening up before me and glistening with possibilities, my father sat me down in the living room. The sponge cake had vanished and the games had been played. My two best buddies, Michael Swanson and Danny Brown, had departed, leaving behind gifts of Hot Wheels race cars.

"There's something you need to know, Terry Paul."

We were all by ourselves there, with the wind bucking up against the windowpanes, and I could tell that the something was nothing trivial because tears were clinging to the corners of his eyes, making me listen more carefully than usual.

"You're almost a man now, Son, and I need to tell you something." Here his voice acted up a bit. "The disease your mother has…well, it could be in you too."

The words hit my body hard, like the big kid in football practice, the center, who thinks he's so tough, only Dad didn't stand there laughing, just sat before me, serious as a heart attack. I could scarcely breathe for a time. Surely he would go back a few sentences and start over with words a kid wants to hear on his birthday, words like, "I know the gifts weren't much, but if you'll look out the window, I think you'll like the color of your new bike." Instead he continued, looking me straight on.

"The reason I want you to know is that…well, they're working on a cure," and here his disposition embraced a glimmer of hope. "We don't know much about it, but I'm sure they'll have one by the time you're twenty. In the meantime, you need to take care of yourself. The doctor says our children are at risk. Aunt Edna says that those who drink and smoke have a greater chance of getting it. I don't know why. But you do what's right and you'll be okay."

For some reason I was tracing the lines on my hands with one of the cars, trying to avoid the urge to plug my ears, I guess.

"What is it?" I asked at last.

"It's called Huntington's."

"What…um…does it do?" I am clumsy with my words sometimes.

"We're just learning about it, Terry. But it is serious. We don't know how long we'll have Mother here." He stopped so long I thought he was finished. "She's crammed more living into her short life than most people who live to be old," he continued. "It's not the years in your life that count, you know, it's the life in your years. Everyone dies. Not everyone lives."

And that was that. He never brought it up again. Just patted my shoulder softly and left me sitting there, wondering what his words could mean and holding an orange Hot Wheels Corvette which, though it was my favorite color, didn't look so hot anymore.

How quickly childhood can scamper from some of us.

The best gift I can give my mother is to sit beside her and ramble on about school and friends and the weather. The night of my birthday I freshened the tattered cloth for Mom's head and felt the sudden urge to smoke and drink and chew big wads of juicy tobacco, or at least to have whatever she had and crawl into bed beside her in the darkness. Maybe bring a spittoon. The wind was still whipping against the window, rattling the panes, something I've loved to listen to all my life, so long as I am tucked in bed. It's the same feeling I get at the sound of the furnace coming on in the middle of a cold winter night, a reminder that things could be worse, I suppose. A reminder to add up my blessings.

I crawled in next to Mom and was surprised to find that I was old enough to think about the good old days. Like when I was eight or nine and Christmas was only a week away. It sounds funny now, but I wanted to be sick that Christmas because people hadn't been all that nice to me lately or even really noticed me, and this would buy me a ticket aboard the good ship Sympathy. I didn't want to be badly sick, not seriously ill, maybe just a broken leg, or better yet, a sprained wrist, but it would swell up something awful and cause doctors to wonder aloud and possibly to shake their heads with uncertainty, whispering among themselves, disagreeing on levels of severity. I wanted my family to be nearby as the doctors discussed this, and I wanted especially to see how Tony would come to my bedside and put a hand on my shoulder and tell me in a faltering voice to be brave.

Then Liz would sit beside me carefully, so as not to shake the bed and say, "How you doing, Tare? I'm just so sorry. Are you gonna be okay?"

And I would respond in a weak little voice, "It won't be long now, Liz. I can see angels—they're setting a place for me at the Christmas table in heaven. The fruit looks so wonderful. Take good care of the parakeet. My Hot Wheels too."

Her shoulders would shake unashamedly. "We don't have a parakeet," she would say. But she would treat me so nicely and nurse me back to health and strength, and I would get all better on Christmas Eve, just in time for them to shower me with gifts.

I'm sorry if you're disappointed at my wanting this, but a boy wants what a boy wants, and rarely is it something he needs. As I remembered this Christmas vision, I was surprised to find myself cheerful, perhaps from knowing I may have some awful disease for real. A disease I could tell my schoolmates about when the time was right. Something to hold over them next time they were mean to me.

With the gradual onset of Mom's illness came a change of church for the Andersons. People at the old church didn't know what to do with the likes of us except stay away. Dad didn't fault them for it. "Most wouldn't know what to say anyway once they got here," he said. "It's not like we could offer them much in the way of coffee and sandwiches." Dad said our pastor, Mr. Frank, had the wrong kind of Bible, one with no verses about compassion and kindness, so we moved on. Our new minister, Pastor Davis, was another matter. He came to visit often and one night brought three of his friends in tow. They poured oil on Mom's head, which was riveting to watch from my vantage point beyond a hinge in the bedroom door. I only knew one of them, Michael Swanson's dad. They seemed like angels to me. Each prayed for healing, and the pastor read from James 5, I believe it was, where it says, "the prayer of faith shall save the sick, and the Lord shall raise him up."

I watched carefully, but she didn't rise. Barely moved for that matter.

For the first few months people from the church brought an avalanche of casseroles, which we tried to stretch into three or four meals each. Dad wrote thank you notes, and we all signed them, me working on my autograph in case I became famous and needed one: Terry with a big loop on the "y."

Sometimes my brothers pull up chairs and sit around Mom's room in silent contemplation. I join them, wondering if being so poor is the reason this has happened, wondering if money could fix anything. "Dear God," I pray, "if there's a way out of this mess, show us, please." Then my brothers get to talking about baseball or football. I find it almost irreverent to talk about a catch Willie Mays made over his shoulder in the 1954 World Series with Mom looking as she does. Or Don Larson's perfect game against the Dodgers two years later. But Mother doesn't seem to mind. Life goes on, I guess.

Your mother is dying, but she understands.

Boys need a diversion.

If they can't have licorice and soda crackers, at least give them baseball.

Four

Sunday

"If God wants me happy, why do I have to sit through church?"

It is not the sort of question one asks on Sunday morning at a quarter past nine when the house is in a panic and your father has just come in from the car, where he has been gripping the steering wheel, resisting the urge to honk. We are moving around quicker now that Dad has made his third trip back from the DeSoto. "What could you possibly be doing in here?" he says, directed mainly to my sister.

On the way to the service most of us are grumpy due to the fact that we have said things about and to each other that we probably should not have, and Dad finally clears his throat and suggests I stop pinching Liz and that we sing something together, which goes over like a ham sandwich in a synagogue. Last time we did this I got to laughing uncontrollably because Dad's voice was fluctuating two or three notes off key. But none of us have the nerve to tell him this. Instead of singing, he addresses my question of having to sit through church, and he addresses it a little sharply, as if he'd like to punch the dashboard throughout his monologue. "This is a big old car, Terry Paul. She squeaks, she rattles, she limps, she grunts. And at times she makes you feel like you might get sick going around the next corner. But she gets us where we're going. Always has. With or without you in it. Kinda reminds me of the church."

I don't have a clue what he's talking about, except that I can't help thinking our car isn't quite that bad, that it has even started on this cold November morning, and that I haven't been sick in it lately. Sickness makes me think of Mother and I wish she were here, sitting beside him so close, like she used to. As we pull into the parking lot, Dad slows down a little and says, "Sorry kids. I lost patience. Let's have a good morning, okay?"

Liz nods and tells me to. Ben and Tony say, "Sure" in unison, as if they've been rehearsing it.

In Sunday school, which starts at nine-thirty (or is supposed to), we discuss sports, of all things. Adam Hanna, a college-aged kid with lingering acne, has spent the better part of October on the first book of Samuel and most of his Saturday preparing the day's lesson on the eighteenth chapter and the story of David and his closest buddy Jonathan. For twelve-year-old boys, we are unusually respectful of Adam partly because he is six foot four and partly because he tells us stories about his tragic life, including the one about losing his middle finger when another high schooler rammed him with a metal food tray in the cafeteria line.

As Adam begins to read this morning's passage, Michael Swanson, little brother to the girl I love, launches us completely off topic by raising a hand and asking Adam why we are not allowed to play sports on Sunday and what he thinks of the regulation. I'm not surprised. Last week Michael asked if it was okay to marry non-Christians if we were trying to get them saved. Adam is caught off guard again, knowing that his response will not be held in the strictest confidence and that if it should differ from the policy of our elders, this could be his last Sunday morning with the boys he has been called to disciple. And so he rejoins the question with one of his own. "Perhaps we shouldn't play sports at all, even on the other days of the week," he says, with just a hint of a smile. "What do you think? Is there a verse that tells us we should?" We have strong opinions on this one. "Sports is a great way of evangelizing, isn't it?" someone says, and "Hasn't God given us richly all things to enjoy?" Except for money, of course.

Adam still doesn't answer, just comes up with more questions. Some real zingers. Are there some sports that are more acceptable than others for believers? Is it easier to act like a Christian while playing Ping-Pong or rugby? Should we play sports against non-Christians? Should we use it as a witnessing tool? Would Jesus play ice hockey? Would He be humble while being interviewed on Wide World of Sports?

I have not spent much of my life thinking about these things, but I am quick to reply: Yes, most definitely He would play. "He would ram people into the boards harder than anyone playing ice hockey," I say, sitting up straighter than before, "but He would do it cleanly." Then I sit wondering if I agree with myself or not. And what the others think of me.

—⁓—

The church of my childhood is richly peopled with characters worthy of a Mark Twain novel, Adam being one of them. But there are others. For instance, there's Dr. Murray Nichols, who is not really an M.D. so much as he is a frustrated evangelist. In his younger years, when he worked in Great Falls, he was so filled with zeal for the Lord that he took to diagnosing patients improperly as a witnessing tool. "You have three days to live, and you'd best get your life in order," tends to stop a person on a dime and cause them to reevaluate their eternal destiny with as much effectiveness as just about anything I've heard of.

Dr. Nichols' first victim was a chain-smoking mother of four who came to him with chest pains and admitted in the cross-examination that her own mother had died of a heart attack at an early age. The doctor could not restrain himself.

"I give you about a week," he pronounced with forced solemnity, "maybe ten days at the most. You'd best get your house in order, Sarah."

Sarah sat there in stunned disbelief, staring blankly at humorous cartoons she couldn't read through the blur while Dr. Nichols cogitated over X-rays and the irregular rhythm of her breathing. She thought of her little brood, the youngest having been a complete surprise last May, and though they were full of beans and a few other things, and despite the fact that she'd hardly slept in five years, she loved them immeasurably, so not knowing how they would survive without her, she began to sob, though the doctor tried his best to console her.

After a few minutes of tapping the X-rays and shaking his head, Dr. Nichols asked, "Sarah, how is your spiritual life?"

His plan met with such astounding success that the good doctor couldn't give it up, until reports began to filter up the ladder and zeal ran smack dab into the Hippocratic Oath. Before he knew it he was out on his ear and ready to accept janitorial work back at Grace Community Church, where you'll find him now, lugging a huge key ring, wearing the same olive-colored pants each Sunday.

Of course Dr. Nichols has made things right now. After all, the church is no place for sinners. "The heart is deceitful above all things, and desperately wicked," I've heard our preacher say, but I'm not so sure. Folks speak of sin always in the past tense here, keeping it a safe distance away. Everyone seems okay, sitting upright, fitting in. Still, there are characters.

There's Blane Wright, Dad's first convert, who met my father when he slammed into our DeSoto one day, smashing the bumper beyond repair. When finally he crept from his car, fully expecting to be punched or at the very least yelled at, he received instead a consoling hug from my gracious father and an invitation to Sunday dinner. He has been to every potluck since.

Eunice Archibald, a recent addition, loved to raise her hands during the singing and sometimes speak in tongues until she discovered she was the only one doing either. Her first day here, Tony leaned over to me and said, "If you're ever in a prayer meeting with people who are speaking in tongues, all you need to say is 'She cometh on a Honda from Anaconda.' Say it real fast over and over. You'll fit right in." I don't know where he gets this stuff, except maybe from the books he reads.

Arthur Tucker, the local barber to most of us, shakes your hand in the foyer after church like he's just handed you a dead fish and never looks you in the eye. He looks you straight in the hair, sizing you up, wondering if you shouldn't have just a little more off the top. Hair is a big deal here. A few years ago, the elementary school that sometimes uses the church facilities invoked clear guidelines from 1 Corinthians 11 stating that hair should not touch the ears, the eyebrows, or the collar (for the boys) and not look "boyish" on the girls. Mr. Tucker could not have been happier. He began attending church that very week.

We are encouraged to support only the Christian merchants in town (even if their prices are higher), so church attendance is good business practice for some, including Anthony Jesperson, owner of the Five and Dime, who loves church potlucks but is no more a Christian than I am Portuguese.

Johnny Miller has the rare spiritual gift of being able to mimic mike feedback flawlessly. He utilizes the gift only when extremely nervous people step up to the podium, people who can't believe during the sleepless nights prior to Sunday mornings that they agreed to share their testimonies, and those who felt such an inner tug toward the front of the church that they had no choice at all in the matter. Johnny usually sits down front, and when he is through tormenting people, they look like northern pike snared on the end of a hook, being jerked around something awful. Ironically, he is always the first one to go forward when there is an altar call, a call for prayer, or a time of rededication.

Mr. Walter Solynka sits near the front too and cups his ear to hear the sermon. He runs our only grocery store by day and tapes a weekly Christian radio broadcast in Ukrainian at night, mailing it overseas for distribution. A quiet and unassuming man, Mr. Solynka moves along the street with a constant cloud of garlic about him. It is so bad that the radio studio must be aired out when he leaves, even in the winter months.

Pastor Davis is perhaps my favorite. Thickening through the middle and topped with prematurely white hair, he has a laugh that shakes him right down to his boots if he gives way to it. He recently celebrated his forty-fifth birthday ("despite threats from my former high school teachers," he jokes), and has been here little more than a year. This is his third church, I've overheard, the previous two having reputations for chewing up and spitting out good men like him. Though he brings his share of quirks and oddments, we love him here. He once paused in the midst of a message to ask us what has done more damage to the church, smoking or gossip, and Ben has been a fan ever since. Dad appreciates the fact that he's poor like our family. The parishioners aren't big givers, I guess, though we do our best.

I don't think you'll be surprised if I tell you that I remember very few of Reverend Davis' sermons. I am quite sure they were fine ones and that subliminally they affected me for the good, helping in some way to shape who I am today, but I was usually doing something else when they occurred. Like drawing my skinny little arms unobtrusively into the sleeves of my turtleneck and discovering that I can turn my shirt completely around. I do remember the odd illustration and things that happened during sermons, like the time Eunice Archibald got up to prophesy or when Billy Sutton came to church having forgotten to put on his shirt and did not remember he had forgotten until we were halfway through the first verse of "And Can It Be?" Perhaps Mr. Sutton was feeling a little stuffy (it was June), so he began to remove his suit jacket. I know it sounds implausible that a man could be in that much of a hurry, but the Suttons prided themselves on punctuality and finding a seat down front.

For the most part, sermon outlines are lost on me, and taking notes does not help. My father encourages us to draw pictures about something that relates to the sermon, but often there isn't much being discussed that lends itself to word pictures. How do you draw atonement? Or sanctification? So we have to make stuff up. My brother Ben doodles gruesome images illustrating some of the more aggressive Bible stories—David holding Goliath's head, Jael driving a tent peg into Sisera's temple, John the Baptist's bearded cranium on a platter—and shows me his masterpieces during serious moments of the sermon.

This morning Pastor Davis climbs the steps wearily, fresh from a late night of preparation and an early breakfast of poached eggs on toast, the poaching having been done by his dear wife, Irene, who plays the organ in an optimistic sort of way, somehow managing to coordinate her hands as her feet seek the pedals, a skill I've always admired. During some of the up-tempo songs like "On-ward, Christian Soldiers," her head bobs back to front like a cork on gentle water, and though several in the congregation have expressed concern about this tendency, she still lets herself go like this.

Her husband begins with the customary humorous illustra-tion ("A woman needs four men in her life: a banker, an actor, a preacher, and a mortician. One for the money, two for the show, three to get ready, and four to go"), after which the doors of my attention are slammed shut. I wonder what it is like to be a preacher, to look out on people you have known for years, some who have confided to you things they would not confide to their own spouses. What is it like to have to fill all that space between eleven-thirty and the final hymn? I can't imagine reading a two-minute testimony; how does he do it?

Pastor Davis quotes frequently from the psalmist and steers clear of preaching directly from the Song of Solomon, something, rumor has it, he learned early in his career at a previous church. The only one who has tackled that portion of the Old Testament is our adult Sunday school teacher, Miss Langford, who never married, and though she interprets the rest of the Bible literally, the Song of Songs is without a doubt a rare exception, a sacred picture of the Divine Lover's relationship with His people Israel, ripe with word pictures and allegory. The Book of Psalms and Samuel are Pastor Davis' staples, and I love it when he apologizes for giving a personal illustration, because I know it will be an inter-esting one, whether or not it enhances the point he's trying to make.

Sometimes he quotes famous poets like Robert Frost, who took the road less traveled by, or Emily Dickinson, who wrote, "Success is counted sweetest by those who ne'er succeed." This morning he quotes from Sir John Templeton:

> How wonderful it would be if we could help our children and grandchildren to learn thanksgiving at an early age. Thanksgiving opens the doors. It changes a child's personality. A child is resentful, negative—or thankful. Thankful children want to give, they radiate happiness, they draw people.

Very few people seem drawn to listening this morning, so he could quote Joseph Stalin or Friedrich Nietzsche and folks would just nod their heads and tell him what a blessing the message was. It's like reciting poetry to radial tires: Go ahead, but don't look for applause.

As we approach Thanksgiving, he is concluding a lengthy series on the topic of Gratitude, which the secretary, Myrtle Campbell, misspelled in the bulletin ("Gratitute"), thus making Pastor Davis' opening few jokes an easy selection.

In our pastor's mind, gratitude is the foundation of spiritual life. "We thank Thee, Lord," is sprinkled throughout his every prayer, and his attitude rubs off on you to the point where, even if you neglected to listen to much of the sermon, you find yourself thanking God for just about everything no matter where you are sitting.

Even I am thankful this morning.

Thank you, Lord, that the service will end at twelve-thirty and not two P.M. We will still have some afternoon left, although it will be boring. I praise You for the hand-me-down bicycle I got for my birthday with its rhythmic squeaks, though I can't ride it in the winter. Thanks for our dark-stained plywood kitchen table that hides the gouge marks I made with my hunting knife. Thank You for gum, though I wish I didn't have to chew it secondhand. Thank You that I am the youngest. That although there aren't as many pictures of me in the family photo album, I am the first to bathe each Saturday night, because by the time my brother Ben climbs in, things are looking pretty murky in there, and there's stuff floating around you don't even want to ask about. Thank You that there's no one coming after me in the family because these hand-me-down pants have known three too many Andersons already. I am grateful that the sky is blue and not green, that fish don't fly and birds don't swim. Thank You that Mary Beth Swanson sits right in front of me in church most Sunday mornings. She is so beautiful. I pray You will grant her the wisdom to marry me one day, although she is one year older. Thank You for Your gracious gift of life, though I don't understand why it's slipping from my mother and why You won't raise her up like Jesus always did, and forgive me if I do not feel badly enough about her illness. And if I'm permitted just one small request in the midst of all this, please make me rich. I'm sorry. I couldn't resist asking.

I am sure others are thinking thankful thoughts too, especially Mrs. Dougherty, two pews in front of me, a huge lady who would likely need two airplane seats if ever she went anywhere. I'll bet she's thanking God for giving her the wherewithal to remain where she is and not excuse herself to go home and fix a thick salami sandwich with double cheese and a triple chocolate fudge brownie with extra icing, but to stick with carrot juice and celery stalks instead.

Tony is perpetually thankful. I know that from watching him. He can't help himself. It oozes from his pores, like garlic from Mr. Solynka.

My brother Ben, who told me that he gave up smoking last month, is probably thanking God for clean air and healthy lungs and thinking, Thank you, Lord, for allowing me to go twenty-eight days without a cigarette, it really hasn't been that hard, not so hard as they, uh, said it would be to uh, oh yes, to quit. I am glad that, uh, let's see, that my hands don't shake as badly as they did a few weeks ago, and I am thankful for coffee and for sunflower seeds, which give my hands something to do. Amen.

Could Dad possibly be thankful? If so, for what? Thank you that my wife may not see another Thanksgiving Day dinner? That I've got a full quiver, and more mouths than I can possibly feed and a job that pays me half what I'm worth?

But the most puzzling thing in all the world is this: That my father is the most grateful man I know. That he has less than anyone to look upon, yet he doesn't seem to know it. He believes that wealth has little to do with money, and he enumerates his blessings often, awakening and crowning each day this way. I've heard him say that laughter and joy grow best in the soil of thanksgiving, and that those who list their blessings daily will grow old with their wrinkles in the right places. And so he lives more in a week than most live in a lifetime, climbing above the valley floor these circumstances have planted him on.

Five

Secret

Winter comes early to these parts, blasting its way in from Canada like an old uncle you're not sure you wanted to see quite yet, the uncle who stayed longer than you thought he would last year and ate too many of your sugar cookies. By mid-November the fluffy white stuff abounds, bringing with it the promise of forts and snowballs and riding frayed inner tubes down the slopes of Mount Baldy—which isn't much of one. Last year on a dusky afternoon I hit a rather monumental stump on my way down and came to such an abrupt halt that I sat in stunned silence for a moment or two checking my limbs to make sure they still worked. Looking about me, I realized I'd just come within an inch of spending Christmas with the angels, and all I could think of was whether or not my friends had witnessed my clumsiness.

Snow foreshadows ice-skating and carol singing and candle making and makes possible the slipping of cold handfuls of the stuff down Mary Beth Swanson's slender neck as she screams with horrified delight. Of course a grown-up finds better ways to show affection, but at the time it was all I had.

I have often wondered what would have happened had I stayed away from the skating rink that fateful Saturday, the day my world changed forever. But I didn't. I tagged along behind Tony, who had beaten me to breakfast and was marching ahead of me to the ice rink, where he would be admired by girls and envied by boys like me whose dream it was to crack the National Hockey League.

I suppose that of all the world's loves, a brother's is the most out of this world. I would have applauded like no one else to see Tony make the big leagues or succeed at anything at all, for I adored him like no one else on earth. I don't think I ever told him so, though I wish I had now.

Tony taught me of history and geography—even Scripture, and he loved, among other things, palindromes, often passing me notes in church on which he had scribbled the latest he'd discovered or one that had to do with the sermon. "You can read them both ways," he wrote. "Try it. Read these sentences backwards: 'We panic in a pew.' See how it works? Try this one: 'Yaweh—the way.' Or how about 'Madam, I'm Adam.'" I studied them for a minute or three and then caught on. "Do geese see God?" was next, and I snickered on this one, drawing a disapproving glance from Dad. Undaunted, Tony passed me the bulletin and I turned it over. It said, "Sit on a potato pan, Otis," and "Go hang a salami; I'm a lasagna hog." Once, during a lengthy sermon, he handed me one that said, "My rear end is killing me." I tried to work it out backward, "em gnil lik sid nera erym," but it made no sense at all.

Not all of Tony's tutorage was impractical. He taught me to whistle when all I could think of was the painful way I had lost my tooth. He taught me to tread water the summer Danny O'Grady threw me into the deep end. And when winter entrenched itself in our landscape, he attached me to a hockey stick and began dragging me around the ice rink, holding onto some vain hope that his skills would rub off on me. He was a natural at most anything, was Tony, and some of it I managed to acquire. By the age of four, I'd mastered the art of gliding around the ice rink without wacking my forehead on the boards. By five I was standing by myself on hand-me-down skates, raising a rubber puck off the ice without having to stand it on edge. And now, at twelve, I imagine he is proud of me, though, like his younger brother, reluctance keeps him from saying so.

There are four seasons here: baseball, soccer, football, and hockey. And if you don't learn to ice-skate come winter, you turn into one of those pale, emaciated children who watch their friends through frosted windowpanes and have to be treated once a week for sniffles. We see snow of some sort almost every month of the year, so the rich own snowmobiles, and the only consolation the rest of us have as they whiz past us on their big fat Arctic Cats is that we are learning to skate, a healthier activity than just holding down the throttle. Small consolation. The truth is, it's not easy staring at happiness through another kid's eyes.

Our outdoor rink is surrounded by three-quarter-inch plywood erected in warmer times to stop pucks from escaping into deep snow banks. Eighty feet wide and two hundred feet long, the rink is shorter than the European versions but regulation for us. Adult administrators from Lone Pine Christian who seem to have nothing but time on their hands turn fire hoses on the frozen ground in late October, and within days it is a pristine sheet of glass, inviting us to carve sweet circles on its surface. The adults have to walk around the glass first, however, stomping it with thick boots, scrutinizing their work before admiration sets in. If they are particularly industrious, they will paint blue and red lines on it and then congratulate themselves over a thermos of hot chocolate.

When we are tuckered out from all the gliding, we lean over the boards and gaze across Franklin's Creek at the Independence Arena, the indoor rink where the pagans play. "Don't envy the man who has everything," my father often says. "He probably has an ulcer too." Ah, but what a sweet ulcer. The towering edifice was built to celebrate our town's hundredth anniversary. It boasts pipes in the ground able to freeze the ice long into March. And bleachers from which the pagan parents can watch their children play on Sunday mornings while we sit in church reminding ourselves that church is a much warmer place but not nearly so warm as the place the pagans are going one day.

We are forbidden to enter the Independence Arena in a section called "Athletic Competition" on page sixty-three of the Lone Pine Christian School Handbook that each student is to sign indicating they have read and will adhere to its principles, God helping them. Signing that statement was the first time I had put a lie in writing, but I did look up certain rules from time to time to research the rationale and soothe my conscience. This excerpt is from chapter III, paragraph two, subsection C:

> Upon recommendation of the administration, students are required to refrain from entering the local arena on account of expense and reputation. It is a place many young people learn to smoke and swear and develop bad associations. We hold our children to higher standards. The outdoor rink is a suitable substitute. We ask those who would challenge this rule to remember that outdoor activity is better for you, builds stamina, and is good for the lungs. For energetic youngsters, we strongly recommend as a substitute for league play enrollment in our intramural program. Please remember Paul's words to Timothy: "Bodily exercise profiteth little" (1 Timothy 4:8).

On our sheet of glass, on our side of town, the big guys have a hoot playing shinny and little kids like me get to skate around the boards and try out our slap shots in hopes that girls are watching and will be duly impressed—unless we fall flat on our backsides. Today I'm hoping that Mary Beth Swanson will be there with that tight little figure skating outfit that I can't believe they let her wear. She should be in the Olympics, she skates so well. She's pretty as can be. And a Christian too. When she shows up, I admit my mind isn't entirely on hockey.

The only other times we cease our frenzied activity are when someone appears to be badly injured, lying there like they are gasping their last, or when the gloves come off and a fistfight breaks out. We crowd around taking sides, watching in amazement as teenagers who sometimes teach us Sunday school punch each other's lights out. It doesn't happen often, but if we are really lucky we catch them using words we have read on the skate shack wall. Words that get painted over within hours but tend to stay with a twelve-year-old kid awhile. Probably the worst language I've heard came along when some of the pagans showed up one afternoon a few years ago and Matthew Jennings, a foul-mouthed pagan who smelled bad and had no business being on our rink, began knocking smaller kids into the boards. My brother Ben grabbed him by the throat and told him to stop or else. "Or else what?" mocked Matthew in a pinched-off voice. I was shocked to hear Ben start swearing right back. He looked so mad you could fry an egg on his forehead, and before you could blink the two of them dropped their gloves and slugged it out. I can see them yet, standing toe-to-toe, belting each other until both were dripping blood and Matt's glasses were a permanent part of his smile.

The skate shack is a humble two-room structure with wire-guarded windows and a locked equipment room in the back. The building looks like it was built by someone who had been thinking a lot about the Rapture of the Church, someone who wasn't planning on staying around to get much use out of it. Clapboard siding torn from an old barn leaks light and heat. The floor is mostly slivers from rounded two-by-sixes, and the walls wear various shades of hospital green, marked up by older kids using hockey pucks for pencils. Sometimes I watch them etch hearts with arrows and initials in them. Once I saw Brian Shelton and Mickey Hanson write threatening things like, "We comin' for you, Mutha," or "Danny Macintosh is Dead Meat!" (the D and M underlined).

Lunch is tomato soup today—not exactly what a hungry boy craves after a morning ice-skating, but Tony finds some soda crackers to give it "some protein." Afterward I beg him to return to the rink with me. "Give me a few more minutes," he says, sitting at the kitchen table rolling a lined sheet of paper into the Underwood.

"What are you doing?" I ask.

"Writing Matthew. Remember him?" His tongue sticks out as he plunks the keys on the typewriter.

I do remember. Matt Jennings, the same kid Ben beat up so badly at the rink, is now a jailbird, which stands to figure. At the tender age of nineteen he's already spent a year in prison for goodness knows what, and for some reason Tony's taken an interest in him. Calls him a pen pal, which makes sense, him being in prison. It's not new for Tony, this fraternizing with the enemy. He's always writing letters to who knows who, sitting at the pressed wood table, squinting at the typewriter. Some names he gets from popular magazines which feature a pen pals section, and he tells them about his faith. He also finds the most unconventional ways to witness. One Sunday he took a cheap radio transmitter he had assembled from spare parts, strung a little antenna to the ceiling, and plugged up the airwaves, blocking out Public Radio with Ralph Carmichael's "Sunday Sing" album. All over town people were livid, but Tony figured it was worthwhile, them hearing the gospel this way. He is pretty sharp when it comes to folks witnessing to him, as well. Last summer two Mormon missionaries came to town, and when they arrived at our house, Tony opened the door and pretended to be deaf. Just stood there, making up his own sign language, moving his lips a little. It was hotter than blazes as they stood there in sweaty suits. One said to the other, "I guess he's deaf," and they smiled and trudged off, adjusting their ties.

"Let's go," I say, craning my neck to read over his shoulder:

Dear Matt,

Thanks for your letter. I'm really sorry for the way this has turned out, and I want you to know I'll be praying for you. I'm gonna try to find a Bible to send you. Hope that's okay. Hope you like reading it. You should probably start in the book of John. And remember: The mind is like a parachute. It works best when it is open.

Sincerely, Tony

"Why would you send a letter to such a jerk?" I ask Tony as we hoist our sticks and skates over our shoulders and traipse along to the rink.

"Why not?" he says.

"I don't know. Just sounds strange, you writing an idiot like that. A guy in prison." The snow makes a scrunching sound as I walk on it.

"It's something I like to do," he says. "Actually, he wrote me first. Told me off something awful. Said he was coming to get me when he got out."

"He did?"

"I knew I had a choice. I could be scared, or I could do something. So I'm doing something. I think he just needs a friend. And I know he needs Jesus."

I just stop and stare as he walks on ahead. This crook's been written off by everyone but Tony. If my brother were a Catholic, he'd be a saint in no time.

<center>~~~</center>

The rest of the day cruises swiftly by despite Mary Beth's absence, and the sun is sinking fast on another afternoon in which I score an important goal into my own net and then shatter my stick on the boards. "I'll have to nail the darn thing together and tape it," I mutter out loud, amazed at my own stupidity, hopeful that no one heard my bad language. About five o'clock I sit in the skate shack, angry and alone, beneath a few slogans that have yet to be erased. Tony has gone home for supper and I am doing my best to join him, but my fingers are so frozen I cannot get a wiggle out of them. I cup my hands and blow on them. Soon they are loose enough to tug at my skate laces a little. But the knot is stubborn. At first I consider leaving the laces done up. I could easily skate the two blocks home on icy roads, but I risk ruining my already badly rusted skate blades. Besides, I've lost enough games for one day, and I'm not about to let a stupid knot beat me. Pulling this way and that, I realize that this is a job for Mr. Skate Tightener, a handy little gizmo my brother Ben crafted for me last Christmas.

Removing it from my pocket, I admire the sharp wire hook on one end. In no time I have the knot undone, but as I triumphantly pull my foot loose and slip on my boots, I see that the skate won't budge. It is wedged into the floor, standing by itself as if by some strange magic. Curious. When I wiggle it side to side, part of the floor wiggles with it, and when I stomp on the floor, it sinks as if to cave in. *Aha:* a trapdoor, about three feet square. Digging the skate tightener deep into one corner, I lift upward. The door opens easily enough.

Darkness jumps out at me, swallowing the pale light cast by two bare light bulbs on the ceiling. I close the lid with a bang. No way am I going down there. Not for any amount of money. Until I discover I've dropped the skate tightener.

Knowing full well that Ben will kill me if I lose it, I open the trapdoor again, prying it up with my rusted skate blade.

In subsequent years I have often marveled that the damsel in distress goes into the cornfield knowing that evil lurks there, that curiosity kills more than cats. Part of you wants her to go home and eat supper and read a book and go to bed. The other part of you knows that if she doesn't go into that cornfield or that attic or that cellar, the movie won't be worth watching.

I take a long look at the skate tightener. It is four feet down, lying in a bed of frozen muck. I try reaching it with my arm. I can't quite. I try picking it up with my hockey stick. It moves farther away.

So, like the damsel, I descend into the cornfield.

Which is to say that I get on my belly and drop my feet into the darkness, fishing for solid ground. It's musty smelling, as if you'd poked your head into an old root cellar, but not as frightening as I'd thought. The light from above falls around my shoulders, and I feel somehow brave, bigger than I am. I pick up Ben's gift with one hand and hold my nose with the other. Suddenly I see within spitting distance the outline of a large hockey bag, and as my eyes continue adjusting to the dim light, I can see that it's dark red with a Detroit Red Wings crest on the side.

It is obviously filled with hockey equipment, but who would leave it here, and why? Was someone playing a joke or evening a score? Are there skates in there? Are they less rusted than mine? I inch further into the cornfield, hoping to drag the bag into the light.

Taking hold of one corner, I pull. It won't budge.

I reef hard on it. Still it won't move.

My spine must be linked directly to my active imagination, for it begins to tingle. Suppose it's a body? Or parts of several. Or maybe just a bunch of heads. The Liberty County Jail isn't far from here, complete with twerps like Matthew Jennings. Real live murderers escape every once in a while. The tingling increases. If Mr. Tucker, our intrepid barber, had left any hair on my neck it would be standing on end, I'm sure. My brain tells me to run, but curiosity has me by the collar. I unzip the top of the bag, close my eyes, and reach timidly inside.

As my hand touches the first one, I let out the breath I am holding and draw a fresh one. Nothing in all my life has prepared me for what I find.

Six

Checkers

They feel like books at first. Small ones. Like those you'd feel at the library if you closed your eyes and ran your fingers over a stack of paperbacks. What are they doing here? Are they valuable? Are they forbidden, like the ones I found in Ben's dresser drawer once, concealed inside a school notebook? I pull one out and squint at it. This is no book. This is Abraham Lincoln staring expressionless at my right ear from a stack of bills. Five-dollar bills to be precise, bound together by a thick red rubber band.

All these years later I can't remember my reaction entirely, but my mouth drops open, I'm sure. I kneel there, staring at the president's face, speechless. Opportunity is a bird that seldom lands near me. You couldn't surprise me more if you told me the Pope was coming to speak in our church. I believe it was William Blake who said, "No bird soars too high if he soars with his own wings," and I am soaring now on wings of my own discovery. I want to yell. I want to laugh. I want to kick up some dust and dance as they do at the liberal church across town. What's more, I'd like to know how much money is in there.

Standing up, I hunch over and kick the side of the bag as you would the tire on a car. *"Man oh man!"* I gasp audibly. Either the bag is cemented into place, or it is unreasonably heavy. How much money does it take to turn a hockey bag into an immovable object? More than a kid can spend, that's for sure.

Well, I've always wanted to be rich. I've prayed to be rich. And I've heard it said that the Lord provides in mysterious ways. But this is beyond my most extravagant imaginings.

Suddenly the skate house door opens, and I hear footsteps tramping across the floor in my direction. I stuff the money back quickly as if it will bite me and the feeling creeps back up my spine. The trapdoor is open. I'll be caught.

The footsteps move the other way. I follow their sound intently with my eyes, from the entrance to the south end of the shack and over to the equipment room. I am breathing again. The padlock jangles, and whoever it is lets himself in. I take one more look at the bag to make sure I'm not dreaming and then hurry over to the trapdoor and pull myself up. Within moments the floor looks exactly as it has for years.

Footsteps crunching on the snow outside offer a brief warning before the door bursts open again. It is my brother Tony, poking his head in. "Hurry up," he growls, the irritation in his voice hard to miss. "Supper's on the table. We're waiting."

"Coming." I zip up my jacket and pull on my gloves. "My lace was messed up."

"What happened to your pants?"

"Oh…I fell," which isn't exactly a lie.

"Fell?" he says, but lets the matter drop as Mr. Peters comes out of the equipment room and greets us. "Howdy boys," he says, looking directly at my right ear. Maybe he's the thief. He never looks at you straight on.

I don't say much on the way home, and if Tony looks me in the eye he'll know enough to ask why.

"Poor Dan is in a droop," he says, out of the blue.

"Huh?"

"It's a palindrome," he laughs, getting no response from me.

"Cat got your tongue?"

"Is that a palin-whatever, too?"

"Nope," he replies. "Just wondering why you're so quiet."

"Oh."

"Uncle Roy's here for dinner. Betcha he'll stay a month."

"Oh." Uncle Roy, who eats my sugar cookies.

"Beat you to the house."

He does. Easily.

—⟋⟍—

Dinner is potato soup, which comes as no surprise. I can smell it while I take off my snow-enshrouded boots and place them atop a fresh section of newspaper. It is the entertainment section, and I look at the forbidden movies: *Rocky, Taxi Driver, Logan's Run.*

No one brews potato soup as thickly as does my sister. Chunks of potato the size of your eyeball floating around in a thick oniony broth—slightly burnt. All these years later I can still taste them.

Some nights we hear potatoes and carrots sizzling in the fry pan. If it is early in the month, Liz sprinkles chopped liver and onions atop them. She has resorted to some rather silly ways of avoiding the adverse effects of onion chopping lately. Once I discovered her clutching a pair of unlit matches between her teeth, tears streaming down her face. When she spit the matches into the sink, she had some harsh things to say about the advice offered in *Good Housekeeping.* I've also seen her cut onions under cold running water, and when this didn't succeed, she began freezing the onions first, but to no avail. "Life is an onion," says Dad. "You peel back the layers, and sometimes you cry."

Uncle Roy is there all right. Mom's one remaining sibling shows up when you least expect him, and ever since I can remember he has smelled like a giant mothball, an odor he alone seems to appreciate. He wraps his old gray clothes in them I guess, which is a little optimistic of him, to think that moths would want them.

I smile politely. "Hi, Uncle Roy." At Christmastime he brings a boatload of gifts, but it's a little early this year.

Liz calls everyone to the table and doesn't interrupt as Ben offers me a small piece of his mind. Mom isn't up to eating with us tonight, but Uncle Roy is eager.

"God is great, God is good, and we thank Him for this food. Amen," we say in metered unison, holding hands. I have yet to see Ben close his eyes during prayer, and Uncle Roy bows his head with the rest of us, though he doesn't pray along either. After the amen he eyes the soup and tells us how he will be heading back to Minneapolis soon, though he has yet to make concrete plans.

I dip homemade bread into the broth and munch contentedly, my mind in another place.

It's obvious what's right when it comes to the money. I know what I'll do with it, but what a shame.

Wouldn't it be nice if we were able to afford cheese to grate over this? Or real butter to lather the bread.

But then again, perhaps my vision is too small.

Suppose that tomorrow night the family arrived to a meal I had flown in from Seattle. Wouldn't their eyes go wide! Just imagine four chefs in white hats scurrying around the table pulling stainless steel covers off trays heaped with steaming lobster. Shrimp on a bed of long rice, some of them battered, some fried. Shucked oysters. Crab legs marinated in garlic butter, succulent scallops dripping with cream, and the chefs pouring the world's finest apple cider (wine is out of the question) from tall bottles into crystal goblets that go clink when you flick them with your finger. *Mama mia!* Wouldn't I be the toast of the family?

Then again, both my brothers hate seafood.

So how about a table laden with wild boar, its mouth stuffed with apple, the rest of it surrounded by fruit? Mangos. Japanese oranges. Kiwis. Maybe a pheasant on the side. Or buffalo burgers with fries and gravy. Or venison. I'd heard that was good. It comes from Australia, I think. How about Mom, sitting in a soft wheelchair with a fancy van to get her anywhere she wants? Maybe her own personal doctor who lives here and a maid to wash our clothes and get me snacks. The old times would be back—the long desserts, the laughter.

"Did I ever tell you about the time I lost an eye?" Uncle Roy is sitting next to me poking at his soup, and apparently it has reminded him of something. Liz glances at Dad and raises her eyebrows. "Yes, I believe you have," she says loudly, hoping to compensate for Roy's hearing deficiency, something I'd heard Dad say wasn't so much a hearing disorder as a listening one.

"So, like I was saying" (my uncle begins most of his sentences this way, even when he hasn't been saying anything for hours), "Sherman Schultz, who lived up at the old Wilms place, got me with a slingshot he made hisself. I was only eight. About your age," he says, patting my knee.

I thrust forth my tiny chest. "I'm twelve," I say, wondering how I got from Seattle to here so soon.

"Came so fast I barely blinked. Entered the corner of my eye and popped the eyeball clean out. I held it in my hand, you know? But there was no saving it. I could still see with it for a minute while it was in my hand, but it's not like a finger or anything. Carpenters pick 'em out of the sawdust and keep cuttin.'"

Uncle Roy clears his throat, which seems to need even more clearing than last year. I've heard the eyeball story before, but never at supper. I am ready for the customary warning against playing with slingshots. Or bows and arrows and sharp sticks. But the warning isn't issued this night.

"So, like I was saying, I don't know if you've ever seen the eyeball cavity. This one was a mess. Not as bad as the time my appendix attacked me and burst all over the place, mind you, but still it was pretty messy."

I set my fork down, the soup having lost much of its initial appeal. Ben has the same idea. But not Tony. He seems to thrive on such things. I watch in disgust as he eagerly cleans his bowl, thrusts it out for more, and asks Uncle Roy what happened next.

And so came the tale of how my bachelor uncle had been playing the violin at church when suddenly he dropped the violin with a crash and fainted dead away right in the middle of "The Old Rugged Cross." The doctor who removed the appendix found it to be unusually yellow with a trace of green and told him it was a miracle he'd survived at all. "Did you know that doctors sometimes leave stuff in their patients when they sew 'em up?" Uncle Roy asks, as if someone will care to answer. "It happens more to fat patients because there's more room to lose equipment."

Liz has already taken the empty bread plate to the kitchen to reload and commences to bang cupboard doors as if looking for something important. I'm sure she is praying our uncle will forget about his appendix.

"Have you ever seen an appendix?" Uncle Roy has forgotten lots of things, but not the gory details of the various maladies he's suffered over the years. "Like I was saying, they pickle them now, you know. For research. They're not that big, about the size of a potato."

Well, that pretty much ends supper for me, while ensuring that my mothball uncle and Tony have all the soup they want, eyeballs and all.

—⁓—

When Liz and I have washed and dried the dishes and I've snapped a wet towel at her hindquarters more than once, I am sentenced to an evening indoors where I am to finish some homework and play checkers with Uncle Mothball.

"So, like I was saying, how you doing, boy?"

"Pretty good."

He takes his hand from a king I've just crowned for him and winks at me. "You wanna see something?"

My answer won't much matter.

He pulls up his mothballed shirt, turns a little and proves to me that the appendix story is not fabricated, that the long line of stitches is for real.

Only once in my life did Uncle Roy beat me at checkers. This is the night. I can't remember the last time I let him corner my lone king, and it isn't only on account of listening to more talk of eyeballs and burst appendixes, though that would be reason enough. No, I am thinking of the money and wondering if it will still be there tomorrow. And though my uncle never lets things get dull around here, my stomach is growling loudly, thanks to him, and I must confess that I have begun speculating on how many of those paperbacks a one-way plane ticket to Minneapolis would cost me.

—⁓—

The money is there all right, salted away, just as I left it the night before. I unzip the bag just to make sure, terrified that it has somehow vanished. I start pulling it out by the fistful, even rolling up a tight wad of it and peeking through the center as if it were a telescope and I a rich astronomer.

I listen for footsteps, and when none materialize, I get down to business, separating the plunder into piles: ones, fives, tens. A small heap of twenties. Some are stacked already, fastened together with rubber bands. Some are flat and new, others old and wrinkly. The one-dollar bills form the largest stack, higher than a loaf of bread before kneeding. I begin counting out the tens, and when I reach five hundred dollars, I let out a stifled gasp and begin stuffing them back into their rightful spot.

I have scarcely made a dent in the pile.

I grab one with Andrew Jackson on it, stuff the twenty into my pocket and creep cautiously outside for air.

It is Sunday afternoon now, so the rink is empty. A few broken sticks lie around the edges of the ice surface, a glove here, a hat there. My head feels suddenly dizzy, like I've just stood up too quickly after a week in bed. When finally I quit chewing my fingernails and sit down on a wooden step to think, a drop of sweat trickles down my forehead, plunges from my nose and lands *splat* on the dusty toe of my sneaker. Remarkable, considering how cold it is.

Well, what would you do if you were wearing my shoes?

You can't just pretend the money isn't there, can you? It's calling your name for crying out loud. It draws you like flies to a pig farm. You can't just take it home, drop it on the table and say, "Hey, look what I found today. What's for supper?"

You know what to do, don't you? You must tell someone imme-
diately and get it over with. But thoughts creep into your head.
Thoughts you've not entertained before but dearly hoped you
would one day. Not even your brother's palindromes can keep
them out. Not "Ma is a nun, as I am," or "Ned, go gag Ogden," or
even "Cigar? Toss it in a can, it is so tragic."

Nothing works.

I thrash about in bed with two voices jousting around my head,
medieval audiences on either side of them, cheering their view-
points.

"We will tell Dad first thing in the morning. That's what we'll
do. We've taken twenty dollars, but we haven't spent it. We'll just
hand it to him. Get it over with."

"We will not, Dumbo. We will keep the money right where it
is, spend it on good things, like…well, like…hmmm…well, perhaps we can tithe some of it to the church. We'll do fifteen percent.
Maybe twenty."

"Are you kidding? We will go to the police station with Dad
once we've given him the twenty. That won't be so bad."

"What, are you crazy? They'll never believe us. They'll think
we stole it. They'll lock us up with Matthew Jennings, who will
beat us to a pulp."

"Be quiet. It doesn't matter. Who said doing the right thing
was easy?"

"Well, give it some thought, but don't say I didn't warn you."

The voices are silent now. But the thoughts still linger. Imagine
the things I could do with a zillion dollars.

My forehead wrinkles as the questions engulf me. Who would
leave a fortune like that in such a place? But if I take it, where will
I put it? What if someone else discovers it too? What if it's stolen
money and the thieves find out I've taken it and come looking

for me? Shall I grab it before they grab me? Will they bury *me* below the skate shack too? Bury me alive with a tiny air hole and a hostage note that was never sent?

This much I'm certain of: If I give the money to the police I'll never see it again. And it's mine, isn't it? Possession is how much of the law?

Such are the thoughts that battle me for sleep this Sunday night, and when I do drift off at last, I dream I am playing checkers with Uncle Roy, who is completely naked and covered in stitches. The checkers are made of dragon gold I found buried deep within the mountains.

When I awake the dream is more real than reality itself. I would sooner believe in dragons than believe that I, Terry Anderson, twelve years old, am the richest man in town. My whole world has been radically altered. The floor has tipped, the mirrors have tilted. If Tony, my palindromic brother, were writing it for me on the church bulletin it might look like this: "Are we not drawn onward we few, drawn onward to new era?"

—ɷ—

Breakfast never tasted better.

I add extra sugar to my oatmeal porridge before Dad notices, and I begin to consider the day ahead. School will complicate my plans for sure, but I now know what I will do with the money. I am grinning and chuckling to myself.

Sometimes you have to go out on a limb. That's where the fruit is.

I will spend the money, of course. What do you think I am, a fool?

Seven

School

Shool has always been an eternity for me, a restless roaming of my imagination, sometimes interrupted by an interesting anecdote from the teacher. Never more so than on this day. School lasts a week this Monday morning. Math class trudges stubbornly toward science, which ambles its way into a lull our teacher calls geography. Important discoveries by Aristotle, Newton, and Christopher Columbus are lost on me. *Discoveries? I'll tell you about discoveries.* If only I could stand before the class—I'd give them a show and tell they wouldn't soon forget. Instead, I pull an HB pencil from my pocket and doodle a snowmobile on lined paper. *Ah, the things I will buy.* I have already visited the skate shack, which is conveniently located right on my way to school, and my pocket is bulging.

Today begins like every other school day at Lone Pine Christian —with Bible reading and prayer. Our teacher, Miss Ursula Hoover, paces before us, reading the Gospel of Luke in preparation for the soon-coming Christmas program and then invites our prayer requests and inscribes them on the blackboard in immaculate penmanship. Her strokes are heavier on the downswing, which turns mere prayer requests into works of art. Sarah Stuart's sister has asthma and her aunt has shingles, which she is asked to explain. Joan Foster's cousin is arriving a few days before Christmas, and she doesn't think he knows the Lord. Michael Swanson almost always has a request. Today he is concerned for one of his cows that is deathly sick and maybe pregnant. Some of the girls snicker when he says this, and Miss Hoover shushes them. I know for a fact that Michael doesn't even have a cow, and I sit here wondering what God does with phony requests. Does He block them out somehow? Does He smile? Or get mad? Will He punish Michael one day? I am quite certain He will, and I wonder what that will look like. Will Michael remain the shortest kid in the class all his life? Will he contract one of the diseases he is always asking prayer for, or merely be smitten with bad acne?

On one occasion when Michael was asked to lead us in prayer, he consumed a full fifteen minutes, delaying mathematics by working his way around the world. By the time he arrived in Africa, he was praying for missionaries whose existence was doubtful, people with names like Ezra Nehemiah, and Esther Job, until finally our frustrated teacher stood up and exclaimed, "Amen!" thereby putting an end to one of the most entertaining prayers ever offered at Lone Pine Christian. Michael sat down reluctantly as if he was expecting a standing ovation. Never was he asked to pray again, though he volunteered often, particularly on test days.

For reasons I still can't explain I raise a hand and tell Miss Hoover that I have an unspoken request, something I've never done before and which irritates me badly when other children do it. What could be so awful that you wouldn't talk about it? Have you done something to someone that is too terrible to mention? Did you have bad thoughts? And if it was unspoken, why would you speak it in the first place?

A metal chain keeps the lid on my desk from collapsing forward onto Danny Brown's pointy little head, which bobs in front of me, offering a tempting target for sighting in my spit wad shooter. Sometimes I stick the big gobs to the ceiling right above him, and one day Miss Hoover saw them hanging there, all dried up. Though Danny blamed me, she insisted she knew who was responsible and had him stand in the corner until he admitted it. I waited in the hallway as he climbed a ladder and chipped them off after school.

The apology was important, I thought, because, though Danny attends our school, he is a pagan if ever there was one and it's important that I be a good testimony to him. His father is a real live atheist—the only one I've ever met. Although I was surprised to find that no horns grew from his head and a forked tail was nowhere to be seen, Mr. Brown is no poster man for atheism either. His beady eyes are small and pouched, like a bullfrog's, and his chin is like a weasel's, running right into his neck without stopping. Mr. Brown sends his son to our Christian school partly to honor the late Mrs. Brown, who died before Danny was old enough to really know her, and partly because Danny was kicked out of the public school and he'd rather the child not hang around the house by himself, although he lives on our side of the creek and would be perfectly safe here.

While the others pray, heads diligently bowed, eyes dutifully closed, I sneak a peek at the row of painted presidents above the blackboard. Lincoln is in the middle, wedged between Washington and Jefferson, who is hanging a little crooked. I'd met Mr. Lincoln up close and personal yesterday. In fact, he seemed to have struck the same pose for the five-dollar bill—not exactly frowning, but not exactly happy either. Perhaps he was impatient having to sit for both the penny and the five-dollar bill, to say nothing of the responsibilities that came with the presidency. I wonder if his friends teased him for having a beard but no moustache, and if he himself had combed the wisp of dark hair that lay across his forehead. I reach for the wad of fives in my pocket to compare.

They are gone.

I reach into my other pocket. Nothing.

I grope for my shirt pocket but my shirt doesn't have one. My desk lid squeaks so I dare not check in there during prayer.

I peek under the desk. Sure enough. How clumsy of me. It must have come out with the pencil.

Danny Brown's foot has corralled the bills and pulled them forward. Reaching down, he picks them up, wide-eyed. I grab his shoulder. Hard.

"Yours?" he whispers, thrusting them my way.

I snatch them from his grasp.

He cranes his neck to look at me, thunderstruck at the goldmine in my hand. I lean forward. "Close your eyes, we're praying," I whisper, and stuff the roll into my pocket. Danny puts his head back on his desk and I squint at the presidents again, hoping their collective gaze will calm my thumping heart.

George Washington is my favorite, but his hair is funny, almost like he'd had it in curlers when they took the picture. Was he miffed at being caught this way? Was he upset with only being on the *one*-dollar bill? Jefferson, our third president, is a handsome man and comes the closest of the three to breaking a smile. None have their mouths open. Did they have bad teeth? Did they forget to brush? Did their mothers remind them often enough? Why didn't they smile? Had they been told there is no humor in the Bible, like Miss Hoover sometimes says? "Be sober," is her favorite Bible verse and is beautifully hand-crafted on our blackboard.

Miss Hoover loves to point at each of the presidents and introduce something they once said to illuminate her point. Like the time she informed us of Benjamin Franklin's words: "Three men can keep a secret if two of them are dead," and then launched into a discussion of gossip, looking often at a few of the girls.

At recess I have some explaining to do. "It's my mom's. I'm supposed to get her some stuff after school." This is good enough for Danny. The little atheist saunters off to a kick baseball game that has already entered its second inning. It is the only type of baseball winter allows us, and I love the game. Love driving the soccer ball with my foot when it is pitched hard by an eighth-grader, then diving head-first into second, which is buried in a foot of snow. But my mind is on other things now. How long will it take to get to Ying's Corner Store? Can I make it back before science class? Why not? Thoughts of candy have me running faster than ever I thought I could. The icy wind blows through my thick hair and excitement surges through my tiny body.

Things will get better than this, of course. But this is enough for now.

—⁓—

Mine is a maple desk with slivery feet, iron scrollwork on the sides, and an inkwell filled in clumsily with a lighter-grained wood. The inside of the lid bears the artwork of my bored predecessors who once carved their initials alongside slogans like "Brian slept here" and "Rosalie McCoy, I love you. Don't go." Everyone knows Rosalie's story, how she had died of bone cancer, her parents unable to afford the right treatments. But no one could say for sure who had written the words. In some way they were from all of us, I suppose. How I wish I had all this money a year ago. Maybe I could have done something for Rosalie.

I push some books aside and my ring of Bible memory verse cards too and then start shoveling candy by the handful from my jacket pocket. Four necklaces. A bag of cinnamon hearts. Twenty

Tootsie Rolls. Twenty packages of SweeTarts. Two small paper sacks filled with sixty Mojos, three for a penny. Two Mars Bars, a Snickers, a Baby Ruth. The desk will overflow if I'm not careful. I've spent less than three dollars, but it is all I dared buy without being obvious. As it is, I rustle when I walk. The pockets of my jackets and pants are ready to burst. Any more and I'll look like a toddler in a snowsuit.

I tap Danny on the shoulder as Miss Hoover begins the arduous task of bringing our science textbook back to life. "Thanks for giving the money back," I say quietly, leaning forward. "Here's your reward." I hand him a necklace laden with sour pastel candies and know I have made a friend for life.

Dave Hofer taps me from behind. "How about some back here?" I hesitate for a moment because Dave is not my favorite friend of late. For one thing, he is bilingual, speaking fluent pig latin, an ability that irritates me to no end. "Utway areway ooyay ooingday?" means "What are you doing?" but how am I supposed to know? Whenever he uses it I feel like clubbing him. It is juvenile and I tell him so.

"Oh ya?" he says, "then if you're so mature why don't you say something in pig latin?"

I say, "Ouya areway an idiotay," and end up getting clubbed myself.

Despite all of this, I pass him a handful of SweeTarts as a symbol of truce. In exchange, he hands me a note. It is written in English, and he has written it himself.

> When you eat your toe jam,
> Don't wipe it on your clothes,
> Just slurp it down real fast
> As you pick it from your toes.

For it's jammed with bugs and protein,
It's best when it is green,
So always eat your toe jam
And you'll grow up fat and clean.

Before I can clap my hands over my mouth I am laughing too hard, and before I know it I am standing silent before the class, stuffing the note into my pocket.

Miss Hoover is a kind-faced woman, though she rarely smiles, perhaps on account of the bun in her hair being drawn so tight. She is uncommonly thin and wears dark stockings with a seam up the back. "She's strict," someone said to me once, and that's what I thought the word meant: You wear that style of stocking, you're strict. My brother Ben enjoys telling of the day Miss Hoover held a folding chair up in art class and told the students to draw the curves and angles as they saw them, and Ben was asked to stand in the corner for laughing so hard over that one. When Wendy Pike and Ronny Green were caught in close proximity near the drinking fountain one recess, she scolded the whole class. "There's been some kissing going on right underneath my nose," she reprimanded. Ben had to stand in the corner again for snorting so loudly. I got the second joke but not the first, and I try not to think of things that will make me laugh as I stand before her today.

"If it's so funny, Terry, why don't you share it with the class?" Miss Hoover says, looking me over like a general inspecting the sorry troops. I stand at rapt attention and don't budge.

"You are chewing gum, Terry. Take it out. Put it in the wastebasket."

I obey.

"If you are going to chew gum, you will bring enough for the whole class." She smiles at the impossibility of this one, but I know better, so I join her in smiling. Her face snaps back to its former state of sobriety.

"Why are you wearing your jacket in class, Terry?" she asks, not waiting for the answer. "Empty your pockets on the table," she commands, expecting prompt compliance. What am I to do? Run from the room screaming? I empty my pockets. More Tootsie Rolls. More SweeTarts. More of everything. And a note which flutters like a badly designed paper airplane to the floor. Miss Hoover lets out a soft gasp at all the candy, then points toward the note. I double over and pick it up. "Read it for us," she commands, strolling over to her desk and leaning against the edge of it, knowing she has me trapped.

I hold the note before me, look up at a horrified Dave Hofer, and then begin to read: "And it came to pass in those days that there went out a decree from Caesar Augustus that all the world should be taxed. And all went to be taxed, every one into his own—" Miss Hoover interrupts me. "That will do," she says, rising to her feet. "I don't know what you are finding so funny back there, Terry Anderson, but you will stay after school for half an hour today. We'll see how funny you find that to be."

I return to my desk, smiling at Dave Hofer and wishing I had the nerve to wink at some of the girls. It's exhilarating, you know— being shot at without being hit.

—⁂—

The gates of Lone Pine Christian give way at three-thirty P.M. (four o'clock for me), releasing a landslide of pent-up energy and mischievous inmates. Many of the children stream into noisy buses whose drivers are eager to sprinkle them throughout the nearby farms. A small cluster of kids from our side of the creek stays to

throw snowballs at moving targets on the playground. They stop
when I approach. For once no one pastes me with an ice ball.

"Hey, do you want something?" I say. They do. Boy, do they
ever. Eagerly they hold forth their hands, like baby robins with
their beaks open. I am their benefactor, giving to those in need,
helping out where I can. Rarely have other children seen such
generosity and never have they been so kind to me.

Michael Swanson, who can pray so eloquently but can also
squeal on you with the best of them, is unusually polite. He even
asks how I am doing and tells me how good a hockey player I am
and that he thinks I have real potential.

"So you still got that old Ski-Doo snowmobile for sale?" I ask
after the others have gone back to packing snowballs.

"Yup," says Michael, looking at my pockets, searching for tell-
tale bulges.

I flip a Mojo in the air and watch him stuff it in his beak. "Is
it any good?"

"It's old, but it's a Bombardier with a 250 engine, so it goes
like stink. We just put a new seat bottom on it, you know. Goes
like the dickens."

"How much you want for it?"

"Oh, I don't know. Two hundred bucks, I guess. It belongs to
my dad."

I am not thinking of where I will park it or where I will say it
came from. I only know how badly I've wanted one all these years.
"Tell him I'd like it," I say. "I'll bring the money tomorrow. It's...
uh...for my brother, you know—he's been lookin' for one."

On the way home I visit the skate shack to check on the loot.
The place is teaming with children, so I pretend to be warming
my hands, and then I saunter over to check on the trapdoor, which
seems to have gone undetected. I stop at the Tastee Freeze once

again to buy a bottle of Coke and stuff it in my pocket. Once home, I will pour it into a glass, drop a quarter in it, and see if it's true what they say, that the quarter will be eaten overnight.

When I tromp through the front door and stamp the snow from my feet, Mother is waiting with a big question mark on her face. It's a rare thing these days to see her out of bed.

"Had a call from Miss Hoover," she begins.

I know the rest, so I think up excuses as she questions me about all the candy.

"I found some money," I tell her. I haven't lied quite yet, have I?

"Five dollars." I still haven't lied. Not really.

"I guess I should have told you about it, huh?"

Mother nods her head. She explains that if I find something as huge as a five-dollar bill, that doesn't make it mine. That possession is really not nine-tenths of the law.

"What if I find a penny?" I ask.

She smiles. That is okay, she thinks. But five dollars is a lot of money, and I should have told her and dad about it. They would have taken it to the principal and had an announcement made, something I would need to do with the remainder.

"What if I find more?" I am prodding a little.

"Did you?"

This is getting tricky. "I wish," I smile, which seems to satisfy her.

"Well, if you ever find more than that, we would take it to the police."

"What would they do?" I'm trying not to appear overly interested.

"I'm not sure exactly. They keep it awhile—two weeks, I think—and if no one claims it, the finder gets to keep it."

"Oh."

"Did you find a wallet with the money?" she asks.

I report that I hadn't. "Is Liz doin' liver for supper?" I ask. I can already smell it, but I'm not hungry. Not one little bit.

Two roads converged in a wood, and I have taken both, trying my best to straddle and balance and dodge and hide, hoping all the while for a merge sign.

—⚊—

Though the school hours drift slowly, the week speeds by, with me waffling back and forth. It's not too late to turn the money in. Or is it? I am dying to ask someone a little more about it, but how? And who?

Michael's dad needs to tune up the snowmobile, so I have to wait, something I'm not much good at these days. I pass the time dreaming of the minibike I'll ride come summertime and sneaking off to the trapdoor, to which I have cleverly tied a string so I can tell if my treasure has been tampered with.

I'm not sleeping as much as I'd like to, with all these decisions to be made, and my homework has suffered for it. On Saturday night, after chores are finished, Dad insists I stay in to catch up. It is too late to go out anyway, and thinking up an excuse good enough to visit the skate shack seems impossible. "I left something there" doesn't sound quite right, and I am hoping to avoid telling any more lies than I must. "Michael Swanson wants to meet me" might work, but what if my mother calls his mother? Deceit is a crooked business. Tricky too.

Homework is a poetry assignment, due yesterday, so I sit down at the kitchen table, chewing on the eraser end of a pencil and hoping it will help me think of some options. My sister is sweeping the floor and keeps whacking my feet even when I move them. I pretend to stab her with the pencil and then throw it at her. She picks it up, snaps the lead from it, and hands it back.

"Dad, Liz broke my pencil," I squeal, which is exactly what Michael Swanson would do. Dad is in the other room and doesn't seem to hear.

I chew on the bottom until I find some lead. Should I write of big sisters, of ice hockey, of flowers? Would Miss Hoover dock me marks if I start out "I really hate my sister, she's fat and she is mean"? How about romance or tragedy or something about dogs? Those had worked before. I try a few of these themes, but they end with eraser shards scattered all around me. My heart isn't in it. All week my mind has been filled with one thing and one thing only.

So I sharpen the pencil with a blunt kitchen knife and sit back down to write about it. I title the poem "Rich Little Poor Kid," writing my name carefully below the title, and begin.

> I found a briefcase full of money
> Just the other day.
> I will not tell you where
> Because I'll give the place away.
> I snatched it up real fast,
> Grabbed it quickly with my hand,
> And hiked to Florida
> With its beaches full of sand.
>
> I bought a great big house
> And a car I like to drive,
> I ate from stainless steel
> And was glad to be alive.
> I lived there on the beach

With a one-eyed hound named Mike,
I sailed a yacht named Charlie,
And I owned a motorbike.

At the door in dark black suits
Came two men that awful day,
They grabbed me from my bed
And swore they'd make me pay.
They said, "We're Slim and Jim
And we hear you got our money,
So we've come to break your legs,
You won't think it very funny."

Well, I'm glad I knew karate
And a few more Chinese words,
And I'm glad my Doberman awoke
To chew those awful nerds.
And I'm pleased to live in Spain now
Where I eat Spam and I snore
While my great big dog named Mike
Keeps one eye upon the door.

For all her whacking me with the broom, my sister truly is a kind soul. She listens as I read it to her and tells me how much she loves it and that if I don't get one hundred percent and a gold star she will come talk to Miss Hoover herself. We are brushing our teeth together in the bathroom mirror when she looks at me adoringly and inquires, "You think you'll be a poet one day, Tare?"

"I already am."

"No, really."

"I don't know." I search her face for any sign she may know my secret. "I think I'll be a pastor."

"What would you do if it just happened?"

"If what happened?" I am examining my front teeth, in case Mary Beth sits near me at church tomorrow.

"If you had that much money."

"I don't know. What about you?"

Liz adopts a faraway look. "Probably the same as the guy in the poem. I'd like to go someplace warm. I haven't been hot since August. And I think I'd buy something nice for Mom. A dress maybe. And groceries and stuff. There'd be more presents under the tree this year, that's for sure."

I snap the water from my toothbrush and set it down. "Liz, um…I wanna tell you something." My mind is whirling, wondering if I should.

Liz drops her toothbrush in the cup, brush-side up beside mine. "What is it, Tare?"

"Can you keep a secret?"

"Of course I can." I have her full attention now.

"I drew Ben's name for Christmas. I might get him a hunting rifle. An expensive one."

"Right," she says, rolling her eyes. "And I bet you'll be buying me that silver ring with my initials on it too. You know, the one in Penny's Jewelry."

—⋙—

I kneel beside my bed to pray. But instead I decide to pour the entire contents of the Coke bottle into a tall glass, slip the quarter into the fizz, and slide it beneath my bed. It could be a useful experiment if ever I need to make some money dissolve.

In the morning, the quarter looks fine—a little shinier perhaps, but none the worse for wear. I, on the other hand, haven't slept so well. I wish the Coke weren't so flat. I could use a stiff drink.

Eight

Guitar

This Sunday morning's guest speaker, Patrick Klassen, has arrived and is in the church foyer, standing beside a table laden with his book, *Satan's Plan for Your Kids,* subtitled *Drugs, Sex, and "Christian" Rock,* the *Christian* having been set apart in suspicious-looking quotation marks. I'm glad to see him here because it's not easy sitting through church wondering when our pastor is going to look directly at me and say, "Hey, Terry, why don't you stand and confess your sins to us? Start with the stealing, then get to the lying. Take your time now."

I know Pastor Davis is unlikely to stoop this low, but our previous pastor, Francis Frank, was certainly capable of such things. You never quite knew what was going to happen when he took to the pulpit. Certain memories linger, still keeping me on my toes. Like the time Reverend Frank stopped mid-sentence to rebuke some young parents, telling them to hurry up and take their screaming child to the "ballroom." He had no reservations about reprimanding a sleeping brother or a teenager chewing gum, or telling someone to sit back down when they likely had good reason to be slipping out to the restroom.

One Sunday about ten past eleven, he asked the Hudson family for a suitable explanation as to why they were late for church. He halted the singing to do this. An awkward silence settled upon the congregation rather quickly as Mrs. Hudson, who had lost her husband a year earlier and was not the sort of woman one should mess with, stood to her feet, gritting her pearly whites. "I believe the Lord takes more pleasure in a family that gets here ten minutes late having had a good morning of fellowship together," she offered pointedly, each word of her oration punctuated by an exclamation point, "than in one that shows up ten minutes early hating each other and acting like hypocrites in the parking lot." After a stony silence, Mort Wainbee, the song leader, clumsily suggested we return to singing "Blessed Assurance," but Pastor Frank did not look like his heart was in it.

On an unusually warm September day, Priscilla Knight got up to sing a rather lively version of "He's Got the Whole World in His Hands," and Reverend Frank rose behind her and tapped her shoulder after the verse about Him having the little bitty baby in His hands. As Miss Knight sat down, flustered and sweating and monumentally embarrassed, he launched into a diatribe against shallow lyrics and modern music.

Pastor Frank is a memory now, but the music debate has not subsided. To say it is a hot topic here is like observing that we have big skies on our side of the mountains or that there's a risk of a blizzard come January. I once overheard Dad observe to Mom that some of the deacons seem to find things in their Bibles that he has not yet encountered, things about the inherent evils of drums and amplifiers and loud music in general. Few issues have polarized our little flock like this one, causing nastiness to bubble to the surface with the stroke of a guitar pick. They say music is a gift, exalting our joys and allaying our grief, but it seems to me it also has the power to make folks around here roaring mad. One man's drum set can be another man's headache, I suppose.

"When David calmed Saul's woes with the harp," one elder pointed out during a particularly heated exchange at one board meeting (these things I learned later), "he did not use a guitar, and it was certainly not plugged in."

I remember well the night Tony and a legion of youth gathered behind the church for a hot dog roast and a record burning. It was mid-September, the same month of Priscilla Knight's final solo, I believe.

The youth group had been studying a book by Bob Larson called *Rock and Roll: The Devil's Diversion,* and those who had come under conviction brought with them shopping bags filled with popular albums, which made quite a pile stacked beside the fire, waiting until the hot dogs were consumed and the coals were just right. A friend and I came to spy through the fence, and though we found it necessary to shield our faces from the searing heat, we still managed to watch The Beatles' white album turn black, a Rolling Stones' record with a cake on the cover melt like icing, and a host of gold records by the Bee Gees, Johnny Cash, and Olivia Newton John go up in smoke. I couldn't believe how fast the vinyl melted, nor could I help but mentally calculate the fortune we could have sold them for and what we could have done with the money. "You don't sell something that's evil," Tony told me later when I posed the question. "You just cause the person who buys it to stumble."

"Couldn't you have helped poor people with the money? People like us?" I challenged him.

"I suppose. But what about the poor people who will buy those albums and be led astray?"

He had a point there, and I wasn't about to argue the matter further.

—⁓—

The first guitar I ever saw in church was brought there and strummed just a few short weeks ago by Louie Corzini, whom we nicknamed Noah. A lanky youth whose trousers never quite touched his shoes, Noah lugged a Gibson archtop to a Friday night young people's event that the pastoral staff managed to tuck neatly into the church basement. It was the first time the young people in our church had heard "O Happy Day" quite like that. Our youth pastor, Davie Foster, was so taken with the instrument that he asked Noah to give him lessons and decided to play it himself as soon as he had learned three chords, which happened to be the very next Sunday. Until this point in our congregational history, the organ and piano had always provided enough instrumentation, with the rare exception of a trumpet solo performed by Ronny Graham, who had a set of pipes and baggy cheeks Dizzy Gillespie would have died for.

The song Davie chose to sing that morning was not the most profound in our *Glad Tidings* hymnal by any stretch of the imagination. In fact, it never quite made it into the hymnal—not even the appendix. Just before Pastor Davis' sermon, Davie strode boldly to the microphone, the guitar hanging from his shoulders by a leather strap that said "Way Cool" in some fluorescent font. This should have been our first clue that the service was about to change gears.

"The Lord's been talking to me lately about the beauty of His Creation," proclaimed Davie, causing a number of people to stir uncomfortably and tug at their collars in hopes of circulating a little more air. Davie was big into hearing directly from God on a regular basis and he had encountered some harsh criticism for it during what seemed like a long six-week tenure as youth pastor. "Um" stammered Davie, "though we are in the middle of winter and there aren't a lot of them around, I was thinking that one of the first things God created was the bird because He wanted to have beautiful music, and so I think music is important and the Psalms talk about a joyful noise and about cymbals and drums and so I wrote this song with that in mind and I hope you like it, the Lord sort of gave it to me. I've asked Noah Corzini to play the bongo drums, so Noah, if you'd come up here, please." Davie strummed an A chord hard as Noah arranged the drums between his knees, and then Davie stopped, as if he'd forgotten something he'd planned on sharing.

"I wasn't able to sleep last night," he confessed, looking down at the Gibson, wishing he'd brought notes perhaps. "I guess because I was thinking about all the needs of the youth, so I got out of bed and just wrote down the words as they came to me, which happened in less than five minutes." He looked up expecting to witness amazement on our faces, as if his story provided ample evidence that miracles still happen. Instead, folks just stared at him suspiciously. And so, strumming a few more chords on the poorly tuned instrument, Davie closed his eyes and began to sing in a sweet tenor voice, switching quickly from A to E to D. Noah cocked his head and hammered out a rhythm.

> You are so wonderful.
> I see You in the flowers,
> I see You in the trees,
> You are so wonderful, oh yes, oh yes.

I could have listened to Davie sing for an hour, the way he put such intense feeling into each note, but as he continued to sing, substituting birds, bees, sand, leaves, flowers, rain, and wind, I realized I was in the minority. Aubrey Fletcher walked out, airing a disgusting snort. Mrs. Grady plugged her ears. Tom Simmons plugged his son's ears. Sensing a general unrest, Davie changed chords and tried to end it:

> There's beauty in the winter snow,
> There's beauty in the frost, you know.
> There's beauty in the morning sun,
> There's beauty when the day is done.

Pastor Davis had been thinking about a winter retreat in the mountains for the past few weeks, something his lovely wife Irene kept telling him he needs. In fact, he was likely kicking himself for his decision to stay now that he was imprisoned on the platform directly behind Davie and Noah, an entire congregation watching his every expression and studying him for body language that might communicate levels of disapproval.

His message seemed a little scattered that morning as he discarded notes long labored over in favor of a friendly talk on orthodoxy and the need for an understanding of the deeper things. "John Huss and William Tyndale were not martyred on account of their feelings toward nature," he said, and I stretched my neck to verify how my favorite guitarist was taking this.

"The lyrics were lousy," Dad said as he eased our DeSoto into the driveway.

"So were the words," agreed my sister, Liz.

Dad laughed. But he wasn't finished. He was looking at me in the rearview. "They were ambiguous, vague, shallow, and I could scarcely hear them. But I like that boy's heart. You can tell he loves the Lord."

I didn't know how to counter this. I could hear the words fine from where I sat. And I kind of liked the music.

—⟋⟍—

This morning, Dr. Patrick Klassen is pinch-hitting for Pastor Davis and his wife, who are at Camp Overflowing, a hundred miles straight west. Mr. Klassen has been lecturing in a nearby Christian college and is a bit of a celebrity, although *Satan's Plan for Your Kids* hasn't exactly been flying off the table in the foyer. Folks gather around to cast curious glances at the book and its author. Dr. Klassen stands nearby, wondering if the three-dollar price tag is too steep.

Snippits of his sermon return to me even now, for he is in his element this day, holding the book aloft and referring to it often. The lights are turned out and the makeshift blinds pulled as we tour sensational slides of rock concerts where teens have been tragically trampled, photos of the Beatles and The Who, and undoctored images of people dancing in the aisles right inside an Episcopal church. I can't remember anything so entertaining in a previous service.

Dr. Patrick is exciting to listen to, for sure. He not only employs multimedia to whack exclamation points onto his premise, he regales us with fascinating studies he himself has conducted. "Extensive research has been undertaken on the effects of music upon both plants and animals," he says, "and I have researched some of this in my own home. I go into it in far greater detail in the book, of course, which you can pick up later two for five dollars, but let me say this. For more than one year I attempted to grow Christmas Cactus, Philodendron, and Wandering Jew in our living room while pounding them with some of this so-called Christian music from Love Song, Phil Keaggy, and the Second Chapter of Acts. Though I watered the plants regularly, one began to wilt within two weeks, another stopped growing altogether, and the third died within four days. Some were bent away from the speakers, as if they were begging to be released from the punishment being inflicted upon them. My friends, if the musical tones and rhythms of this music have that kind of effect on the cells of life-forms like plants, then imagine what they are doing to our children."

A growing murmur of amens wafts through the room, as do shuffling of feet and "I told you so" nods. Patrick's assertions have not always met with such approval, so he rubs his hands together and keeps the information coming.

"Even more startling are the findings of a Dr. T.C. Singh, head of the Botany Department at Annamalia University in India. His experiments conclude not only that classical music and musical instruments such as the violin cause plants to flourish at twice their normal growth rate but later generations of the seeds of musically stimulated plants carry on the improved traits of greater size and denser foliage. The music actually determines whether or not these plants will evolve in an upward pattern."

One glance at my father and I can see he is unimpressed by the reference to evolution, but he listens carefully.

I sit wondering how loudly these people played which kinds of music. Did they turn the Rolling Stones up loudly enough to make the plants bend in the breeze? But there is no question period, not that I would take advantage of it, of course. Tony cranes his neck my way, drops one corner of his mouth and whispers wryly, "I've heard that opera music can shatter wine glasses."

I smile.

"Opera is where the fat lady gets stabbed and instead of dying, she sings." Tony is funniest in church. He even scribbles more palindromes on an offering envelope: "Oh no! Don Ho!" and, "Golf? No sir. Prefer prison flog."

Amazingly I am more interested in the sermon than my brother's notes. In fact, I wish Dr. Klassen would speak here more often, maybe every Sunday. There isn't a lot of scriptural content to his message, but that's okay because he tells us things we need to hear in a way we won't forget. Besides, I'd certainly rather hear a message on music than one on wickedness or the eighth commandment, "Thou shalt not steal." The great music debate is a welcome reprieve from the guilt I've been feeling lately.

Before Dr. Klassen concludes, he tells of another experiment in which a teenage boy and girl who had never met previously were getting acquainted in a cozy room with soft music playing in the background, not knowing that their reactions were being observed and recorded by adults in an adjacent locale. This seems odd to me but not to Mr. Klassen.

"When classical music and soft ballads were piped into the room," says the Doctor, who has lots of notes but uses few of them, "they talked in a friendly sort of way, but were somewhat aloof. When pop music and jazz or the rumba were played, they quickly developed a much 'friendlier' attitude and began holding hands and putting their arms around each other. When the music changed back to classical and ballads they would again become more formal and reserved. If the music would swing back to jazz and pop, formality would give way to inappropriate familiarity."

His conclusion is succinct: "Is this music a bane or a blessing? I'll stick with the former."

On the way home, Dad is looking at me in the rearview mirror and not saying much. There are vertical question marks on his forehead. Ben says some rather unflattering things about the message, and Tony interrupts to tell Dad that he'd like to be a researcher like Mr. Klassen.

"Can I do an experiment involving music?"

"*May* I," corrects Liz.

Dad says it's not a problem. "So long as it's not too loud," he adds with a rearview wink, and by afternoon, sure enough, Tony is lugging a pothos plant into our bedroom and setting it in the corner by a cheap tape deck he has borrowed. He pops in a brand-new tape by Chuck Girard and cranks it up until the windowpanes vibrate.

> You ask me why I keep on smilin'
> When all the world's in such a mess…

I have never heard words like this teamed with music this catchy, and I sit next to Tony, my back against the cold wall, wondering if the music is slowly killing me and if I'll feel noticeably weaker when I arise. The guy on the cover of the tape is badly in need of a haircut, but the music is captivating. Tony confidently air-guitars to "Rock and Roll Preacher" and hums along with more mellow

> Sometimes alleluia
> Sometimes praise the Lord
> Sometimes gently singing
> Our hearts in one accord.

It's a far cry from the country music I prefer, sung by Tammy Wynette and Charlie Pride on my favorite radio station, KFAC. Or as Tony calls it, "Krud For All Cowboys."

"Not a palindrome," he adds sarcastically.

—⁓—

Often at night Tony reads aloud from a devotional book he has tucked under his pillow. Tonight, before he switches off the lamp beside his bed, he reads from somewhere in the Psalms, "Let the words of my mouth, and the meditation of my heart, be acceptable in Thy sight, O LORD, my strength and my redeemer."

The words make me glad I haven't bought the snowmobile yet and that it's not too late to turn in the money. I will do it tomorrow. I will tell Dad at breakfast. The music is playing near the plant. "Lay your burden down...take your worries to the foot of the cross...and lay your burden down." The plant may be wilting, but the music keeps the voices from arguing in my head and helps me drift off to sleep.

Nine

Brigade

Monday morning arrives right on schedule, bringing with it unending possibilities. I lie there considering them and staring at the darkened ceiling. Though I should be locating a white flag and planning my surrender, I find myself thinking once again of snowmobiles and candy and the adoration of my classmates. "If Ben wakes up in the next five seconds, I'll give it back," is the fleece I lay out before God. But Ben sneaked out again last night, and he's sawing logs on the top bunk, so I might as well say, "If a fat man in a red suit comes down a chimney (which we do not have) bringing me a minibike, I will give the money up."

Dad is already at work when I arrive at the breakfast table, which is a sure sign I should at least wait until later today to tell him about the money. Uncle Roy is there, mooching from the refrigerator, but there is no way I'm confessing anything to him.

At school, Michael promises the snowmobile by Wednesday, and the butterflies are flying fast around my stomach as I sit in English class wondering if Mary Beth Swanson will accept a ride from me come Wednesday. "Hang on tight!" I'll yell as I squeeze the throttle hard. She will scream and clutch me tightly about the waist. I must remember to dab a little of Ben's cologne on my neck

97

or maybe buy some of my own with the growing wad in my
pocket.

—ᘉ—

Tuesday night is the annual Wild Game Banquet sponsored
by the Christian Service Brigade—our church's answer to the Boy
Scout meetings held in the arena across town. Few boys on this
side of the creek miss out on the weekly meetings, and death is
too feeble an excuse for avoiding the yearly feast. Christian Service
Brigade sounded pretty good to me from the moment I first heard
about it. It was a chance to discover the art of tying knots and
setting things on fire, though my mother kept reminding me that
it was also a chance to learn about Jesus.

Normally we gather each Friday evening between seven and
nine-thirty, commencing in September and saying our goodbyes
in late May, by which time we will either be promoted and
bedecked in more badges or scorned by those who are. We are
expected to be there on time, dressed in the appropriate attire and
rank, with our uniforms clean and wrinkle-free. I have advanced
to Company Section, and I wear my green-trimmed attire proudly,
though it has no badge yet (I am still working on my first—for
Woodsman). Sadly, the uniform seems to be shrinking, the sleeves
riding higher than I wish they would, and the pants I keep tugging
downward when I think no one is looking. Before long, these
things will only fit Noah Corzini.

Captain Jake Guenther, a lean man who works as a contrac-
tor by day, begins each meeting with the "fall in." Then the roll
call, a short prayer, and the recitation of our purpose statement:
"To advance Christ's Kingdom among boys and promote habits

of obedience, reverence, discipline, self-respect, and all that promotes a true Christian manliness."

We are to have memorized this by heart, and most have, though I find it necessary to pretend for much of it, having chosen instead to memorize this year's motto: "Sure and steadfast."

The remainder of the evening is spent on instruction in Christian faith, first aid, safety, crime prevention, physical recreation, local history, and camping. Boys are encouraged to work toward various badges and awards or take up a particular sport, hobby, or musical instrument. A year ago, in my fervor, I decided on the trumpet, but my practice time was deafening, my notes sour. It's a good thing there were no plants nearby. Tony asked me to play "Far, Far Away," or "Down by the Firehall," but I'd not heard either piece despite his insistence they were both timeless classics. He told me to practice in the DeSoto, but that is not something you look forward to, not in the winter, and my interest was buried somewhere, with Tony's full approval.

To Mr. Guenther, the Brigade program is deadly serious, as serious as anything we will ever do in our entire lives. So serious that if you so much as snicker during inspection or lose interest during Bible study, he will single you out and glare at you. If the glaring does not work, he has been known to yell until everyone in the gymnasium drops what they are doing to stare. Mr. Guenther is the Paul Bunyan of the Brigade. He has more stamina than people half his age. I have watched him do one-armed push-ups and bench press three of the chubby kids all at once. Field trips proved that he can out-fish a raccoon and out-climb a mountain goat. Sewn to the arms and chest of his uniform is every badge the Brigade has ever issued, and if he maintains his current pace he'll have to knit them to his pants. He can light fires in a downpour, tie fifteen different knots in a shoelace, and tap out Morse code, I've been told, though he has yet to need it.

Once the troops have been lined up and inspected, he bellows, "Atteeeeenshun! March!" And we do, to our designated stations in the four corners of the gymnasium: me to the North Pole, others to the East, South, and West. There we do an unsteady pirouette and face the middle of the room, where our captain stands rigid, already saluting. At the command of Lance Corporal Danny Higgins, we sing our theme song as if we are rallying for an invasion of Normandy:

> Brigadiers, all join together,
> Rise as men, be strong.
> By the grace of God go forward,
> Shout the triumph song.
>
> Forward to the far horizon,
> Though the road be long,
> 'Til from every tribe and nation
> Echoes back the song.
>
> Bright and keen for Christ our Savior,
> Glory to His name;
> Brigadiers to serve the King,
> His wondrous love proclaim.

At a campout this past June shortly after the singing was finished and the prayer time begun, some of us North Pole boys slunk away from the fireside to discover the wonders of inhaling smoke through rolled-up copies of the *Grace Chronicle*. Gregory Stonehocker was just beginning to teach us about smoke rings, for which the Brigade gave us no badge, when Mr. Guenther was somehow alerted to our activities. He hastily put down his accordion—the discordant exhalation audible from a hundred yards—stormed from the campfire, and then lined us up and began yelling at us in a voice that would have earned the attention of my stone-deaf Uncle Vince in Mississippi. Captain Guenther had a deep gravelly voice that surprised you coming from one whose long narrow face was broken into longitudinal strips by an even longer nose. When he got mad, the nose reddened and flared noticeably and his nut-brown eyes were almost lost under a tangle of darker eyebrows.

Mr. Guenther told us loudly of the shame our parents would feel when they discovered what we'd been up to and that he should probably just fold up the tents and take the well-behaved boys home for ice cream and leave us here to practice the things we'd learned, but that we likely hadn't learned anything all year so we wouldn't survive the night anyway, we'd be eaten by wolves, or die of smoke inhalation, and maybe that was justice, we'd learn our lesson then.

By the time he tired of arraigning us, we had been stripped of every honor possible, informed of the great tradition of the Brigade, how the Cross for Heroism—something we'd never see—was introduced in 1902, and how the very first camping trip held at Tighnabruaich on the Kyles of Bute in July, 1886, was something those boys knew enough to fully appreciate, being Christian boys, unlike us.

Gregory Stonehocker boldly interjected, "I'm not a Christian, Mr. Guenther, but I think that one day I would like to become one."

That changed everything. Mr. Guenther stammered a little and apologized a lot, and before a minute was out we found ourselves back around the fireside, prodigals who were part of the group once again.

But tonight all of that is forgotten. Tonight is banquet night and we are at ease. No marching. No saluting. No singing. Just lots of eating, the only menu being wild game, shot by none other than our fearless leader, whose motto is, "If I can shoot it, you can eat it, and you *will* eat it. In fact, you will have something of everything, and you will finish that something, every last lick of it. Or else."

Two long tables of meat adorn the center of the stuffy gymnasium. Each dish is carefully labeled, and we can't believe our luck. Cougar Stew, Roast of Bear, Beaver Jerky, Fried Moose, Elk Burgers, Deer Meatballs, and Roast Rabbit with Carrots (the only vegetable present, Mr. Guenther being an unmarried man).

My eyes are so big, I cannot help loading up on a little of everything and going heavy on the Cougar Stew. It's been a full year almost to the day since I've seen a feast like this, and the meals at home have been a little lean of late.

Now, I don't know if you've ever sampled any of these delicacies, but they tend to taste the same after a while as if the great hunter cured them all in the same smoke shack or boiled them in the same pot. Pretty soon you find yourself chewing more than swallowing and wondering if you are biting into actual carcass or if it is indeed the meat. And if you haven't had the best of days or haven't slept as well as you might have the night before because you've had something bulky on your mind, it can become too much for you. Suddenly my stomach informs me that it has accommodated all it intends to, that if I send one more scrap of anything its way, I may have a revolution on my hands and perhaps on the table and the floor too. But what to do? I have finished most of the moose and bear, but the cougar and beaver linger on my plate, large and obvious items I must do something with.

I look around me for a solution. Any solution.

A cool breeze is blowing just over my shoulder where some-one has cracked open a window. The window is two feet behind me, a narrow crack, but it will have to do.

Now all I need is a distraction.

It comes in the form of Mr. Guenther sliding his chair back and standing to his feet. "Men," he yells in his gravelly captain's voice, snapping us to attention, "I have a few people to thank for all of this."

Everyone looks his way and I realize it is now or never.

I push my chair back slowly, my eyes never leaving him. Then, lifting the paper plate with one hand, I fling it over my shoulder right at the crack.

It is a fine toss. A major-league toss.

I am still confident the meat would have made it.

Had it not been for the screen on the window.

—⟋⟍—

If you considered Captain Guenther uncouth after he caught us blowing smoke rings at the campout, you'd be blushing to hear him now. He leaps over his table and stands before me, trembling, the veins on his neck threatening to pop. Boys all around him are fighting off snickers, examining the contents of their own plates and wishing they'd had the nerve to do the same.

He rants. He raves. He barks like a drill sergeant. He calls me an ungrateful wretch, he tells me what children in Africa would give to have such abundance, and he dubs me a sorry excuse for a man. His nose is positively bulbous, reddening by the second. I can't help looking at it. It fascinates me. I hardly notice as he brings into question every sincere act I've ever committed and bans me from the Brigade forever. "Never," he hollers, "will you be admitted in here again, acting like that. Never ever. Shame, shame, shame." I am trembling now, wondering how far he will go, wondering what he will tell my poor dad. "But," he says, ever the champion of second chances, "if ever you come back to my Brigade, you will clean up your act, and you will get a new uniform before Friday, one that fits you, Terry Anderson. You look pitiful. Now go on, get out of here. Someone clean up this mess."

Whirling on his army boots, he marches rapidly from the room.

—ᴍ—

Funny how the theme song rattles through my mind as I pull on my hand-me-down coat and step into the winter. "Forward to the far horizon, though the road be long." Seems fitting. The tune sticks hard. Funny too that it is not so much the banishing that slays me; it is the comment about my uniform. Where will I, the poorest kid in the room, lay my hands on money enough to obtain threads that fit? Twelve years of poverty does that to you, leaves you weighing a problem when the solution is right there, reaching out to smack you.

The skate shack is abandoned tonight since most of the boys are in the gym. The bare lightbulbs are aglow however, so I sneak in and pry open the trapdoor to examine my treasure. The light is barely sufficient. I unzip the Red Wings bag and walk my fingers over the money. My money. How does one begin to count such a sum? I pull out a bundle of twenties and tally them, two at a time. There are one hundred. At least one hundred. How much is that? I wish my math was better. I pull five twenties from the bundle, roll them like a cigarette and stuff them in my coat.

I should buy new uniforms for all my friends, bribe badges from the good kids, and get my sister to sew them on for us. She would be so proud. I could pay her a dollar an hour. Maybe more. But then they'd find out, wouldn't they?

How does a boy contain a secret so large? It bursts within him, leaving him aching to tell the world. It blinds him, too, leaving him unaware that what he has stumbled upon may bring down more trouble than he thought possible.

Back home, I stuff the rolled-up bills deep into Ben's drawer, behind the forbidden paperbacks. There's no way I'm leaving it in my pockets or my drawer. Tomorrow I'll think of someplace else.

My hand brushes a pouch of tobacco that smells sweet to me. There's a funny-looking pipe too. Maybe I'll try it out sometime.

—⁓—

The pothos plant Tony has been serenading is deader than a floor tile. It could have been the music. It could have been the lack of water. Or it might have something to do with the fact that Dad came in here to air the place out and it is covered in frost now. I try to warm the big green leaves with my hands, but they are more brown than green, the last vestiges of life having given them the slip.

"Some things you can't resurrect," says Tony. Liz pokes her head around the corner. "I told you so," she grins.

"Do you have a plant I can borrow?"

She almost runs to her room, then returns with a smaller one. A spider plant, she calls it, and she tells Tony what he's been doing wrong. Tony places it a foot from the window this time. "Maybe the preacher was right," he says, "but we'll give it one more chance."

"Liz," I say, following her to her room.

"Yep."

"Can I come in?"

"*May* I come in," she corrects me.

"Close your eyes," I command, as I push through the door. "Now open them."

Liz isn't used to me herding her like this, but she concedes. Opening her eyes, she stares speechless at a silver ring with her initials on it, E.A. "It's like the one in the catalog, only better," I say. "I, uh…did some work for Mr. Swanson, and he gave me some money."

"Oh Tare, you're just the best. Isn't it just great how God just supplies for us? Thank you, thank you." And all of my troubles are smothered in my sister's hugs.

Ten

Slim and Jim

Each and every night, without fail, my father kneels by my bed and beseeches me to crawl from beneath the covers and join him in prayer. "There's something about this position," he says, as I dutifully place my elbows on the bed covers and fold my hands beneath my chin. "It helps you remember you need help to get up." It also helps me remember that the floor is cold in winter and I should be wearing socks.

Tonight, after another full day of conniving, I watch Dad shut off the music, smile at the spider plant, and prostrate himself beside me. I am pretending to be asleep, but I can see him through my squinty eyes.

Prayer is tedious work for me. I begin with reluctance and finish with delight. The prayers I pray are pretty well memorized, and I deliver them rapid-fire as if I have someplace I need to be: "Dear Heavenly Father thank you for this day bless Uncle Roy help Mom feel better give me a good sleep help the missionaries in Jesus' name amen." Dad doesn't chide me for using no commas or periods. He just pauses a moment, then prays eloquently in a steady, confident voice, entreating God on my behalf, asking that my tongue be kept from evil and my lips from speaking lies. Sometimes his arm is about my shoulders, sometimes not. But always he finishes the prayer this way: "May the Lord bless thee and keep thee, Terry. May He cause His face to shine upon thee and be gracious unto thee. May He lift up His countenance upon thee and give thee peace. Amen."

Something magical happens when that prayer leaves his lips. I know when I hear it that all is well, or at least that it will be one day. And I wonder why Dad isn't a minister of the gospel as he once said he wanted to be. I'll bet it pays better than his job, and he surely has the prayers for it.

One summer vacation when we were driving southward, staying with relatives until the hints grew too obvious, the transmission in our car blew up. I say blew up because I heard the noise myself from the backseat where Liz and I were seated just out of reach of Dad's big right hand. At first it sounded like someone grinding coffee beans, only louder. Then there was a high-pitched whir and a loud clunk that sounded to me as if a very large and necessary component had fallen from the car and thunked the highway. We were somewhere in the middle of Utah between Beaver and Fillmore, I think—not quite what you're hoping for in your hour of need—but somehow we managed to coast to a gas station, only to discover that there was no garage there and the pumps had been closed for years. Dad climbed out, poked his head under the car and stood up looking like he'd just seen a ghost or maybe a whole roomful of them. It is a frightening thing for a child to see his mechanic father bearing such an expression, so I slouched in the seat, behaving myself entirely for the first time in hours.

Dad climbed back into the car and lay his head upon the steering wheel. Then his back stiffened and he sat straight. Taking my mother's hand, he began to pray, simply reminding God that we needed to get to Phoenix before nightfall, that relatives were expecting us, our wallets were getting thin, and we could sure use a little help. What happened next, I have trouble believing to this day, but I saw it with my own eyes. My father turned the key on the old DeSoto, and it started as if fresh from a tune-up. He nudged it into gear and the car crept forward. I sat in the back wondering if he shouldn't stop right now and pray that she would never run out of gas.

Nine hours later we were in Phoenix.

Sometimes when Dad thinks I am asleep, he kneels quietly beside me, lays a huge hand softly on my hairdo and prays quite another prayer. The urgency is much greater in this one. He punctuates the sentences with heavy sighs, asking God that I would encounter the "vacancy of worldliness" and get sick on it early in life. He implores God to keep me from being comfortable, asking that I "not live a life of ease but one of danger" and that when it comes along I would meet it with courage and steadfastness, whatever that means.

It's quite an earful for a twelve-year-old boy who's trying not to move and whose conscience is beginning to poke him hard, but such is the prayer he offers this night as I lie against a lumpy mattress with my eyes closed, wondering if that cougar stew will stay where it should. To help me forget his words, I think of my sister's adoration and of my love of snowmobiles and my gift of poetry.

But the prayer keeps coming.

"Protect him from hollow religion. There's so much of it around here," Dad implores, and I know he has a front seat in the throne room of heaven. "And if ever he turns his heart against Thee, dear Lord, may it be like he pulled the shades on the sun itself." He then asks God to allow me a tiny glimpse of just how depraved my heart is so that I'll know it is deceitful above all things and desperately wicked. He prays that my sins (if I am harboring some) will track me down and find me out and that God's discipline will accompany His love.

It is not the sort of prayer one is eager to hear when he has had the temptations of the world laid at his feet. I must admit that by the time my father says "Amen" and flips off the light, leaving me alone in the dark, the roll of bills in my brother's drawer and the bundle beneath the skate shack are growing heavier, and it takes some time convincing my eyes to shut.

Above all others, the thought that begins to rear up and overtake my mind is of Slim and Jim, the dreaded villains of my poetry, and the things they will do to my tiny body when they discover I've made a discovery.

Tony arrives along about nine-thirty P.M., when I should be sound asleep, climbs into the bottom bunk on the other bed, and begins munching an apple loudly.

"Come on, quit it," I nag.

"You'll never guesh whosh getting out of prishon," he manages past the big gob of apple in his mouth.

I can't guesh.

"Matthew Jennings."

"The guy you've been writing? The guy Ben beat up?"

"That's him. Remember last summer, when I told you about the Jennings family?"

"No," I say a little huffily. But I do remember. Last August as we sat around a campfire in the dark, wishing we had a larger bag of marshmallows, Tony had recounted a story he said was true. A story of stolen treasure. One a child doesn't soon forget.

"I thought you made that one up."

Tony splits a huge chunk off the juicy apple with a sharp row of incisors. Five feet away I can feel it squirt. "No way," he says. "But it's just gotten better. You want to hear about it?" Well, of course I do. I'm just not sure I want to hear him tell it here in the dark. He sounds like he's talking to a four-year-old.

"You won't get scared now, will you?"

"Nope," I say a little too quickly.

I'm not about to tell him that I am afraid of almost everything. Of Mom dying. The disease that waits. The darkness in the middle of the night when a dream cuts short and you find that you're the only one awake listening to unexplainable noises that may include your own raspy breathing. Afraid of reaching for a light switch and finding something else there. Something squishy. Afraid of silly things like the wheels on my grocery cart going in different directions or the front tire coming off my bicycle as I round a gravel corner. Or getting caught and jailed for this secret I carry.

I am thankful that Tony has left the door open a crack. The hall light is a welcome companion as he revs the story up again, adding details I don't recall from the August telling.

"You asked me how I can write a guy like Matt," he says. "Well, you find out someone's story, and it changes things."

Raised on the other side of the creek, Matt Jennings was one of the pagans, one of the Townies, as we call them. On the day he was born, his father was absent on account of men not being allowed into the delivery room at Grace Municipal and also because he happened to be an inmate in the state penitentiary at the time. Mr. Jennings spent much of Matt's life incarcerated there for armed robbery among other things, and they only let him out in hopes he'd lead them to the stolen treasures he'd buried beneath stone fences and behind flimsy walls in Shell service stations.

On Matt's eighteenth birthday, his father was released from Liberty County Jail along about supper time. "One of the problems with releasing these guys from prison," says Tony, "is that they get to feeling so free that they start peeling off all their clothing without even knowing it."

"What about in the winter?" I interrupt.

"Oh, it's worse in the winter," Tony insists. "You see, it gets so cold that the prisoners get confused and think it's warm, and they peel them off twice as fast. They sometimes find 'em frozen in the snow, clad in nothing but their birthday suits."

I'm not buying any of this, and I tell him so.

"Hey, did you ever put your hand under the cold water tap and think it was hot?"

Come to think of it, I had. Especially when I'd been ice-skating and my hands were half frozen.

"Well, after the bumpy bus ride into Grace," Tony continues, "Mr. Jennings put his clothes back on and marched straight to the First Street Bridge over Franklin's Creek. He glanced carefully over both shoulders (a habit he'd developed through the years), and when he was satisfied that no one had followed him, he got on his hands and knees and crawled under the bridge. Minutes later he emerged, brushing dirt from his pants. He was wearing a very guilty expression and had a bulge in his jacket about the size of a bag of jewelry that had gone missing from Penny's Jewelry four years ago to the day."

"Did anyone see him?"

"Nope."

"Then how do you know this happened?"

"The police report. And from these letters Matt's been writing. Do you want me to finish or not?"

"Yeah. Do."

"No, I don't think I will," says Tony stubbornly. "You can't interrupt a good storyteller. They get thrown off their rhythm."

"I'm sorry," I plead. "Finish, please?"

He sighs heavily. "Well, okay, but no more interruptions."

"Okay, I won't, I promise."

"Well, Mr. Jennings was wa—"

"No way will I interrupt you," I say, grinning. "Wouldn't dream of it."

Tony grabs his pillow and heaves it at me. I can hear him chuckling.

Dad arrives at the door and tells us to pipe down, that our sister has a test tomorrow and is trying to sleep. Then he shuts the door.

"*Aha*," says Tony. "Did I ever tell you about the headless cannibal who has a key to our house?"

"Yes, you have." My voice is a little trembly. "Tell the other one. The one about Matt."

Tony takes another crunch on the apple, chews thoughtfully, and resumes. "Well, all that time in prison and Mr. Jennings hadn't seen his son, but he hoped to that night. He wondered if his boy would recognize him. Would he be glad to see him or run the other way? What had he become in four years? What did he look like? Did he have a beard yet? He couldn't wait to get home and find out. First, though, he would stop at the Draft Choice Bar to gain strength to face Mrs. Jennings.

"Down the street he walked, grateful it was a Saturday night and the shops were empty of people with their endless questions." Tony inherited the storytelling from Dad, I guess. "Mr. Jennings stood looking in shop windows, thinking of the treasure beneath his coat. Surely it was enough to change things. He remembered his favorite piece, a thick gold band crowned by a huge opal offset in silver. He would sell the rest and keep this one.

"In the bar, he sipped from a frothy mug, compliments of Mr. Olson himself, and wondered what he could say to convince his wife that he'd changed for good and would steal no more. She'd heard that a hundred times."

"You ever been in a bar?" I ask, forgetting I'd promised not to interrupt.

"No."

"Oh. Sorry."

Tony doesn't seem to mind and returns to his tale.

"The bar was empty except for four kids about his son's age who were seated at a nearby table, each of them staring down the barrel of a loaded whiskey. *Huh—guess the bartender is more concerned with cash than underage drinking laws,* he thought. Mr. Cramer undid the drawstrings on the jewelry bag and peeked inside. A smile graced his cheeks. The opal ring was there. Among other things.

"The electric clock above the fancy bottles was creeping up on eleven when one of the kids, who wore a green plaid logger's shirt, offered to buy old man Jennings a drink. He gratefully accepted. One led to two, which led to a couple more, and before long the bar was growing blurry and the ceiling was moving counterclockwise. The next thing Mr. Jennings knew, the bartender was slapping him gently on the face and helping him up off the floor.

"An hour had disappeared, and the place was empty now," Tony continues, clearly enjoying his role as storyteller. "Mr. Jennings patted his jacket and let out a groan. The bag of jewelry was gone."

My eyes were wide. This was better than television, especially if you'd never had one.

"It was a dejected man who walked two blocks to a strange place he called home. Was the place green or blue? He couldn't remember. He kept patting his coat and shaking his head and telling himself that he had all he needed: the love of a patient woman and a son who would grow up and make something of his life.

"He tapped at the door and opened it slowly. A dying fire was on the hearth, and the room looked so cozy, so inviting. The young man who stood there looked vaguely familiar. He was wearing a green plaid logger's shirt and fiddling with a ring on his right hand. It was a beautiful ring. A thick gold band crowned by a huge opal offset in silver. 'Hi,' he said. 'I'm Matt.'"

My eyes widen at the ending. "You made that up," I charge.

"No I didn't. What's more, Matthew Jennings gets out of Liberty County Jail pretty quick. This week I think. I'd like to follow him, see where he leads me."

Tony keeps talking but I'm not listening. It isn't so much the story that scares me as it is the truth: Whoever salted away the money beneath the skate shack will come looking for it, sure as giraffes have necks, and I'd better do something. You didn't need to have much between your ears to know where the money came from.

Tony sneaks along the floor, and I'm prepared for him to jump up and frighten me. Instead, he clicks the tape player back on. I hope it isn't the selection he played last night. But it is. I'd rather listen to something by the Rolling Stones or even Dolly Parton, something that doesn't set off these voices in my head.

If I find any relief at all in Tony's story, it comes from knowing that others have sinned too, that others would stoop as low as I have. But I'm fooling myself. Matt is from the other side of Franklin's Creek. Expectations are higher over here. On this side I seem alone in my sin. Here in this house, I'm surrounded by saints. I know this as surely as I know that the only voice I'm listening to tonight is the one telling me the obvious: "Hide the treasure somewhere, Terry Anderson, and hide it fast."

Eleven

Snowmobile

How does a twelve-year-old boy go about hiding a zillion dollars in a small town where everyone not only recognizes him, they stop him on the street to ask how his mother is doing each time he walks past? Very carefully, that's how. You wonder how much you can hide in your coat without attracting stares or spawning rumors. You can't put anything in your hat because bigger kids love swiping it in the school yard and filling it with snow before cramming it back down on your rumpled head.

The how is what occupies my mind as I help clear our cracked sidewalks of fresh snow in the early morning hours, and by the time I leave for school a plan is beginning to vibrate around my tiny brain, though it looks bleak (the plan, that is). A dozen dreams clouded my sleep last night. In one, I removed the money slowly, like Uncle Roy when he slips into a swimming hole—an inch at a time. The thief stood by, never noticing my thievery. There's my answer. The thief won't notice if I take just a little. Why not be content to take a thousand dollars or two and abandon the rest? But the thought of leaving that much behind is too much for me. The money is mine now. Surely I will be haunted by a hunger for leftovers, lured back weekly to examine the remains, to swipe a few more of the crisp bills. If I am to tamper with the spoils at all, I cannot just dabble at it.

It is all or nothing.

My eyes look down at the sidewalk as I walk past buildings with rich histories a boy doesn't pause to consider. The church with the steeple that was shipped from England in the late 1700s. The dentist office Peter Hawkins purchased for back taxes in 1957 when the truth emerged that old man Welch had been slipping too much anaesthetic into the injections so he could pick patients' pockets while they slept off their pain. My eyes are still on the sidewalk where I once found a nickel. But what is a nickel now? When you're as rich as I am, it's not worth the effort of bending down to pick it up. I scarcely notice the fog as it drapes the evergreens with thick frost or the children who grunt their hellos in the school yard or jostle rudely past me, forgetting that only yesterday I was their benefactor. Normally I would join a small cluster of boys who are telling illegal jokes over by the pull-up bars. Or on days as cold as this one, we would stand around pretending to smoke cigarettes, our warm breath launching artistic smoke rings into icy air. But today I go straight into the building before the bell rings, a first for me.

The school is virtually free of children, but my stomach is filled with the same flock of butterflies I've grown accustomed to now. Teachers are in their homerooms, dutifully mixing the day's poison, so I slip undetected into the boys' washroom, making certain it is vacant as I press onward to the farthest stall. Standing atop the wobbly lid of the white American Standard, I push a corner of the false ceiling tile upward with one hand and withdraw a few paperbacks of assorted bills from my coat pocket with the other. More are zipped into my notebook, on which is scrawled the initials of the only girl I've noticed all year—M.B.S. Less than a minute later I have rid my coat of two thousand dollars, a delightful and terrifying burden. Reeling off ten feet of toilet paper, I clean my footprints from the lid and flush.

My Timex is getting ready to nudge nine when Michael Swanson eagerly meets me at the drinking fountain and elbows my ribs.

"Ouch," I respond.

"Did you get it?"

"Get what?"

"Don't be stupid."

"Yep, I got it. See you at recess."

As I head for class, I find myself wondering what nameless, faceless taskmaster is commanding me, against all I know to be right, to keep pushing forward, recklessly crowding myself toward disaster? I do not know.

Ten-fifteen is recess, my favorite class of the day. Far from the game of tag, I pay Michael in cash. All fives. Precisely forty of them by both our counts. I feel like a character in one of those movies where shady people in trench coats and fedoras exchange newspapers near the Eiffel Tower, oblivious to the headlines, oblivious to other people in trench coats.

Twice before lunch I ask to be excused from class so I can visit the restroom. The first time it works without a hitch. When I am in the hallway and no one is looking, I rush from the school, returning to the restroom exactly eight minutes later, my coat pockets stuffed with more of the tainted cash. The second time I raise my hand, Miss Hoover saunters over to my desk while the others are working out math problems and tells me to wait 'til lunch.

"But I've really gotta go," I plead.

"But you just did."

"But I…um…well, I mean it this time. Really. I don't feel so hot."

She eyes me suspiciously. "Well, you hurry. Your math marks, well, they're not adding up." Then she waves her hand and I am off.

By afternoon recess, the pile of cash above the commode has grown to the point that I fear the ceiling is beginning to sag a little. Time to find another spot, I tell myself.

During the final period, I stare out the window and mull my options, which are few. I could bring the stuff home and hide it under my bed. This is possibly the dumbest thought I've had today. How about burying it in the backyard? Na. Have you ever tried to dig here in winter? Badgers can't. How about loading the whole thing on the snowmobile and finding a place in the hills—

"You are chewing gum again, Terry Anderson," Miss Hoover interrupts another dumb idea. "Did you bring enough for the whole class?"

Her arms are folded in triumph.

I stand to my feet.

"Yes," I boast, "I did."

As the class looks on in wondrous amazement, I tramp up and down the aisles, pulling out pink packages of Double Bubble (complete with silly Pud cartoons) and handing them to astonished and admiring classmates. Miss Hoover is speechless. She just stands watching me. I think to this day there was the slightest trace of admiration on her face.

—⚬⚬—

4:00 P.M.: I am sitting behind the handlebars of the first snowmobile I ever drove, or owned, or sat on for that matter. What a marvelous machine! A real beauty! If I had postcards of my smile, I could sell them for a dollar. The only item I can remember coveting this badly was a Honda 50 minibike that Brenda Thompson won in some sweepstakes contest, thereby earning her the envy of the entire town of Grace for at least a week. But I was destined only to gape at it as she drove past with me waving and her not caring and me knowing she would cover it with a tarp and lock it up at night without giving me a second thought.

This time I will do more than gape. I will ride like the north wind. I wish Brenda could be here to see me smile. I'd spray some snow on her, maybe.

4:03 P.M.: Michael Swanson explains to me the intricacies of the polished engine, how to adjust the carburetor for different kinds of weather, and how the oil-gas mix should be just so. I am not really listening. I am itching to climb aboard this spectacular snowmobile. "Topped her up for you," he says. "Just pull the rope like this." And I do. She roars to life. What a fantastic machine!

4:08 P.M.: Michael takes me for a short spin, yelling instructions way too loud over his shoulder: "It's so cool, you'll think you've died and gone to Havana!" Other kids are watching us, and I'm sure they can see the haughty grin I am trying to hide. "You tell your brother how it works," Michael bellows, and suddenly I remember. Oh yes, I told him this was for Tony. I better keep my lies straight, or I'll be in trouble.

4:14 P.M.: Finally, I am flying solo, reflecting on all that is right with the world. What a day! Sun is shining but not brightly enough to hurt the eyes. Ah, something magical occurs when a boy finally acquires something he has longed for all his life. It causes him to climb off the object of his affection once he is beyond eyeshot of his friends and just stand there and stare at it, listening to it idle, blinking with delight. As I do so, I find myself wishing I could goose the big cat into our backyard and call Tony and Dad and Ben and take them for a spin. I would offer Liz a slower ride, and she would hang on tight and maybe scream when I give it a little extra throttle around corners. I wonder if Dad would let me take Mom. How I wish I could wake up tomorrow morning and pull back the blind and gaze at my treasure for a minute, just so I won't have to pinch myself too hard. All day long this splendid snowmobile has filled my thoughts, crowding out all else, save the hiding of the money itself, and now even the bitter wind stinging my face cannot squelch the warmth of the grin that is stuck there. All of my imaginings were not this good. The sense of freedom, of power, of importance—each overwhelms me separately, then all at once, bringing a rush of physical pleasure. To make matters even better, the big beauty has a small storage compartment where I can smuggle some cash if ever the need arises. Merely revving the engine turns good-sized hills into mere gopher mounds. Words can't do it justice. Can life get better than this? I shall christen her *The Mary Beth*.

4:19 P.M.: The snowmobile hiccups a couple of times before stalling altogether. Climbing off, I squeeze the throttle with one hand and yank the rope with the other. She sputters and roars to life. Ah, what a dream machine!

4:20 P.M.: The snowmobile hiccups a couple of times before stalling altogether again. I hold the silly throttle and pull the crazy rope. Again. And again.

4:29 P.M.: After the three hundred and thirtieth pull, the stupid thing belches and eventually starts. But it sounds sick, like a dog that needs to eat grass. I climb aboard quickly and I'm off again. I squeeze the throttle all the way, but she seems slow, sluggish. The wind hits my face until the tears come, sliding back to my ears, then turning to shards of ice and breaking off. This cheap old contraption could sure use a taller windshield.

4:32 P.M.: Losing power quickly, which is just as well. Whenever I slow down after cruising fast, the snow sprays up and filters down my neck, causing me to shiver. Wish I could pull the hood of my hand-me-down parka tighter, but it's busted. If this crazy thing stalls again I could freeze to death out here. Would like to put this ugly beast out of *my* misery.

4:35 P.M.: I bring the blasted creature to the crest of a hill and sit shivering, surveying the bleak countryside. What happened to the sun? Suddenly the fields and forest I love are about as dazzling as the dessert menu on a lifeboat.

4:36 P.M.: An ugly thought presses to the surface, one I've been trying to suppress since yesterday. What will I do now that I have one more object to hide—a rather bulky and obvious brute I am beginning to hate? Tell my brothers I found it? That Michael gave it to me? Probably not. Both require follow-up lies. For now, my only option is to hide the lousy monster in the woods and walk home. Shoot. How I've been longing to show it off.

4:38 P.M.: I squeeze the throttle gently and it quits. Dead. I climb off and kick the stupid varmint. Hard. I hold my foot and dance on the other for a while. The pull-start mechanism hardly budges now. Wish there was a cliff to push it over. Better yet, I'll take it back for a refund.

4:52 P.M.: More kicking (followed by a lengthy battle with Tourette's Syndrome, during which I rename her *The Lucifer*). Finally, the ugly critter starts. I turn sharply to the left and ease her down the hill toward the frozen waters of Franklin's Creek. The skis knife through the snow faster than I thought possible, and I am sinking into an enormous drift. I rev the throttle hard and pull her out, but a cloud of icy snow descends upon me. The fiend takes on a life of its own, rocking from side to side, picking up speed. Can't find the brake on this degenerate beast. I wipe at my eyes in a vain attempt to clear the blur.

Good thing for me.

The wiping allows me to see the poplar tree moments before impact.

—⁄⁄⁄—

The limp home is a long and cold one, what with me dragging one bum leg behind the other and trying to nurse a bruised ego as well. I don't limp or shiver as noticeably when others pass me on the sidewalk. Thankfully there aren't many of them. Sometimes the worst thing about getting hurt is not the pain; it's the wondering if anyone saw how silly you looked when it started. But no one saw me. Not this time.

Though the tree has scarcely a scar, the snowmobile is a wrinkled heap of scrap metal now, one ski bent like a limp wrist, the yellow body crumpled, the windshield lying in the snow twenty feet away. I will have some explaining to do when they see the growing lump on my eye and cheekbone, I'm sure. I'll think of something, I hope. My spirits take a leap when I come through the door. Ah, carrots and potatoes. The sizzle and aroma catch my dismal spirits off guard. Not to worry. All will be fine.

"What happened to you?" Liz is wiping her hands on an apron when I come into the kitchen.

"My snowmobile hit a tree." Dumb things come to me sometimes, so I say them.

She laughs. "You okay?"

"Yeah. But I'll never play basketball again. Almost got my eye poked out."

She looks at me and shakes her head. "Chinook's coming."

"Who?"

"A Chinook," she says. "I can tell by the size of my headache."

"Sorry," I say. "What's for supper?"

I've got a headache too. A whopper. But there's no way I'm talking about it. Not now. I am just relieved she's dropped the subject of the bruising around my eyeball, and hopeful no one else will pick it up.

—〰—

Before bed, I experiment with some of Liz's Cover Girl, one of many items she leaves in the bathroom. It covers the bruise a bit, but still I wash it off. I've got enough problems without showing up at school looking like a girl. Besides, I'm surprised at how small the bruise is anyway.

A plaque above the mirror says, "Thou God seest me." I look away.

In every room of our house, including the bathroom, Scripture verses hang on the wall. You can't get away from them. Most are courtesy of Raymond Van Horn, owner of the Book Nook Christian Store down on Main.

Through the years I have been spanked while looking up at Psalm 56:3, "What time I am afraid, I will trust in Thee," taken a bath staring at Psalm 69:1, "Save me, O God, for the waters have come up to my neck," and stood gazing into an empty fridge below Proverbs 13:25, "The righteous eat to their hearts' content, but the stomach of the wicked goes hungry." I prefer the magnet Liz stuck to the fridge door, "Lord, if you can't make me thin, make my friends look fat."

The plaques began arriving a few short days after Dad fixed Raymond's late-model Buick and Raymond announced that although he couldn't come up with the cash, he could offer some attractive wall hangings as payment. Just last week, as if Dad knew every little thought going off in my head, he mounted Proverbs

12:28 above my bed, "In the way of righteousness there is life; along that path is immortality." It's hard to ignore, staring out at you day after day from thickly lacquered imitation oak.

Once again sleep is slow in coming. It's not just the plaques that plague my mind. It's those two voices arguing again. And thoughts of the snowmobile don't help. How will I fix it? How will I hide it? Will I keep accruing larger objects as I go? Hiding the money is one thing, but this problem looms even larger. Is the money cursed? Did God make the Ski-Doo crash? Maybe someone will steal the thing overnight. I'd like that. It's a mechanics' dream, really. Someone could fix it up and paint it, and no one would know. It wouldn't surprise me if one of the pagans stole it. But the answer to my dilemma is closer than that. It's as close as the weather.

—⁂—

Three or four times a year Chinook winds creep over the Rockies from the leeward side and crawl across the prairies like the green slime in a low-budget horror flick. Named after the Chinook Indians, who lived along the Columbia River and told stories of "the great south wind" or "the snow eater," the winds have been known to create instantaneous and drastic temperature changes you'd think were limited to faraway planets. Today my sister is right. I can tell looking at the windowsill, munching a shallow bowl of lukewarm oatmeal. If pressed, I'll bet Liz could almost predict the exact hour the winds would descend.

"We're almost out of oatmeal," my sister says.

"Huh?"

"I was just looking in the cupboards, and there's almost nothing there."

I am too busy thinking of the snowmobile and the Chinook. Already it has wiped the windows clear of frost, and you can hear water dripping from the eaves. I've seen Chinook winds squeeze the thermometer 40 degrees upward in an hour, melting a foot of snow in a single day. Already the temperature has reached 45 degrees, which doesn't mean you don shorts and look for mosquito repellant, but it does beckon you outside to pack snowballs and lie in wait for neighbor kids.

Our weather station once recorded eighty-mile-an-hour winds that flung railcars from the tracks and tipped a semitrailer over on its backside. Lingering Chinooks can infect trees and tulips with spring fever and confuse them into blossoming in January or early February. Liz believes the high-velocity winds are responsible for migraine headaches, sleeplessness, mood swings, severe depression, and in some people, late onset acne. In Switzerland, she says, the winds are called *foehns*, and law courts recognize that fluctuating barometric conditions can drive people temporarily insane, rendering them no longer responsible for their actions.

Dad says that when he was a boy, back when a snowstorm was a snowstorm, the drifts were so deep that Sunday mornings they would ride their horse-drawn buggies to church across the hard-packed snow with nothing but tall treetops for road marks. The only hitching post folks could find was the church steeple. Parishioners had to dig tunnels through the snow to get inside, so only the truly faithful were there. One Sunday, while services were underway, a Chinook blew in, and by benediction time the snow was gone, and horses were dangling off the church roof.

"A good Chinook," Dad maintains, "can give the guy on the front of the horse frostbite and his passenger sunstroke."

Call it temporary insanity, but today the skyrocketing temperatures put me in mind of a plan to rid me of my albatross.

The limp is gone, and I break into a run as I head back to the damaged poplar tree and the scene of yesterday's snowmobile mishap. The snowmobile starts all right, but most of its life is gone. Lifting and heaving and grunting awhile, I pry it away from the poplar enough to start it in a southerly direction, easing the injured cat carefully out onto the ice above a particularly deep spot in Franklin's Creek. Back and forth I go, placing the heaviest rocks I can carry on the seat of the ugly beast.

As I stroll to school, I notice with satisfaction that the west winds are unrelenting, and the snow has turned to water cascading down the street in torrents.

By six o'clock, when I go back to check, the snowmobile is gone save for the tips of the skis. By morning it will be sunk as deeply as the Lusitania. I can't believe my luck.

Twelve

Ghosts

T here are things I haven't told you, things about this house."
Apparently Tony is hoping to raise what little hair I have
on the back of my scrawny neck with another one of his
spine-tinglers now that the evening has reached Spooky Hour and
the sky is moonless and none of us can sleep.

"Creepy things Dad doesn't want you to know," says my big
brother, whom I cannot see on account of the room being cat-
in-a-coal-cellar black. There is no way I am gonna be scared
tonight. Not a chance. Not if I can help it. I have had a bad enough
day as it is, what with lugging cumbersome rocks around and sinking a snowmobile. I weigh my options: Do I plunge beneath the
covers and plug my ears, humming something softly to myself?
Or do I listen in a detached sort of way, constantly reminding
myself that this is fiction, the product of a hyperactive imagination and the devouring of too many issues of the *Alfred Hitchcock
Mystery Magazine?*

"When we first moved in here," Tony continues in a quavery
voice that seems to surprise him, "there were strange things going
on at night that…well, caused me to wonder, I guess. But it wasn't
until I talked to one of the Jacobsen twins, who lived here before
us, that it all began to make sense. I think his name is Arty. Arty

128

Jacobsen. The other one was Marty, I think. Or maybe Bart. I can't remember. They're about your age, Terry."

"I thought it was a boy and girl and their names were Jekyll and Heidi," says Ben, hoping the humor will help.

"No, they live farther down the street," says Tony. "Anyhoo, do you want me to tell you? Or should I just try to forget about it?"

Ben says to hurry up and tell, but he doesn't say this in an eager sort of voice, not the voice you'd use when you want your Grandma to read another Christmas story before bed. Tony can tell you some eerie tales if he sets his mind to it. Like the time he told us about a guy whose plane crashed in the mountains, and he had to eat his own arm.

I bury my head momentarily, but if I have one major fault it is that I am passionately curious.

"I know I've told you other stories and tried to make them sound true and all, but this one is honest to God. Really. Cross my heart and hope to die, cover me with chicken feathers and watch me fry."

"Sure," says Ben. "Whatever—just hurry up and tell it, you dope."

Tony clears his throat first. "You know what it's like when you're in that no-man's-land between consciousness and sleep and something happens that whams you awake and you don't know what it was or who it was and whether or not it's under your bed or right beside you but your heart's a-thumping like it's about to go out of business?" When Tony is excited his sentences run on awhile.

Neither of us answers, but I know of what he speaks. I've been there.

"Well, little Arty woke up like that one night in the pitch dark right in this very room and heard a voice calling his name, and at first he thought it was Marty, but it was coming from the hallway.

'Arty, Arty,'" hoots Tony, sounding like a cross between an owl and some creature that's not properly medicated.

Ben starts to laugh.

"Smarten up, you egghead," says Tony. "I'm serious. This happened. I'll prove it later."

Ben smartens up.

"So like I was sayin'—"

"Now you're sounding like Uncle Roy," says Ben.

"If you don't want me to tell it, I won't. Maybe you're too scared."

Ben laughs at this, a brave yet unconvincing laugh.

"Little Arty told me all about it the day we moved in here," Tony begins. "He was standing across the street and wouldn't come in. Says that on that night, he pushed back the covers and coaxed his little feet across the floor toward the voice in the hallway. He was glad for the night-light his parents kept there, but suddenly it flickered and went out like a match in the wind. Arty's eyes blinked, and he hoped he was dreaming. That's when he saw the glow that seemed to come out of the attic above him. He'll wish all his life he'd just gone back to bed or crawled in with Marty or Bart, but he didn't. He lifted his eyes to the attic door. And what he saw there, he hadn't seen in his worst nightmares, and he'd had some doozers." Here Tony pauses, either adding to the suspense, or reliving the drama himself.

"What was it?" I am too scared to speak, so Ben asks this for me.

"It was an old man's bony hand, dangling from the crack in the attic door and scratching against the wall. It didn't seem to be attached to anything, but the index finger was motioning him nearer. Arty couldn't help himself, he told me. Said it was like he was in some nightmare where the bad guy is chasing you and your feet are cement, only this time the bad guy was calling him and there was nothing else he could do but go."

"See, that's crazy," says Ben. "Why do people do that?"

"I wish this last part wasn't true," says Tony. "I wish he'd never told it to me."

I wish some things myself. I wish Tony hadn't started spinning the yarn in the first place. I wish I didn't have to go to the bathroom so badly because if you think I'm going out into the hall tonight, you've never been more wrong. I wish the story was finished, but it isn't.

"When Arty got right below the attic door, an old man's face appeared. He knew that face. He loved that face. It was the face of his grandfather who'd just been buried a week before. As if that wasn't enough to stop his heart for a year, another face peeked out and smiled at him. It was the face of his brother Marty, who he thought was back in bed. Or maybe his name was Bart—I wish I could remember. Anyhoo, Arty lost it then. Ran into his bedroom screaming. Went completely loco. That's where his father found him, shaking Marty by the shoulders telling him to wake up, that he couldn't be dead. Marty was pretty surprised himself. He hasn't been the same since."

Ben and I are silent for a minute.

"You m-m-mean Marty was upstairs and in his bed at the same time?" I manage.

"That's what Arty told me."

I try to process this, and sheer terror sets in no matter what I tell myself. It's worse than lying awake and trying to figure out when eternity will end, knowing things can't continue forever.

"You said you could prove it," said Ben. "How?"

"I'll show you the scratch marks on the wall in the morning."

"Ben," I say in a timid little voice, "would you mind coming with me? I have to go to the bathroom."

I sleep little this night. An hour. Maybe two. It's hard to tell when you're sleeping with your brother and you can't see the watch on his arm. But when the peace of sleep finally settles across my little body, I dream that the ocean has arrived just to the west of us, flooding Seattle and the whole of Washington and Idaho, washing right into Grace and turning her into a coastal town, actually a grand little island with tropical sand beaches and parrots in the palm trees. The only thing missing is Gilligan, whose absence is not recognized, for we have no television. Our radios, however, have nothing but static on them. Nothing else exists save our little island of about a mile square. Mary Beth Swanson is somewhere in my dream, but sadly she plays a minor role. Everything else is perfect. I have never been happier.

—⁓—

Friday morning finds me sitting in school nursing a Chinook hangover and wondering what in the world to do with the remainder of the money. Less than a week and the thief will be released from Liberty County Jail and I am running out of hiding places. My desk? Impossible. The janitor would find it, or bills would come fluttering out while I rummaged around, trying to find my Bible memory verse cards. Our car? Not an option. Where in the car? Under the spare tire? We change our bald tires too often. Dad will find it. Wouldn't that be something? How about the bank? Just go in and open up a savings account. Start with a small deposit. Tell them Uncle Roy died and I've hit the big time.

"Boys and girls," Miss Hoover interrupts my daydreaming. "It is time for us to write out the Bible verse we've memorized."

Uh-oh. What to do? I haven't had a decent mark since first grade.

I fish around for my verse cards, a stack of a hundred three-by-three cards held together by a stainless steel ring. I locate them easily. Some of the kids take them home or study them in the school yard during recess. I have been doing other things the last few weeks.

Carving the words carefully, I write "Bible Memory" at the top of the page, mindful of the fact that Miss Hoover gives marks not only for accuracy but also for penmanship. Very carefully, with loops she will be proud of, I begin to write in King James English: "These nine things…" and that's as much as I can remember.

Glancing about the room I lift the lid carefully and slide the stack from my desk, trapping it beneath one leg. The other children are writing, stooped in diligence. No one seems to notice. I lift my leg to see what I've forgotten, which is just about every other word. *Aha*, now I remember. I begin to write, checking only when necessary:

> These six things doth the Lord hate: Yea, seven are an abomination unto Him: A proud look, a lying tongue, and hands that shed innocent blood. An heart that deviseth wicked imaginations, feet that be swift in running to mischief, a false witness that speaketh lies, and he that soweth discord among brethren. My son, keep thy father's commandment, and forsake not the law of thy mother. Bind them continually upon thine heart, and tie them about thy neck.

I cock my head and squint happily at the paper. It is the first time this year that I have referenced a Bible text correctly, Proverbs 6:16-21, and it is a brilliant achievement. Depending on my penmanship, my mark could reach 95, maybe even 100—the first for me in a while. Well, let me be honest—the first for me *ever*.

I would be less than truthful if I told you that I didn't notice those words or that my conscience wasn't nagging me during all of this. In fact, lately I seem to be a tourist in my very own body. I know what to do, but I don't do it. I know what not to do, and I do it profusely. I blunder on, while my conscience comes behind me, shaking its head.

I've heard Pastor Davis say that a quiet conscience sleeps in the loudest thunderstorm, but an uneasy one is a sharp stone in your shoe. He may be right. This stone has been irritating me since I bought that very first candy necklace. But the more the two of us argue, the more victories I win, and the more victorious I become, the more I begin to rationalize that given my circumstances, who wouldn't do what I am doing? I really have no choice.

My conscience started to unravel with the smallest sin. And that sin has made a hole I can stick my head through.

For the first time in my life, I feel as if the foundation of all I've been building is crumbling beneath me. In fact, I begin to doubt the truth of the very verses I have written. As I squint at them once more, I fully expect the words to vanish like they were written with disappearing ink.

—∞—

Friday nights are reserved for youth group. It is held in the church sometimes, but lately we meet in Davie Foster's basement, where the cookies and punch are more plentiful thanks to Davie's new bride, who rarely leaves his side except to get pencils or Bibles or anything else he might need. All the teenage girls (except for

Mary Beth, I think) have crushes on him. Ironically, his wife is a best friend to all of them.

We were hoping to play an exciting game of smuggling Bibles past security checkpoints, but the weather is too cold. Instead, Noah Corzini is here with his guitar and flood pants. Tony is sitting up straight; he brought his Bible. Michael Swanson came with my little atheist friend, Danny Brown. Mary Beth is faithful in attendance too, and I am glad.

She sits across from me on the other side of the Ping-Pong table, which partially obscures my view of her, so I will have to be content with just her top half and the toes of her tennis shoes. During prayer I squeeze my eyes almost shut and then rest my elbows on my knees and my fingers on my face, parting them just right so I can watch Mary Beth unawares. Her eyes are closed, but this doesn't stop her from looking magnificent. She is the most beautiful girl I've met, strong but by no means too big, persistent but not annoying. The slightest gap splits her two front teeth, her blond hair is drawn into pigtails, and Prince Val bangs curl over her forehead. What would she say if she knew I loved her? That I'd never loved anyone else except my mother? That I'd been sneaking a peek at as much of her as I could see while she didn't know it? Would she laugh and whisper something silly to an older boy? Or would she be flattered and flushed?

We go around the circle, sharing prayer concerns so that we can "bear one another's burdens," as Davie puts it. I have an unspoken request. I look at Mary Beth when I say this, and her brother, Michael seems surprised too. We sing some new songs tonight, and I like one called "Happiness Is the Lord," although the elders have insisted the last verse be changed from "taking a trip that leads to heaven" because of the obvious reference to drug use. Instead we sing, "taking a journey."

Tonight's topic is martyrdom, and Davie begins to wax eloquent on the subject of persecution, referencing a very thick book called *Foxe's Book of Martyrs* that is only partially understandable to a boy who is already severely sidetracked by the view across the Ping-Pong table. Davie talks of laying down our lives for God and asks probing questions of us. "Is the Christian life all about being comfortable? What about where the Bible says that we should take up our cross and follow Jesus? What does that mean?

"The truth is," explains Davie, "the Communists are only a missile away. They could be here any day, and we need to think of these things. If they bury us up to our necks in dirt and stand around with their shovels full, ready to pile it higher, would we renounce the name of Christ or die with honor like the people in this book?"

Tony is taking this stuff seriously. I can tell by the look on his face and the eagerness with which he flips through his Bible, searching for something he knows to be there.

One of the older kids chimes in. "I'd die before I'd give in to those Commies." He seems angry, as if he knows some of them personally.

But Tony isn't so sure. "You haven't been there," he says. "I don't know what I'd do. Maybe you don't know 'til it happens, and I hope it doesn't."

Commies makes me think of a form of physical torture my brother Ben once inflicted upon me wherein he straddled himself atop my body in the living room so I couldn't move my arms and pounded his knuckle gently on my sternum, tap, tap, tap, until I was ready to die. He called it Commies, and I can't imagine anything much worse. Not even Chinese water torture, which I hope Ben never hears of.

I know what I'd do if they buried me and threatened to finish the job. I'd recant. Then recant about recanting after they let me go. I don't think I'll suggest it though. I wonder what Mary Beth thinks. I would do anything to save her pretty little hide from the Communists, this I know. I would offer them big bundles of American cash. That would do it.

Suddenly I am thinking of the money again and I find myself starting to squirm. Less and less do I fit with these people surrounding me. These saints. I find myself wanting to be somewhere else. Anywhere else. All this talk of persecution and taking up crosses and bearing one another's burdens is enough to make me want to run someplace and hide. I am surprised to find that I am beginning to want none of the things Tony wants. I don't know if I'll ever have the nerve to tell him, but this stifling and sequestered church stuff is all right for old people whose best years are behind them—maybe even my brother if he wants it—but not for me. Not now.

Some can wait for streets of gold. I want to laugh and dance and do some things on the streets down here. I want to choose my own music and buy my own stuff without having to hide it and maybe watch some television without adults choosing the channels. I want to blow a few smoke rings and taste a beer or two and kiss this bombshell on yonder side of the Ping-Pong table.

The stuff I'm hungry for they don't dole out in church.

More than anything, I'd like my mother back—the way she used to be. If God is around, why doesn't He do His part? Where is He when you need Him?

With the final prayer, I stride into the icy air of a winter evening and feel a welcome release from the stuffy Bible study. Free will is a wonderful gift. So why not exercise mine? The truth shall set you free, they said. And they were right. The truth is, there are more than enough people around here to keep up the charade. Why don't I do things my way?

The kind of freedom I'm sensing is startling. I understand those released prisoners who want to peel off their clothes. "Rules," I've heard our pastor say, "are the rails beneath your train. You'll skid a ways without them, but not in the direction you'd hoped." For the first time, I'm convinced that he is wrong. Suddenly I have the desire to boast about my prize. To tell someone. But who? You don't tell your brother you've found all this loot, not when he's walking alongside you headed for home whistling "It Came upon a Midnight Clear."

I'll tell the prettiest girl on earth, that's who. Maybe ask her to elope with me tomorrow. I grin at this sudden rush of silliness.

The hard snow crunches beneath our feet, and the darkness reminds me of Tony's story last night. I shudder. The tale has stayed with me all day. The bony hand. The frightened child. A thought pops into my mind like a lazy fly ball to center field. The thought causes a smile to creep across my face, and I can't keep it from spreading.

The perfect hiding place for the money is closer than I thought.

—m—

Tony's spider plant is thriving amid the playing of the Christian rock-and-roll music. A new tape is in the deck, from Randy Stonehill, another guy with way too much hair. Arthur Tucker, our barber, would love to get ahold of him. He attacks the guitar like our pastor's wife attacks the organ, singing,

> We are all like foolish puppets
> Who desiring to be kings

Now lie pitifully crippled
After cutting our strings.

Liz claims the plant has never looked better and that Tony
should turn the music up a little, just to confirm his experiment.
I wonder what other lies I've been listening to in church.

Thirteen

Philanthropist

D ad is sitting deep in his favorite chair, having just flipped on the lamp beside him to the brightest setting, which is the third click. Dinner is history, the dishes washed by Liz and me, the frying pan scrubbed of lightly singed potatoes and carrots, save for a few mulish streaks. This day has passed like the others for me, stuffed with strategizing and sidestepping and a new resolve to carry this thing through. I've been watching my father for some time now, wondering how long I can stand the suspense and why he won't put down *The Daily Bread* and glance at the mail pile, for Pete's sake.

Finally.

Thumbing through the stack of mail, he whistles softly and shakes his head. Another bill. Yesterday I overheard him tell Mother, between huge sighs, of another creditor on the doorstep. "We have enough money to last us the rest of our lives," he said, "unless we live past the end of the month." His comments set me to thinking. Tonight the urge to spy over his shoulder almost overtakes me, but I stand in the doorway, feigning thoughts of other matters.

There are four envelopes, three of them bills. I should know. I checked earlier. The fourth I am familiar with, and when he reaches for it, I cannot watch, so I leave the room. But *not* watching is worse. Quickly I return with a *National Geographic* and sit down, faking an interest in pygmies in Uganda (although their outfits are intriguing), peering over the top of the magazine. Dad is staring at the envelope in his hands like my mother does when receiving a birthday gift. Why won't he hurry it up? He turns it over twice, shakes it once, scrutinizing every nook and cranny, studying every word. The typewritten address is to Mr. Anderson, Box 117, Grace. There is no return address and no stamp, which is not uncommon in our community. People drop mail in neighbor's boxes often enough. Inside the envelope is a note. It is typewritten too. It simply says,

> Dear John,
>
> We knowed you might be needing this. God bless y'all.
>
> A consarned brother and sister.

Tucked inside the note are ten crisp twenty-dollar bills that flutter to the floor. Dad lets out a startled gasp as he picks them up one by one. He hollers "Praise God, from whom all blessings flow." It is partly sung, mostly yelled. He leaps to his feet. The energy he displays makes him a dozen years younger. Thumping me between the shoulder blades, he charges into the bedroom with the news.

"What? What is it?" I call out, running quickly after him and lunging onto the bed, looking over his shoulder.

"You won't believe it, Ruth! God is so good! Look here." Dad waves the money before her, takes her hand and kisses it hard. She smiles awkwardly and he leans over to kiss her mouth. "Let's

thank Him right now." He grabs me with his other hand and we
bow our heads.

"Dear Father, Thou hast provided once again. May we always
remember what we receive and forget what we give. Bless the hands
of those who sent this. Amen."

I am not really listening now.

I am squinting proudly at the twenties.

—m—

The easiest part of all of this is the giving. The toughest part
is the hiding. I sneak bundles of bills from the skate shack when
I can, but it's not easy work. Usually someone is in there, and sometimes the someone is two someones, couples who should not be
alone and certainly should not be kissing. There are rules against
this kind of behavior, laid down clearly in our handbook, but if
you think I'm squealing on the offending parties, you're wrong.
A boy in my shoes doesn't go around looking for enemies. Nor
does a skunk point his paw at others and say, *"Whooie!"*

As it turns out, the safest hiding place in the world is not
beneath my bed as I once believed.

The safest place is about eight feet above it. In the attic, home
to mysteries and rumors and who knows what else.

My brothers won't go up there for all the beans in Boston if
Tony's story is even halfway true. By the time we bring down the
screen windows in the spring, I'll have thought of someplace else.
But how to get up there without getting noticed? As Tony says,
"Where there's a will, there's a lawyer." There's also a way, and I'm
determined to find it.

—m—

On Tuesday I awake with a dreadful touch of the flu and lie in bed moaning. It's probably the cookies Davie Foster's wife baked. I had seven of them four nights ago. While Ben and Liz and Tony are trying to get into our one and only bathroom, I am in there throwing up something awful. If you've heard someone similarly occupied, you will know that it tends to quiet you down and help you determine not to express anger toward them for making you late for school even if you are hopping around with your legs crossed, as are four other people in our one-bathroom house.

Did you know that if you rub the silver tip of a thermometer hard enough, the friction can cause the mercury to reach temperatures of a hundred and two? It's true. But you have to rub it fast. Did you also know if you lock the bathroom door and place two or three washcloths in the plastic cottage cheese container you use to rinse your hair, fill it high with water, and dump it into the toilet while making horrific gagging sounds, no one at all questions whether or not you are sick enough to stay home for the day?

That is precisely what I am up to this morning. By nine o'clock I am lying on our lime green Naugahyde sofa listening to Aunt Teresa records, my favorite story being the one about the monkey at the zoo who couldn't escape though his cage door was wide open. Trouble was, the creature kept reaching back into his cage for a juicy apple and hanging on to it until the zookeeper found him there, clutching the apple tightly, unable to pull his hands through the bars because he wanted it. The poor little guy chose Granny Smith over freedom.

Mother sits beside me, lightly patting my shoulder like she's burping a baby, her hands trembling and me feeling guilty for keeping her out of bed. Her eyes flutter a lot, especially when the sun is bright, and she stammers as she talks to me, sometimes leaving big holes in her stories on account of the memory loss that comes with the territory this disease occupies. I have seen her stand in one place for an hour without going anywhere or doing anything, and my heart aches as if it will burst. Dad comes along with his strong arms and carries her to bed.

"I love you, Ruthie Anderson," he'll say in a tender voice, rubbing his whiskers against her soft cheek. "You're the ice cream on my cake."

She laughs like she's in tenth grade. And tells him she has a craving for cake and ice cream.

"You mean like you did when you were pregnant? Uh-oh!"

She laughs again. "Bring me some, Dear," she says, and dad passes along the command, "Get some ice cream quick, Terry Paul, your mother's gonna have a baby."

But there is no ice cream to be found.

Except when Dad starts looking. I don't know where he gets it.

Once I was standing before our fridge trying to find something worth eating. There was half a bottle of milk (minus the cream), a loaf of cracked wheat bread, and some garden vegetables best before a long time ago. The freezer above contained nothing more than a tray of ice—I looked, I saw it. But when Dad brushed past me and opened the freezer door, his faith was greater than mine. He pulled from it a fresh carton of Goodrich Vanilla, "Serving Sweet Memories Since 1932," and took two spoons to the bedroom, leaving me dumbfounded and blinking. Either I was blind or he was a magician. Take your pick. "You gotta know how to look," was his only explanation.

Wonders never cease.

"Terry," says Mom, shaking me from that majestic memory. "Terry," she starts up again, then waits a minute as if she's lost her place in a book. "When I was a girl in the late twenties back in New York, I dreamed of singing on the radio one day. My dad built ours from parts he found and parts he bought, and we used to listen to music in the evenings from places like Schenectady and Pittsburgh. Mozart was my favorite."

"I didn't know Mozart was a town," I say.

Mom has a delightful little laugh, a chortle, I guess you'd call it, and she opens her eyes briefly when she draws upon it. Then she stops, perhaps reliving old times, perhaps losing her place again. "What was I saying?" she asks, still smiling, and it frightens me to think this fate could ever be mine.

"You were talking about the radio and about Pittsburgh."

"Oh. Did I tell you I was captain of my high school debating team? I loved the excitement. The crowds. In eleventh grade we won the championship for our district, and I was elected class president and valedictorian the next year."

"Did you go to college?" I'd better ask something sensible.

She pauses again. "I had to stay home and care for my father. We were still recovering from the Great Depression then, and Dad had been without a job for quite a while. He began dropping things and causing accidents and not getting along with people. He had three brothers with the…with it, and that's when he found out he was much like them. His father and grandfather had already died of it, you know."

"When did you know you had…it, Mom?"

"I think you were four when we knew for sure, Terry. It was in the news the year before when Woody Guthrie, the folk music star, died from it. You know who he is? Woody Guthrie?"

"Nope."

"He wrote 'This Land Is My Land.'"

"Oh, we've sung it in the car."

As Mom talks, I am aware of deep emotions within me, the same emotions I entertained while reading the end of *Where the Red Fern Grows*, and I want her to go on like this forever, smiling widely and talking of happier times. I wonder what it would be like to have her come to my hockey games or make supper and read me a book before she tucks me in. The last time she asked me to fish down a book was four or five years ago. The book was lodged between Robert Louis Stevenson and Mark Twain. It was called *Suzie's Babies*. The cover advertised "a charming story about a mother hamster and the birth of her young that will help parents explain with reverence and wholesome frankness how children are born"—hardly what I would have picked had I done the choosing. It told me how Mr. and Mrs. Hamster waited until they were married before deciding to have children, and she explained in startling detail how the little ones came to be.

I pull my mind back to the topic at hand. "Mom, isn't there something they can do for you? I mean, any treatment or something? Or are we too poor?"

The smile is gone and her eyes stop twitching just for a moment. "No, Terry. There's nothing we know of. But you know something? God is with me. Sometimes I wish He'd take this burden away, but I guess He's just gonna give us the strength to carry it." She says this, not like some faraway preacher on the radio, but as my mother, as one who lives with it every day. "Sometimes it feels like He's locked the doors of heaven," she adds, "but I know He's there. You must too, Son. And there's something else. I get to pray more often than most. I pray for you many times every single day. God's got something down the road that will surprise you an awful bunch."

With that, she stands awkwardly to her feet and doesn't move for a solid minute. I don't know if I should help her or just wait, so I wait.

Aunt Teresa finishes a story about missionaries in Borneo, and when she does, Mom is off to her bedroom, where I know she will spend the rest of the day.

I listen to a few more stories and then tiptoe down the hall to see if she's sleeping yet. I'm in luck. Her head is propped against two fat feather pillows, and the nightstand is a small pharmacy. A plaque above her head reads, "He ransoms me from death and surrounds me with love and tender mercies." I stand in the doorway looking in on her with no small degree of shame. Ah, Mother. What chance does a sinner like me stand when there's such a saint in the house?

I turn my back and return to the living room. Quietly I raise the lid on the plywood cabinet that conceals our record player, and lift the repeat arm. This side of the record will play over and over while I'm gone.

—m—

The skate shack is empty of course, honest kids being in school, tugging on pigtails and scratching in notebooks. Fourteen trips (I counted them) with my brother Ben's backpack does the trick, and before an hour is out I have crammed the underside of my bed full of greenbacks, leaving an empty Detroit Red Wings hockey bag on the frozen floor of the secret tunnel. Then I think better of it. I may need the bag to hide the bills. On the fifteenth trip I fold it neatly at first, then stuff it into Ben's pack, making a mess of the job.

Only once do I break a sweat. On my final expedition, Mrs. MacDonald comes around the corner in her late-model Ford and pulls over to ask if I need a ride and what I'm carrying. "Just paperbacks for my mother," I reply, which is the closest I've come to telling the truth in a while. "Thanks anyway, but I need the exercise."

As she pulls away, a chilling thought rattles me. What if she tells my mom? A kid doesn't bring books home in the morning to a mother who hasn't been able to read in years. My mind overflows with what ifs. What if Mrs. MacDonald is waiting for me when I get there? What if the record begins to skip and mom gets up? What if she calls dad? "Don't think about it," I tell myself out loud. "Think of other stuff. Think Ford: Found On Road Dead. Fix Or Repair Daily."

———〰———

From an under-stuffed kitchen chair I reach up and pull the ringed handle on the attic door in the ceiling of the hallway. Mom is still asleep, and it's nearing eleven o'clock. I have less than an hour before the family arrives for lunch. The attic door won't budge. I pull harder. I hadn't anticipated this. I tug hard with both hands. The door starts slowly at first, then swings downward as if the reluctant hinges don't appreciate the interruption. A foldout ladder is attached to the door, and thankfully it is well oiled against squeaking. I guess that's why little Arty or Marty, or whatever his name is, was so surprised.

Only now does the sheer terror of Tony's story slam into me. The ghostly grandfather holding his cloned grandchild. What if Gramps is still up there, cloning more children? Cloning me or my brothers? Will Tony and Ben be up there waiting for me?

"Think Ford," I whisper. "Or Chev. Cheap Hutterite Escape Vehicle."

The humor helps for sure.

Our attic is shrouded in mystery. Always has been for me. It is my brothers' job to bring the winter storm windows down. It is my job to stand at the bottom and hope against their dropping them. I am the weather forecaster, just waiting for something to fall.

But not today. Today I glance around, owl-like. This is my first time on our top floor, and I am surprised to find my own breath up here in the cold.

No wonder. Suffused light struggles in through a shuttered window at the north end of the attic. There is no glass on the window, just a badly ripped screen. Another window guards the south side and a brighter alpenglow leaks through it, spreading sparse light on the floorboards, which made walking up here safe. Off to each side between the rafters is sawdust and insulation, dusty and dark. No boards there. Just floor joists. No coffins or bodies either. Not yet. Where shall I hide the dough? I notice that my hands are shaking. No time for that. "Think Ford," I say, a little louder this time. I try to remember the others Tony has told me about on the evening radio show. "Pinto. Put In New Transmission Often. Volkswagen. Virtually Worthless."

Back in my room I transfer money by the armload into the hockey bag and lug it up the stairs. By the time I've reached Pontiac (Plenty Of Noises That Irritate And Clank), half the pile is gone from beneath my bed. By the time I've thought of a few others, like Dodge (Drips Oil, Drips Grease Everywhere), Beetle (Battered Everywhere Expect To Lose Engine), and BMW (Bavarian Manure Wagon), I've only a trip or two to make and I am back to Ford (Found on Roof Decaying, Fast Only Rolling Downhill).

The hockey bag is hidden now behind a large cedar chest on the west side of the attic, just above my room. The chest is filled with memorabilia and historical news clippings. I should know. I snooped. The bag fits neatly across three or four sturdy two-by-twelves, so there's no need to worry about it crashing down in the middle of the night.

With the ladder up and the attic door firmly shut and the under-stuffed chair in its rightful spot under the kitchen table, I check on Mom again. She is stirring a little but seems to hear nothing. It is quarter to twelve. The troops will arrive soon, hungry as wolves. I grab a piece of bread from the fridge, climb back into my Toronto Maple Leaf pajamas, and crawl under the quilt on the sofa.

I can't help the grin. Tonight my father will find another envelope buried with the others in our mailbox. A thicker one this time. His talk of selling our old DeSoto will cease, and our grocery troubles for November will come to an end. Maybe I'll figure a way to buy him a new car. A Dodge Royal Monaco. One with a 440 automatic and the six-way power seat for the driver.

The record has skipped to the beginning for the umpteenth time, and Aunt Teresa is talking again, telling the story of the monkey who couldn't escape. The one who wouldn't let go of the apple. The record begins to skip, playing over and over the voices of the other animals in the zoo: "Let go of the apple and run!"

I nudge the needle forward.

"Stupid monkey," I say out loud.

—ɯɯ—

The money I've hidden behind Ben's tobacco and paperbacks is missing tonight, and there's a somber conference going on in my parents' bedroom. Cupping my ear to their door, I listen. Much of it eludes me. Ben has done something serious, this much I know. He is sorry, he says, but Dad is equally insistent. "This is the third time, Son, and we have to protect him. You must leave tonight." I wonder what he could possibly mean, and I can hear Mother's soft whimpers. "Ben," she sobs, "we love you, Son. Please don't go." I can hear Uncle Roy attempting to make a point, and Tony is in there too, trying to play peacemaker.

I pull back from the door just in time. A stubborn and resolute Ben strides past me and into our bedroom.

I follow and sit on my bed in terror, about to lose my brother. "Why?" is all I can ask, as I wipe away the tears.

His eyes flash anger my way and his red hair seems darker somehow. Yanking clothing from his drawer, he stuffs it hastily into a small and tattered suitcase. I watch him slam the forbidden paperbacks in there. The pipe too.

"I must go, Terry," he says, and for a moment he offers me a compassionate smile. "I'm leaving with Uncle Roy. You take good care of your mother."

Fourteen

Revival

Folks from as far away as Riverton attend the Friday evening revival service, trudging their way through icy streets and packing our little clapboard church out into the foyer. More than two hundred, by Dad's estimate, many of them complete pagans. I can't remember anything this large taking place in our church.

Though I am anything but eager to attend, Ben's absence has brought more silence and gloom to our house, and this is the only show in town.

Far south of here in the month of July, the meetings began. But the Baptists delayed them from moving north long into August by following the preacher's advice and getting revived. The Methodists had them next, then the Presbyterians, who held them over for a second blessing. By the time the revival reached us, winter had too. It's a cold place to host almost anything, and Ernest Murphy, the revivalist, has been dreaming of warmer climes all this week, hoping to wind things down in time for Christmas back in Ireland.

The meetings started with barely a flicker on Monday but were fanned into flames last night when a local farmer, Mel Hutchinson, came forward to lay down a burden he'd been lugging around since the night he graduated from high school. The entire town knew about that night. The tragic accident. How they found his charred body a hundred feet from the truck, barely alive and wreaking of alcohol. Two girls in the backseat had met eternity in the terrible crash, and although Mel lost his license for a year, it wasn't punishment enough for those whose opinions were shared openly over free refills at the Garlic Grill. Nor was it punishment enough for Mel. Shunned by most, including members of his own family, Mel turned to alcohol as his only handrail during the unsteady journey to middle age. He knew whiskey wasn't the answer. But it sure helped him forget the questions.

Married now, with two daughters of his own, his life was a bundle of ironies wrapped up in contradictions. The one thing he couldn't bar the door against was a praying wife, and just last night, as I was examining the thriving plant life in our room and thinking of the treasures overhead, all those incongruities met their match when he came forward and knelt in confession and an endless flood of tears. Rarely does good news travel as fast as bad, but it's been happening all day. Now other praying wives have been coaxing husbands out of basements and bars to come hear the voice Mel Hutchinson heard last night.

Normally I try to scare up a game of fox and geese or hockey on Friday nights, but Dad insists I make this pilgrimage along with Tony. "I'd rather you not miss this, Son. Come with an open heart; you never know what God will do."

The decision is made easier when I find out that Mary Beth Swanson will be here. I've been thinking about that sweet little gap in her teeth all day, and the blond curl on her radiant forehead. Twice I saw her in the hallway, and once she smiled at me and said, "Hi!" I was too shocked to respond though. It's something I'm working on.

Mary Beth is unarguably the most charming girl in the eighth grade—the whole school, for that matter. As if her beauty isn't enough, she carves the most beautiful circles in the ice once she pulls a pair of figure skates onto her tiny feet. Last winter she fell as she skated past me, letting out a delightful gasp at first, then a desperate scream. I glided on over to her and applied the brakes, dropped my hockey stick and extended my thin little hands. I wish that just once everyone on earth could experience the look she proffered me. And I suppose it was that look that had been luring me to the revival meeting since Liz informed me that Mary Beth would be present this memorable night.

Sure enough, she chooses a pew with her parents, directly across the aisle from me. If I lean forward just right and pretend I have to scratch my right ear, I can turn and see her cherubic face. She sure isn't hard to look at, that's for sure. What shall I buy this girl I love? A locket for both our pictures? A soft sweater? A yacht?

Her brother, Michael, is there, wedged between his parents. Shall I tell him the truth about the snowmobile? He's already been asking how she works, provoking more lies from my imaginative mind.

I sit between Dad and my big brother, bored as usual. Tony is wearing navy blue pants tonight. Flared ones. I scratch on them with a Bic pen and notice that the ink matches the pants. "Hey, cut it out," he whispers, putting a finger to his lips. You'd think this would be the ideal place for one of his palindromes, like "He lived as a devil, eh?"

I wish Ben were here. At the very least he'd write something lame, like "Bible stands for Basic Information Before Leaving Earth." Something to make me think about something else. He never did fit here, however. When they found out about the cigarettes, church folks wrote him off or just plain ignored him as if he was permanently damaged merchandise. It doesn't help that he's always trying to quit, always having his last one.

Tony doesn't seem his usual mischievous self tonight, and the only element of humor comes when Reverend Davis takes up the offering. "I have good news, and I have bad news,"our minister grins. "The good news is we have enough money to pay for the expenses of this dear traveling minister. The bad news is it's still out there in your pockets." People laugh and give generously.

The introduction is brief. Pastor Davis lists Reverend Ernest Murphy's credentials, though they aren't really important, he says. What is important is that God has been using him to light a match to three states in the last six months, and the fire is now raging out of control. Our pastor leads in a short prayer, and Mr. Murphy, a kind-faced, red-headed man with a strong Irish accent seizes the stage, introducing his only daughter, Sharon, a dark-haired jowly girl with serious eyes. Sharon quickly takes to the organ, pushing levers, but she's no match for Irene Davis, I quickly conclude. The visiting preacher's wife is shorter than her daughter, more pie-faced and weather-beaten. Quickly she straps herself to an accordion, and you can tell she knows how to use it.

I've been expecting someone a lot larger and louder than Mr. Murphy, perhaps a lumberjack-like preacher shouting through a megaphone, more like John the Baptist. But when the singing is done, I soon understand why the people love to listen to him preach. For one thing, Reverend Murphy's brogue is smooth as silk, and even better, he keeps his message brief and to the point, peppering it with succinct questions and interesting stories, far from what I've been dreading.

"Top of the evenin' to you," he begins with a smile, and no one is quite sure how to respond.

I lean forward to see what Mary Beth is doing. She is listening intently.

"If you remember my preaching tonight, I have failed," says Reverend Murphy, that rich silk voice shrouding the sanctuary. "You go away talkin' about Ernest Murphy, and tonight will have been a disaster, a calamity." This throws me for a bit of a loop until he explains himself: "I don't want to be remembered. I want God to be remembered. You leave here rememberin' what God did in this place, and the prayers of a host of holy people will be answered."

Amens are hardly commonplace at Grace Community Church, but they are this night. Mr. Murphy speaks eloquently of the brevity of life and of trains bearing down on us while we are battling to start the stalled car, caught like a deer in the cross-hairs.

I don't think I have ever felt more temporal than I do listening to him preach. My life has become a mere breath, a fading flower, withering grass, and Reverend Murphy has ample Scripture verses to hang these images on. One glance over at Mary Beth and I know we'll be a while. Tears are streaming down her lovely cheeks and matting her blond curls together. I wonder what a thirteen-year-old like her has to cry about. But when Mrs. Murphy and her daughter take to the platform to favor us with a duet, "O Love that will not let me go, I rest my weary soul in Thee," and then, "Softly and tenderly Jesus is calling, calling, O sinner, come home," I find that tears have visited my own face too. I wipe them away stubbornly. No way am I falling for this.

"The gospel is a lifeboat, not a showboat," says Reverend Murphy, relieving his wife of the microphone. "When God comes down, things happen that I cannot explain. People thirst for Him more than for alcohol; they long for Him more than pleasure. The grip of sin is broken. Reconciliation is sought and granted. Material things take their rightful place, and spiritual things capture people's hearts. We treasure usefulness to God over career advancement. We watch a wave of divine grace wash over the church and spill into the streets. That is what happens when God comes down. And He's doing it tonight, friends, He's doing it tonight."

It is the first time I've heard my dad say "Amen!" out loud in church. It's not that he's as reserved as the others, it's just that he's more likely to lift his hands to heaven very quietly, which brings a lot of stares our way. Most people here think that raising your hands is something you do only when shot at with live ammunition or when taken captive.

I shall always remember my father's face this night.

The wrinkles seem gone, as if the burdens he carries have been momentarily lifted by the sacredness of the evening. His King James is beside him, worn from use. I carefully open the covers, which threaten to fall apart. Notes are etched in the margins, arrows and colored pencil markings point to passages and preachers' favorite sayings. Dad bows his head in prayer as one by one, folks begin walking to the front and forming a line that snakes away from the right side of the podium. One by one, with shaky hands, they take the microphone from Reverend Murphy, who stands behind them, encouraging their halting confession, offering Kleenex and sometimes a prayer or a warm hug. A few confess to being envious of others, some to greed and lust. I'll admit that it is fascinating stuff, and I almost feel guilty for listening in.

Nathan Lewis, who owns the butchershop, confesses to lying about the steer he said had uttered prophesies in Hebrew just before being butchered, and Mrs. Gorman admits that she didn't really have relatives living in New York City at all, it was just her way of sounding cosmopolitan. Three folks from across the creek come forward for salvation. They are weeping. I wonder what I would say if I took the microphone. Would they even let me? Would they even listen? There's no way I would be serious, not after my recent resolve to simply endure this show. I picture myself clearing my tenor throat and saying, "I was a rebel. I was a thief. I stole things. I lied. And then I was saved at the age of four." Would they laugh at me or look disappointed? The more I listen the sillier it all sounds. Each new confession brings relief to me. Maybe my own sins, if you can call them that, aren't so bad after all.

An hour passes, and it seems to me that the genuinely penitent have had their say and that the rest are merely succumbing to peer pressure or making stuff up. An hour of this and a man gets restless, so you can imagine how a twelve-year-old boy feels. Think of yourself when you were my age. I tap my Dad's knee and wriggle past him. "I need a drink," I explain.

Dad's forehead is furrowed again, like a washboard, and I can see that he is looking in Michael's direction. I wonder why. I have to jostle past a hundred people on my way through the foyer and down the stairs, but finally I make it. Coming out of the restroom, I find Mary Beth, and the next thing I know we are standing together at the drinking fountain in the pale glow of a bare light bulb and she is blowing her nose into a hanky that must be her father's.

It is a magical moment for me, being this close to her.

"Pretty good, hey?" I say, pointing up toward the sanctuary.

She looks at me blankly as if I have just described the sun as a lukewarm object. Perhaps my inclination to say dumb things around beautiful girls got its start that night. I do not know.

Then she smiles.

I press the button on the fountain and hold it down for her. Mary Beth steps closer, roping her golden hair behind her head and stooping to take a sip. I can smell her perfume. Avon perhaps. Her angelic face is soft, powdered I think, and her lips arch upward at the corners in a perma-pressed smile.

"Thank you," she says in a sweeter voice than the choirs of heaven use.

"No…thank you," I stammer. Again, I don't know why.

"For what?" she wipes the corners of her mouth daintily.

"Um…for…well, for coming down here, I guess. I…uh…I wanted to talk to you." Nothing else comes to me, but I must keep talking. I must make it up mid-sentence, only knowing I can't stand it if she leaves me here or makes me sit upstairs for another hour of increasingly boring confessions.

"About what?"

"About being…well, I'm sorry for, um…I'm sorry for…for liking you so much. I need to apologize. Will you forgive me? I'll st—"

To this day I can't believe what happens next, and I think you'll be surprised too.

She claps one hand over my mouth and smiles at me as if I have just given her a store-wrapped Christmas gift. The smile continues to sneak across the rest of her face, and I don't think she knows it. As surely as I am alive she glances around to make sure no one is looking and then grabs me by the ears and pulls my face down to hers.

In retrospect, it wasn't the best kiss I've ever received. It needed practicing, but it was the most unexpected one ever and a little dangerous too, which made it all the sweeter.

What would her father think? Or her brother?

"Don't apologize," she says when she has finished with me. "It's rather nice to be liked, and I hope you won't stop. Maybe I'll marry you one day."

It would be fine if my day ended here, but it doesn't. We walk hand in hand from Sunday school room to Sunday school room, me in a dream world walking on air. Nothing on earth matters anymore. Not my marks in school, not Fidel Castro's Communists invading from Cuba, not being picked last at all the sporting events in my brief history—not even the money stashed away in our attic. We stand together looking at Bible pictures hanging on walls. I cannot believe the vibrant colors. They spring to life like never before. Samson wrestling a fierce lion. David twirling a sling. Jesus bouncing a child on his lap. And I know without a doubt that God loves me again and that I need to repent and that I will do that just as soon as we climb the stairs together hand in hand. The future is brighter than it has ever been before. Folks upstairs are not the only ones being regenerated in this place. When all is said and done, I know that I will take good care of this woman, even if I am poor like my father, even if I'm not a millionaire.

We don't say much, Mary Beth and I (good thing for me), but as we stare at Solomon with a baby in one arm and two mothers tugging at the other, a dull but decisive thud wafts through the floorboards from somewhere overhead.

Then a high-pitched wail, followed by the scurrying of a hundred feet.

We run together up the stairs, and I know two things. I know I am finished holding Mary Beth's hand. And I know something terrible has happened in the sanctuary.

Looking back, it's strange how quickly one of the best nights of your life can turn into the very worst. The door of destiny swings on small hinges, I suppose.

Fifteen

Coma

A true story, only partially related to this one: My father was a corporal in the Second Great War, fighting for a free Europe and a world without Hitler, hoping to come home with all his limbs intact. He'd been married to my mother less than a year when he climbed aboard a locomotive and left her sporting a brave façade on a train station platform. When I was a child he would occasionally relate stories to us of the bright and varied characters he fought alongside, of time spent in a hospital with men who had lost touch with reality, of exotic places he'd been like Rome and Manila, but mostly he remained silent when the topic of war arose. I always wondered why. Until the day I discovered—while pulling from the old cedar chest in the attic a fold-out army hat and a baton they used for who knows what—a news clipping he had kept for good reason:

Miraculous Escape As Wrong Man Shot

London. March 14, 1942. For 68 days Corporal John Anderson's only contact with mankind was the pair of hands that shoved food and water down to him in a pitch black hole in the ground. But the American soldier was joyfully reunited with his wife yesterday after escaping from his Japanese captors in the

Philippines two weeks ago. During a tearful reunion with his bride of eight months, Anderson told reporters he credited his survival to the power of prayer and the ineptitude of Japanese marksmanship. "I've always believed in God, but I had never needed Him like this," said Corporal Anderson. "I know now it is a miracle that I am here at all."

Anderson appeared in good health despite two months in captivity and a jungle march that should have resulted in his death. Because of intense darkness, however, the guard standing next to him was shot by mistake.

"They shot the wrong man," Anderson reported, as his wife broke down in tears. "I believe it was God's hand, but it was dark also, so I guess that didn't hurt either."

Born near Seattle, Washington, to a British father and an American mother, Anderson enlisted in the 2nd Battalion, 131st Field Artillery Regiment and was shipped to Java in the Dutch East Indies in January. The regiment became known as the "Lost Battalion" when it was forced to surrender to the Japanese.

Anderson's cell was a hole in the ground, measuring four feet by six feet. A chain around his neck prevented him from standing up. The only sound was the drip of water leaking from above, the only light a candle, and his toilet a crude bucket next to his cot. Once a day, a pair of hands lowered food and water to him through an opening. "You try to remember Scripture in a place like that. You think of your wife," recalled Anderson. "Every image I have of my childhood passed before me in the dark."

On January 30 Anderson's captors pulled him from his cell and forced him and a dozen other prisoners to march through the jungle. When they stopped suddenly, he knew he was going to be shot. "I saw them taking rifles off their shoulders and pulling the bolts. I had two choices, pray or run, and I decided to pray."

The captives were blindfolded and pushed down a steep trail. By the time the shooting was done and his captors had left,

Anderson knew the gunmen had shot the wrong man. He was the only American left alive.

I don't know exactly why the story ended here or why I tell it to you now except to say that all his life Dad seemed to land on his feet like one of those Siamese cats after falling from a tree. He often told us stories of how he was nearly electrocuted, burned, crashed into, or marooned. For some reason I began to take an active interest in these stories during the weeks following that awful night and the days preceding Christmas, when hope seemed to be the biggest liar I'd ever bumped into.

Most ten-year-old boys wouldn't give you a chipped penny for a trip to the hospital, even if they've slid into home plate and fractured an arm. Or a nose. Or both. But for the next week or so, that's where I find myself at least twice a day: walking spotless hallways in socked feet, smelling antiseptic smells, and sitting in overstuffed chairs from which a kid can't quite reach the floor. The nurses are kinder than your average grown-ups, and one in particular takes an active interest in my interests. Her name is Anna, and she brings me soda pop—Orange Crush—whenever I ask, which is often.

"Your parents…well, they're special to me," she whispers, leaving me to wonder what she could possibly mean. Anna is our neighbor to the north, but I rarely see her. Barely into her thirties, she has a narrow face, partly hidden by wispy brown ringlets cut short and lying wet, as if surfacing from a swim. I'm surprised to be noticing these things. What would Mary Beth think?

Tony finally got ahold of Uncle Roy in Minneapolis on Saturday, hoping to tell Ben of the tragedy. But Uncle Roy says he's gone. He's not sure where.

Whispered conversations tell me that something akin to death itself has visited Dad. Perhaps something worse. The conversations are frequently interspersed with a word I haven't met before—*coma*—which, I come to learn, is what Dad is in. I piece the details together from the debris of conversation, most of them hushed, all of them fragmented.

"I can't believe it," one of the visitors tells his wife as they stand gaping at Dad, unaware of my presence on a chair in the corner of the room, oblivious to the fact that Dad might hear them. "It's the strangest thing I've ever seen in church."

"Not really," she whispers. "Remember that time with the baptismal?"

The couple then treats me to a delightful story that takes some of the sting from my day. They try not to snicker as they recount it. She interrupts him often, correcting certain details. Seems that long before I was born, two men and a woman from the other side of town were converted. Of course the whole community turned out to see them baptized, and they weren't disappointed. The church had only one dressing room at the time, which was designated for the lady. The makeshift men's dressing room, a few feet from the baptistery, was simply a thick blanket that shielded the male participants from view. The first candidates for baptism were the two men, followed by the plump lady, who had some trouble getting into the baptistery and even more getting out. Finally, thanks to some vigorous pushing by the minister, she emerged. A few feet away, behind the blanket, one of the men had already wriggled out of his wet trousers, while the other was attempting to do so. The first gentleman extricated one leg and gave the other a spirited kick. His foot skidded on the wet linoleum and into the baptistery he went, taking the large lady with him, both of them landing solidly on the poor pastor. As he fell into the pool, the recently baptized man sought something to break his fall, and all he could find was the blanket, which left the other recent convert, a man who had been exposed enough before the community lately, standing there stark naked. Someone yelled, "Hit the lights!" and an excited usher cranked them up higher.

The couple has to leave the room, they are laughing so hard, and Tony comes in.

"How's it going?" he asks, barely above a whisper.

I am only finding a few puzzle pieces so far, I tell him. Obviously the strangeness visitors refer to, the strangeness I missed, took place while I was busy romancing Mary Beth Swanson in the church basement, gazing at colorful Bible pictures and planning our future together.

If only I'd been upstairs, perhaps I could have done something.

But Tony says I couldn't, says he saw the whole thing.

Apparently Michael and Mary Beth's father had shuffled forward to stand in line with the other penitents, something which came as a shock to me, to think the man had anything to confess. Mr. Swanson was the head usher, the lead deacon, the top choice to fill the pulpit whenever Pastor Davis was due a weekend off. He was also a large man. "Has more chins than a Chinese phone book," Tony told me one day, before having to explain what he meant.

Mr. Swanson stood in line that night, waiting for the confessions of the others, but when he reached the microphone, he could not coax a word from his throat. Just stood there, looking down, his shoulders heaving with regret for something the congregation was waiting to discover.

Finally Dad stepped into the aisle and walked to the front to be of support. The two met to the side of the pulpit right on top of the trapdoor to the baptismal built into the stage floor. Reaching out an arm, Dad placed it about Mr. Swanson's shoulders. The act seemed to bolster the man, and he began to share something he'd clearly been thinking about awhile. "I have been in this church eighteen years now. I have preached from this pulpit things I believe to be true. But—" he broke down at this point, unable to continue.

Dad moved closer.

Mr. Swanson began to sob uncontrollably, his broad shoulders shaking as if he were trying to control a runaway rototiller.

The wide trapdoor had been built to withstand a lot of things—trumpet solos, the children's choir, the moving of the Steinway piano—but not this. Suddenly and unceremoniously it gave way beneath their feet, swinging sharply downward. Mr. Swanson fell forward, grabbing the edge and slithering his huge frame back onto the platform. Unfortunately, Dad didn't fare so well. He plunged about four feet downward, whacking the base of his skull on linoleum and wood joists and landing facedown in about two feet of stale but reddening water. Most in attendance just sat there stunned, unable to react to something that could not be happening. Tony was the first to reach Dad and pull him out. He cleared the way as three or four men carried my father up the aisle. People's mouths were agape, many had an arm outstretched, as if wanting to help. Dad was bleeding profusely from a wound at the base of his skull.

No one paid much attention to Mr. Swanson, who was following Dad, limping badly. The limp was not caused by the neglect he was feeling nor the burden of guilt he was bearing, but by the fact that he had just ruined his left knee. "His leg sounded like a man crunching peanuts," says Tony as we sit in the waiting room, him telling me the story once again. It's the first time I've laughed all day, a vengeful laugh for sure.

Well, it was the benediction to the revival, you might say. A most unusual one, and the news traveled through Grace like a gasoline fire. Many showed up at the hospital. Most were turned away.

Now I understand why I'd been ordered into a doctor's office within an hour of the tragedy. "We need to take a quick blood sample," the doctor had said. "It will pinch a little, but that's all."

"Why?" I asked, clutching my arm.

"Your father needs blood right away, and if your mother is right, you may have the right type. Roll up your sleeve, be brave."

As one nurse descended upon me with a huge needle, the other issued me two sugar cubes. I rolled them around my gums. The needle hit me hard, but didn't connect. After four tries, an older nurse came in. Her hands shook a little, but she found a vein and my arm began to tingle. The quick sample wasn't so quick, and soon they were filling a plastic bag with my blood. I searched for distractions. A cartoon on the wall showed someone else getting pierced with a massive needle. It said, "No pain, no gain," which is not what you're looking for, not in my situation.

I find myself holding my arm again as I sit beside Tony, reliving the painful memory.

"I feel like an orphan," I tell my brother. "Dad's as good as gone. Ben's missing. Mom's not much good. What are we gonna do?"

"I don't know," Tony admits, shaking his head. "Haven't a clue. But we'll be okay. I...uh, went up at the revival too, you know."

"What for?"

"Just needed to get some stuff right."

"What about the confession?" I ask. "You know. Mr. Swanson. What do you think he was gonna say?"

"Half the town's wondering that," says Tony. "Others are wondering if it was really an accident or if someone rigged the baptismal."

"Come on," I protest.

"Yep. People don't have much to talk about in a small town, so they make stuff up."

"Tony, what's the deal with Ben?" I've been waiting for the right moment to ask this.

He pauses, weighing his options.

"Ben did some things he shouldn't," he says slowly, carefully. "You know that tobacco?"

I nod my head.

"Well, it's not tobacco, it's Mary Jane."

"Mary who?"

"It's drugs. Marijuana. Plus he stole some money. Not a lot. He said he didn't steal a thing, but it was in there with the drugs. A roll of twenties. A hundred bucks. It wasn't the first time either."

My upper arm is throbbing again.

On Saturday afternoon, Dr. Mason knocks on our front door to meet with the four Andersons who still live at this address, all of whom are staring down the barrel of a grave new world. In solemn tones he speaks of the severity of the situation and inserts words I do not know. Words like *obtundation* and *stupor* and *stimuli*. He explains how consciousness is defined by two fundamental elements: awareness and arousal, and that in Dad's case both are out of order, though they are quite certain some degree of awareness remains. Most of it is medicalese, but I'm able to understand enough to get the picture: If I thought we were in trouble a week ago, I didn't know what trouble was.

"First the good news," says Dr. Mason, glancing about the room, perhaps thinking there should be more of us. "Your father has had a traumatic head injury and oxygen deprivation, or anoxia, which almost always leads to permanent brain damage. The brain swells and pushes against the skull, cutting off blood supply."

"This is good news?" I mutter, still aware of the sting in my arm.

Dr. Mason nods his head. "He is not feeling any pain," he responds kindly. "From what we know, those who wake from a coma recount experiences ranging from absolute darkness to partial awareness, much like a dream during sleep. Some have vivid perceptions and hallucinations, but we believe they're not feeling anything in this kind of sleep. In most cases, the coma lasts less than one month. A comatose patient who is still alive after ten days has a good chance of survival, and even after several weeks, partial or complete brain function tends to return naturally. So the best we can do for now is care for his body while the brain heals itself," he adds. "We are thankful he is alive. But I need you to know that at the very best, he will emerge from coma with lingering difficulties in speech, memory, or movement. At worst, the coma will transform into a vegetative state. You should know that recovery from such a state is unlikely after three months, and after twelve months it is exceedingly rare."

I am hoping he'll never reach the bad news.

"Well, w—what can we do?" stutters Tony, who has suddenly found himself thrust to the head of the table, a role he wasn't auditioning for. "I mean the family?"

"Well, you can visit him and read to him and talk to him during certain hours. He may be able to understand you. We just don't know. So be careful what you say."

"Anything else?"

"Well, Tony, I suggest you start looking for work. I hear they could use a good waiter over at the Garlic Grill. Your brother's been working there I know, but…well, he's gone I hear. You can take home about two dollars a day in tips, you know."

"What else will you do to help?" asks Tony, and I am surprised at his maturity.

Dr. Mason is looking at Mother with deep concern written on his face. "Everything we can, Son," he answers softly. "Everything we can."

Sixteen

Rodeo

Dad is lying flat on his back when I visit him just before dinner. I try not to look at him as the nurses turn his body, gently exercising his lifeless limbs. They check monitors and hang liquid-filled bags that drip fluid into his bruised arm. When they are through, I sit by his bed, surprised at the quiet, with nothing to do but wait. Tony will spell me off soon, but unless I think of something fast, I'm doomed to spend the hours trying to forget what's happening to my life, or Ben's mysterious disappearance, or the fact that Matthew Jennings is about to pay me a vindictive visit once he's released from prison.

I tug my chair closer to Dad's bed and wriggle my feet onto it. A nurse named Anna is on duty tonight, and though she's old enough to be my mother, I can't help being flattered by her attention. "Tell him stories," she urges me, placing another Orange Crush within reach before scurrying from the room. And so I do. As best I know how, I begin to tell a man who cannot hear, a man I can scarcely bear to look at, a story of summer. A story he may never remember—even if he does wake up.

"Dad, I…um…have always loved the rodeo, so I wanted to… um…remind you of it," I begin awkwardly. Dad doesn't move. I pull my feet from the bed and gaze out the frosted windowpane, beginning the story again, trying to remind my father of warmer, happier times.

The closest we ever get to a traffic jam in this town is the last weekend of July between six and seven P.M. when the rodeo comes to town, bringing far more trouble than it's worth, many believe. It's the only time we're permitted to enter the Independence Arena, which reeks of tobacco smoke and something that must be alcohol.

Our former pastor used to give his annual Rodeo Warning message the Sunday preceding the show—Exodus 15:1 was his usual text (I will sing to the Lord...The horse and its rider He has hurled into the sea")—and on Thursday night my father sits us down to tell us where these people come from and what kind of lives they lead and how we should be cautious and stick together and avoid all appearance of evil. But on Friday night when the last dish is dried, I am off like a dirty shirt to see if I can find proof that this show is better than last year's. Have they really added an extra barrelman and a faster merry-go-round like my brother Tony says? Will "the world's smartest elephant" really sign autographs? Will the Fat Lady hypnotize an alligator and get him to bark like a dog while Bucky the Clown plays "She'll Be Comin' 'Round the Mountain" on the harmonica using only his nose?

I don't say these exact things to my father, but I do all I can to set the mood and take him back, if really he is listening.

Three summers ago the undisputed highlight of the rodeo was the greased pig chase, an event that had the whole town buzzing for weeks afterward. An unusually ornery pig was selected that year and greased right up to its earlobes. When the hoard of hollering children descended upon it, something snapped deep within the pig—his natural boar-like instinct, Tony claimed—and the pig turned on the unsespecting youngsters, oinking wildly and biting some of the smaller ones.

Pandemonium is a mild description of what occurred next. Sixty or seventy kids all screaming and crying and crawling over one another in a panic to get to their angry parents as a possessed boar stampedes them through the mud is a sight one doesn't soon forget. A rather fast-thinking bull rider raced to his truck as the confusion spread, and before anyone advised him otherwise, he was pursuing the pig with a loaded rifle. "Ready, fire, aim," was his motto, and the audience was plugging its ears and covering its eyes, and only the bravest among us watched in horror as he shot the poor pig dead, putting it out of *our* misery.

The organizing committee debated alternatives to the pig chase during the winter months, I've been told, some of them making ironclad cases as to why the event should be banned for good. Finally a mild-mannered farmer named Bart Stolzfus volunteered to personally ensure that more caution be exercised in the selection of the pig. They could even have one from his barn. Bart hadn't spoken up in a meeting since he had tendered his personal convictions regarding the impropriety of female clowns, so the rest of the committee was surprised enough to trust him entirely.

Thus it came about that on opening night at next year's rodeo I found myself standing with a crowd of children ten years of age or under (and a few who lied) as we were herded into the middle of the arena floor, trying to be careful what we got on our shoes. A tiny piglet was standing stock still where center ice lies frozen in the winter, and the announcer towered over the poor creature, securing it by a red collar and a tight leash. Drawing the microphone too close, his voice boomed and echoed throughout the aluminum-sided building. "When I say 'chase him,'" he instructed the few of us who were listening, "you chase him," and when he

released the pig and hollered "Go!" into the screeching microphone, we did, albeit with some reservation. Most of us had
witnessed the events of the previous year rather closely, and we
were not eager to get bitten or shot at. As we cautiously approached
the tiny animal, the pig merely stood there shivering, a frightened
shadow of his feisty ancestors.

He was a humble pig. His tiny head was down and his shoulders hunched, as if he was wondering where to go or who to ask
for help. I was the first to reach poor Piglet, so I merely bent down
and picked up the slimy little guy, patting him like he needed
consolation. He acknowledged the comfort I extended by oinking appreciatively as if I had just rescued him from some great
evil, and perhaps I had, judging from the looks of envy on the
faces of the other children.

After more squealing from the microphone than we would
ever hear from the pig, a disappointed yet somewhat relieved announcer tried to cheer himself up by saying, "Well now, it looks
like we have ourselves a winner," and the winner was me. I
received a bright yellow ten-cent token and in no time at all
decided to blow it on cotton candy. As I tottered from foot to
foot eagerly watching them heat and whip and wind that sugar
onto a paper cone, I knew that money might not buy you happiness, but it could buy cotton candy, and for me that was close
enough.

My favorite nurse is standing behind me without my knowing. I wonder how much she has heard and what she thinks of
my storytelling ability. Pulling up a chair of her own, Anna sits
down beside me, a kind smile on her face. "I mentioned your
parents have been a help to me," she says, blowing at the ringlets
matted to her forehead with one corner of her mouth. "Would
you like to know how?"

Are you kidding? Of course I would. But not yet. The Orange Crush is backing up. "Be right back," I say, excusing myself.

The restroom is squeaky clean, and I leave it that way after soaping my hands and gritting my teeth at the mirror. I poke along the hallway, recalling what I already know about her family.

Annabelle, as her friends call her, lives in a tired two-bedroom house one door north of us with her husband of thirteen years and three small but energetic little powder kegs who are always within a whisker of detonation. I'll be honest: They are irritating children, are the Greisons, short, flattened children—all of them boys—with pointy heads and bulging eyes that look like they might leap from their sockets if given half a chance. Their names are Isaac, Elijah, and Jacob—big footsteps to follow, Tony says. From between slats in the fence they watch us like lizards whenever we play baseball or football or ball hockey, and when the ball scoots over or under the tattered fence, they strike like lightning, grabbing it and running into the house, squeaking with excitement. Once I can remember Mom having a conference with their mother and returning triumphantly, carrying the football. But more frequently she returned empty-handed, shaking her head, and we were forced to stand on our side of the fence, glaring between the slats at the Greison boys, who looked out the window through beady eyes, thumbs in their ears, wiggling their fingers and sticking out their little lizard tongues.

I rarely saw Mr. Greison, but when I did he always called me by name and once even stopped to show interest in my world of sidewalk bugs. His first name was Bob, though I never used it of course, and in the summer he worked the night shift at the seed plant. Bob's hands were always grimy and his overalls tattered as if he got them from the missionary barrel at the church. Despite these things, you could see his cheerful countenance coming a block away, though at times you had to stand on tiptoe because he was so short. Anna had always seemed an unhappy soul. She had frightened eyebrows which always made me feel sad. Her smile rarely came to the surface, but when it did, two large dimples appeared in her peach blossom cheeks making her unusually pretty, an apparent conflict with some inner theology of sobriety. Approaching middle age too fast, Anna always seemed destined for a collision of some sort.

I am in my sock feet, so Annabelle doesn't hear me reenter the room. Good thing. She is already telling my sleeping father about the collision, and I can tell that she is crying. I backtrack through the door and stand against the wall, eavesdropping.

"I missed the events Terry spoke of that opening night of the rodeo because I was trying to corral my three little cowboys, who never seemed to ride in the same direction at the same time," she says, letting out a sniffled laugh and pulling tissue from her pocket. "When they finally sat still long enough to watch the world's greatest trampoline act (a family of nine dressed in red, white, and blue doing astounding flips, loops, and dives), I probably looked like a calf that had been roped once too often and was looking for another line of work.

"After the final event of the evening," she continued, "a friend noticed my exhaustion and offered to take the children home and put them to bed. Her kindness surprised me."

I slouch to the hall floor and listen as the story unfolds, wondering why she could be crying.

Mrs. Greison tells how she sat all alone in the vacant bleachers, watching the clowns rehearse for the next day, leaning against the wooden ledge behind her, feeling relieved and grateful for the reprieve from her domestic duties. Raul Seville, world-renowned champion calf-roper and winner of two hundred dollars that evening for dropping a calf in nine seconds flat, saw her sitting there by herself and climbed over the boards and into the stands. "Howdy," he said, easing himself onto the seat in front of her and tipping his hat. "Come here often?" Annabelle grinned and then quickly composed herself and wondered how she looked.

He was a tall man, was Raul, with broad shoulders like a water buffalo, a handsome head set defiantly on his thick neck, and dark skin which belied roots in Texas or Mexico or possibly even South America. "Quite a night," said Raul, putting an elbow on the back of the seat in front of her. He spoke with just the hint of an untraceable accent while stroking his thin moustache thoughtfully. "Makes it all worthwhile to know there are pretty ladies like you watching."

"I…uh…thanks," Anna managed, hoping her cheeks weren't blushing. "Were you in the show?" Annabelle caught herself covering her wedding ring.

Raul laughed. "You might say that. I almost own the dang thing by now. I've been doing this since I was twelve, you know. Don't do it for the money anymore, no ma'am, just love to make people happy. I see kids laughin' and hangin' onto their parents' hands, and it makes me know I can go another night."

Annabelle was charmed by this southern gentleman, but she was no fool. Standing hesitatingly to her feet, she said goodnight and then smiled self-consciously, prompting her dimples to appear.

"What do you do?" asked Raul, standing too. Annabelle turned to face him, noticing that his brown eyes were level with her blue ones though he stood a foot below her. She forced herself to look away.

"I'm a photographer," she said, shocked that the lie came so easily to her lips, the first one she'd told in years.

"Oh. Who do you work for?"

"The local paper here...and sometimes *National Geographic.*" She couldn't believe her mind would think such a thing and her mouth would say it.

"Wow!" exclaimed the cowboy, as if someone had just aimed a different colored spotlight at her. "You're some piece of work." He shook his head and grinned as he said this. "I'm sorry, I didn't get your name. I'm Raul."

"Anna," she said, extending her hand, which the smooth cowboy pulled toward his face and kissed gently.

"Say, is there anything open this time of night? I'm starving."

Annabelle knew she was blushing now. "You could try the coffee shop a block south. It's called the Daily Grind."

"Care to join me?"

"No." Annabelle glanced nervously about her. "I...um...I better not."

"I understand," said Raul, "You're a wise woman. I wouldn't go out with me either if I didn't have to." His friendly laughter echoed throughout the building as he pulled from his pocket a ticket for the next night's show. "You're coming back I hope," he said, handing it to her. She extended her right hand and he covered it briefly with his left one. "It's been a real pleasure," he murmured softly, holding her hand a little too long. He asked her exactly where the diner was, and she patiently answered before pulling her hand away, turning and nervously hurrying off.

I sit quietly in the hallway, hoping no one will come along, wondering if Annabelle has ever told the story before, saddened to think that she's forgotten my existence.

"I'm ashamed to tell you this, Mr. Anderson," I hear her say, "but I walked home slowly that night, looking up at the stars and realizing how bright they were and asking why I hadn't noticed them in years. I knew the answer. I'm stuck in a dead-end marriage with a husband in absentia and three crazy kids I don't even like while I watch opportunity knock on everyone else's door. The streets were almost empty, and I was surprised to find that my feet had turned themselves around and were walking south toward the coffee shop and that my body was following them almost involuntarily. One of my hands even took a ring off the other and shoved it into a pocket of that light yellow sweater. *You be careful, Annabelle,* I reminded myself as I pulled the sweater from my arm and draped it about my shoulders. *There are no secrets in a small town."*

They sat across from each other at a small table in the Daily Grind, her nursing a soda and he some thick dark brew. Thankfully, the place was vacant, but still she kept her back toward the window, slumping a little just in case. *It's perfectly harmless,* she thought. A cousin from out east, she told the manager.

They spoke of life on the road and the loneliness of motherhood and of faded dreams both had entertained as children. She avoided questions about *National Geographic,* and when the silence came, he told her he'd been reading a few wise philosophers lately and he was learning intriguing things.

"Like what?" she asked, genuinely interested.

"Well, I'm learning to live each day with passion," he said, sitting a little straighter and leaning forward. "Too many people sit on the sidelines of life, waiting for some great opportunity to come to them. You gotta grab it or it might be gone. It's not too late to learn new things if you're willing to be a beginner. When you're a beginner, the whole planet opens up to you, ya know what I'm sayin'?"

She nodded her head.

The seasoned cowboy stroked one corner of his handlebar moustache and continued. "I'd like to make a change, do something new, but I'm afraid of taking risks. That first step can be the most frightening, but sometimes it's the most rewarding. We have to keep moving forward, opening new doors, doing new things. Curiosity leads us down new and wonderful paths. You aren't running away if you're running toward something better, you know?"

Annabelle wasn't sure where he was going with all of this until he told her he was hoping to take all the money he'd earned over twenty-two years of riding bulls and roping calves and buy a piece of land, settle down, and maybe make a steady living writing cowboy poetry. He just happened to have a few such poems in his pocket, but of course he didn't want to trouble her, but would she care to hear one? Why, of course she would.

Raul said he used to write funny stuff like "You're the Reason Our Kids Are So Homely," and some of his rodeo pals liked them. He also claimed he wrote "Get off the Stove, Granny, You're Too Old to Ride the Range," and someone turned it into a country song making all sorts of money that was rightfully his. He wrote serious material too. This one he would give her when he was done, so she could have it, maybe even memorize it.

Opening a yellowed sheet of lined paper, Raul cleared his throat and began somewhat sheepishly.

> Some like the light of a big neon sign,
>   I like the prairies and takin' my time.
> Some like the smog and the noise of the city,
>   I like the mountains and sunsets real pretty.
>
> So give me the pine trees, the antelope, the dew,
>   Hand me a guitar, a mandolin too.
> You keep your concrete and stoplights, my dear,
>   Give me a horse and I'll ride out of here.
>
> Some like the city girls, that's who they choose,
>   Their late model cars and their fancy hairdos,

I'll take a country girl with eyes full of blue,
A smile that's so pretty and a heart that is true.

Give me the sky streaked with wood smoke at night,
Folks singing country as I turn out the light.
There's fire in the whiskey and beans on the stove,
So let's raise a toast to the ones that we love.

Bob wouldn't be caught dead reading poetry, thought Annabelle, and he certainly never wrote any. He sometimes told stories to the kids, and he once read books to her—back when they were first married. But those days were long gone. He was too tired lately. He arrived home at seven each morning and was asleep by five after. Sometimes she watched him lying there and thought of what was and what wasn't and what could be were she able to rewrite the script.

"You didn't like it, did you?" Raul had noticed the faraway look in her eyes.

"Oh," she leaned forward a little, "it was wonderful. Thank you. I—" she stopped mid-sentence and drew back slowly. "I really must go." Raul covered her petite hands with his large leathery ones. "No. Thank *you*," he said. "I'd really like to see you tomorrow night. You could come by my motor home after the show, maybe talk some more, hear a few more poems."

Annabelle admitted to my father that she could feel her pulse racing as she left the café. I wondered if I should go get a drink or listen some more. I decided to stay. The story was sounding familiar. It was sounding like mine.

This time her feet headed north without turning back. A thousand thoughts raced along beside her, both thrilling and torturing: *What should I wear? Is this wrong? Who will babysit tomorrow night? What in the world am I doing?* She slowed down to make the sidewalk last longer. On either side of the street, pine trees whispered softly in the breeze. Lightning flashed faintly in the distance, revealing the ragged edges of thunderheads peeping over the hills, growing larger and angrier—like wild animals roused from sleep.

At home, Anna tiptoed about the house like she was in a ballet, trying not to waken the kids. Her youngest, Jacob, was asleep in the kids' room, one hand curled loosely about a stuffed bear, his mouth parted, a question mark in the lines on his forehead. Pausing, she knelt by his bed out of habit, but no prayer came to her lips. She dare not touch the child while entertaining such thoughts. Was she crazy? *No,* she thought, *just confused.*

About midnight the rain began to fall. She drifted into a fitful sleep and dreamed of a stonecutter at work in a quarry. He hammered away at a rock, fifty, a hundred times, without so much as a crack appearing in it. Finally, on the one hundred and first blow, the rock split in two. She woke in the middle of the night, wondering what it meant and listening for the kids. The only sound she could hear was the rain.

At eight in the morning she awoke again to find Bob's side of the bed empty. Where could he be? She found him in the living room flat on his back with three children leaning up against him in a variety of postures. Bob was telling them a story, so she sat in the overstuffed recliner and listened. Perhaps it would help her nod off again.

The old story was true, Bob claimed. He had heard it in church when he was a boy. It involved a farmer in Montana who worked hard to support his family. One day he stopped plowing his field and stood wiping his brow, squinting at the horizon. In the distance, another Model T Ford was headed for the train station. How he longed to join them. They were leaving home to join the gold rush. But not the farmer. There was work to be done. Fields to be tilled.

Livestock to be fed. Yet the promise of a fortune in gold kept him awake at night and turned his menial tasks to drudgery.

"Who's menial?" asked little Jacob, who was tracing the lines around his father's cheekbone.

"It means boring."

"What's valuable?"

"Well, like the diamond on Mom's ring." Bob turned to look at Annabelle. "It's a valuable rock. Show him, Honey." Annabelle's eyes were closed, and she left them that way, pretending to sleep.

Bob continued the story a little more quietly. "One day a complete stranger with a big red hat on came up and offered to buy the farm, so the farmer agreed with a handshake. Finally he was free. He bought supplies, hopped a boat to Alaska, and headed for the mountains. The search was long and painful. Trekking mile after weary mile across tundra and ice, across frozen rivers and through mountain passes, the farmer searched for the elusive gold. But none could be found. Weeks turned to months. And months to years. Finally, penniless, sick, and utterly depressed, he gave up in despair.

"But back home, the man with the big red hat carefully tilled the ground and while taking a break one hot day, dipped that red hat in the creek to cool himself off and scooped up a dull but promising stone. Carrying it to the farmhouse, he placed it on the mantel."

"What was it?" asked young Jacob, still tracing the lines.

"Why don't you just shut up for once in your life!" yelled his older brother, Elijah.

Annabelle almost opened her eyes, but thought better.

"Don't talk like that," chided Bob. "Apologize or I won't finish the story." Elijah did and his father continued.

"That very night, a friend noticed the unusual rock over the fireplace and picked it up, turning it over and over in his hands. 'Do you know what you have here?' he asked the farmer with the big red hat. 'This has to be one of the largest chunks of gold ever found.' And he was right. Before long it was discovered that the creek bed was full of the precious metal."

Annabelle sat perfectly still, lost in the story. Her eyes were squeezed tight, her right hand concealing the absence of her wedding ring.

Exhausted, Bob excused himself, and despite the boys' pleas for another story, walked quietly past Anna and crawled into bed. Annabelle made a breakfast of toast and cold cereal for the troops and then went to the bedroom, sat on the edge of the bed, and watched her husband sleep. "You are a good man, Bob Greison," she said softly. "A saint, maybe." Walking to the window, she drew the blind on the morning sun and quietly began the search for her ring.

—⁂—

I am still slumped in the hallway, an undiscovered little voyeur. The hospital is almost empty of visitors, and I am so glad. I wonder how Anna would tell the story if she knew I was there. Would she tell it at all?

Her voice is much softer now, and I must strain to hear it.

Annabelle called the Daily Grind the minute it opened at nine. No one had seen a ring. Could she come look for herself? Of course she could, but there was little point. The place had been vacuumed and swept that very morning. To complicate matters, there wasn't a spare seat in the house with the 99-Cent Saturday Morning Buffet Special, which included one helping of Canadian back bacon and

Richard's all-you-can-eat golden hash browns. She was welcome to go through the vacuum bag, they said. And, yes, the garbage too.

The morning search turned up nothing except the realization that there was only one place left to look: Raul's motor home.

Babysitting was hard to find, but at last Annabelle promised a neighbor girl a dollar, and she couldn't refuse, even if it was the Greison kids.

The rodeo began with a bang and ended with a whimper, and when the final fireworks had faded, no one seemed sad that it was over except those who had to clean up the place. Annabelle sat by herself between two very noisy and obnoxious strangers who stood often and managed to encroach on her space whenever they sat down. She was used to it. *I feel like deli meat in a sandwich, gazing out past the thick slices of bread on either side, barely able to find the star of the rodeo,* she thought. When she finally found him, the feelings of last night began to surface, and she wondered if she was hoping to see Raul later to find the ring or hear more poetry.

Raul left the arena quickly, and Annabelle followed when she knew it wouldn't look obvious. Trembling and glancing about her, she knocked quietly on the first motor home door she came to. A middle-aged man in a dirty T-shirt and dirtier jeans pried it open and peaked out. "Can you please tell me which is Raul's?" she asked nervously. He wasn't sure at first, but then he remembered. "Oh, that one," he said, aiming a half-empty beer bottle at an aluminum-colored Airstream. "I'm just hoping for an autograph for my son," she told him, but the door was already shut.

Where do all these lies come from? she wondered as she hurried toward the motor home.

It sat in the shadow of a large poplar tree, two propane tanks perched aboard its tongue. Six feet wide by twenty feet long, its aerodynamic shape made it look futuristic, like something they might build in the eighties. Bumper stickers cluttered the back. "Work is for people who don't know how to fish." "It's lonely at the top, but you eat better." "Vegetarian: Indian word for bad hunter."

She hesitated. Twilight had arrived and with it the promise of darkness. Backing away, she circled the park twice, wondering. *What will I say? What will he do? Why is my heart beating so fast?* She knew the ring was only an excuse. Picking her way past mud puddles, she approached the Airstream again. A lone light shone through the curtains, inviting her in. *I must be crazy,* she thought. *I really should go home before it's too late.* Again she hesitated. "He called me pretty," she said out loud. "I haven't heard that in five years. I show Bob a new dress, he says, 'What's for supper?' Raul made me laugh. Bob hasn't told a joke since those moron jokes in high school." Before she knew it, her hand was tapping the door.

There came a scurrying sound inside the motor home, then whispering, and then the door opened and Raul stood before her in a bathrobe. She blinked and averted her eyes.

"Annabelle," he said quietly, "this isn't a good…can you come back later?"

"Who is it?" demanded a high-pitched female voice behind him.

Annabelle exhaled quickly as if she'd been punched in the stomach. Then she lurched backward and almost fell. Tears blinded her eyes as she stumbled away, not noticing a deep puddle until she was halfway through it. Then she thought of the ring. No way. She wasn't going back. Not for anything. But what would she tell Bob?

She was surprised to find him home when she got there. He was sound asleep on the sofa, their youngest dozing on his chest. She stood there, watching them sleep, and then knelt beside the sofa and prayed for the first time in days: "Forgive me, dear God. Please forgive me."

Opening her eyes, she saw Bob frowning up at her. He reached out a hand and brushed a tear away from her cheek. "What is it?" he whispered anxiously.

"Oh, I was just talking to God...and wondering...do you really love me?"

"Of course I do. Why would you say that?"

"Because you never tell me. And you're gone so much."

Bob was silent for a minute. "I'm sorry, Annabelle. I thought you knew."

"I need to hear it, Bob. I need to know you care."

He pulled her face toward him. "I...I...guess we Greisons were never much good at saying these things, but...I love you, Annabelle. I have since you smiled at me on the hayride twenty years ago."

She smiled again. "You mean the day you stuffed my hair with straw?"

"Yup. I can't believe you married me. You have made me a happy man."

"But Bob, I would never know it because you never say so."

"I'll do better," he said.

They talked then of work and of temptation and of a love that lasts through the dry times. She told him everything, and he stroked her hair and pulled her close. Then she offered to take little Jacob to bed.

"You'll be back, won't you? I'm supposed to work in an hour, but they owe me some time off."

"I'll be back," she smiled.

I'm sure other things happened that night, but responsible readers like yourself are not interested and would likely skip to the next chapter anyway.

Before you go there, however, you may be wondering what happened to the ring. Well, as I listen from the hospital hallway, she tells me. Six weeks later, while searching for a dress she hadn't worn in a while, a dress that Bob told her she looked especially pretty in, her hand brushed up against the ring, which had been snagged by the diamond and was stuck to the wool of her light yellow sweater.

In the months following the departure of the rodeo clowns, Annabelle discovered, among other things, that she had a gift for writing poetry. Sometimes she reads it to Bob. She was reciting one of her favorites to my sleeping father as I came into the room trying to act as if I hadn't heard a thing.

> Fools seek happiness in the distance,
> The wise discover that it grows best
> Beneath their own feet.

"You were gonna tell me about my parents," I say as I sit down beside her.

"Oh yes," says Annabelle. "I have…well, our marriage has been a struggle. Your parents have been there for us. One night when you were much smaller, your mother saw my Bob walking past with a suitcase in his hand and yelled out the window, 'Don't go away mad, Bob!' She was joking of course, but that stopped him in his tracks, for he *was* going away mad—he was going away for good. We spent that evening with your parents, and many more evenings, talking of the struggles of a marriage and what it takes to bring it to life. I can tell you that without them, Terry, I'd be very alone."

I am looking at my father, this giant of a man who now seems so feeble, so helpless. All day long, Anna informs me, people have been filing past him. To confess their sins. To say thank you—or goodbye.

Annabelle stands to leave and then pats my knee and blows at her curls again. "These are tough times, I know. May God bless you, Terry Anderson."

She tiptoes away and then pokes her head back through the doorway. "Oh, I almost forgot, Terry. Your mother prays for me every day. Has for years. Those requests are a sacred trust. When temptation pulls at me, I can never quite forget that your mother is praying for me."

Oh boy. I know exactly what she's talking about.

Seventeen

Hospital

Tony was right. Mr. Swanson does have four chins. At least four. I count them this blustery night as I sit around the dinner table at Michael's house, where I've been invited to my very first sleepover, Annabelle's confession still ringing in my ears. What a feast. Three whole pizzas. Homemade, of course. After all, you can't buy pizza in a town this small.

All that's missing is Mary Beth. Michael informs me his sister is at a sleepover at a friend's house. Just my luck.

Mrs. Swanson has generously scattered ground beef atop the pizzas and sprinkled lengthy dashes of oregano, something I have never tasted before. I watch wide-eyed as Michael's dad puts away fourteen slices (I counted) all by himself while the rest of us combine to finish the other ten. The image of him gorging himself reminds me of the time last summer when I saw him standing at the ice cream freezer of our grocery store, rubbing his hands and gazing through the icy door with anticipation and perhaps a twinge of doubt, wondering if there was enough in there to meet his enormous cravings. He has a wonderful laugh, does Mr. Swanson. "Fat people need to laugh," I've heard him say, "Nobody wants to hang around a miserable fat man." But there's no laughter tonight. "I'm so sorry about your father," are the only words he says, and you can tell he means it.

Though I haven't eaten since breakfast, I can't even finish one piece of pizza. It's tough to eat when something's eating you, so I pass the rest of mine under the table to Michael's black Labrador pup, Harry.

We pass the evening playing Chinese checkers, and when I finally beat Michael, he pulls out the chessboard and creams me. Bedtime is ten o'clock, but he finds ways to delay it. I'm wondering if I could get away with calling home, just to check on things and maybe talk to Tony, but I decide not to risk letting my friend think I can't handle things alone. We climb in about eleven, and Michael flips off the light and shows me how he can play his rock-and-roll collection without his dad knowing. He plugs a microphone into the speaker outlet of a light tan Philips cassette recorder, and remarkably, a tinny sound escapes the front of the mike. He carefully places it between our pillows and we listen to Elton John and then Rod Stewart. I've never heard anything this wild. This would kill plants for sure.

"How do you get away with these?" I ask, clearly impressed.

Michael grins and switches on the bedside lamp. He has labeled the cassettes: "George Beverly Shea," "Beethoven's Fifth," and "Great Hymns of the Psalmist."

"What if your dad catches you?"

"He'll beat me," says Michael, not having to think long.

"My dad used to spank me too," I admit, "always with 'the board of education on the seat of understanding,' as Tony puts it. But now that I'm twelve, the board has been retired." I laugh. "Tony used to hide wooden spoons behind the bookcase, and once I watched him bury a leather strap in the garden, between rows of peas."

Michael is quiet. "I had quite a collection of tapes, you know? Stuff like Evie and the Imperials. Christian stuff. Used to hide them in the closet. Dad found 'em and smashed 'em with a hammer. I watched him. I like *this* stuff now."

I wait until he turns off the light before I ask the burning question: "What do you think your dad was gonna say the other night?"

An uncomfortable silence ensues, during which I ponder changing the subject.

"I don't know," Michael replies at last.

More silence.

He turns the volume down on the Philips. "Don't tell no one, but my dad gets real mad sometimes. Gets so angry he just leaves the house." Michael is lying motionless beside me, hands behind his head.

"Why?"

"I don't know. Something sets him off. My mom opened a letter last Sunday. He got pretty mad."

"Opened a letter?"

"Yep. Dad doesn't allow nothing like that on Sunday. Says it's work. Doesn't allow me to go swimming or look at the Sears catalog neither."

"Why not?"

"'Cuz of bosoms. Says I'll learn to lust there. Talks about the temptations of the flesh."

In some roundabout way, his response brings me back to my original question. "What do you think he was gonna tell the people at church, you know, when he stood up?"

"I don't know." Michael yawns widely. "Haven't a clue."

He rolls over and faces the wall, leaving me to ponder life in the Swanson home and to wonder if I'd choose a dad like Michael's over a dad like mine—one in a coma. Mr. Swanson. The man who pastes gawdy magnetic Bible verses to the side of his car. The one who stops kids in the street to pray with them, only to discover they've tiptoed away and left him standing there by himself, praying out loud. Didn't he preach once on anger? What a jerk! Suddenly I am ashamed of my thoughts. He is a man of God, a preacher, a deacon. Maybe he'll be my father-in-law one day.

"What would you do if you had a million dollars?"

I ask the question with a knowing smile, squinting at the ceiling, trying to see it in the dark. I'm not quite sure if I'm looking for advice or an accomplice. I wait for the answer, and when none comes I start to tell Michael of my own dreams. How I would buy stuff for my friends and my family and cure my mother and maybe my dad too, and wipe out disease everywhere and buy a brand new motorcycle, and before long I have decided to swear him to secrecy about the money.

"I…I…found something. Beneath the skate shack." My words come in short bursts. "Money. Lots of money." I tell him of the delight of it all, of the endless possibilities, and of the challenges, the hurdles. How it isn't working like I'd hoped, how my brother Ben is out there somewhere paying for both of our sins. And how I cannot tell a soul about my secret.

Michael is speechless and I'm not sure why. I nudge him and he rolls over, his mouth wide.

Then he starts with the tiny snores.

I plug his nasal passages and he sits up straight. Then lies back down.

I'm a little upset, to be honest. He hasn't heard a thing I've said for fifteen minutes.

Dozing off to Elton John singing "Goodbye Yellow Brick Road" is a new experience for me, and when he finishes the last song on side A, the tape clicks over and over, the automatic shut-off button having worn thin.

I stab at all six buttons with my thumb before the machine shuts down with a loud click. Michael lets out a snort. I lie there, staring at nothing, alone with thoughts of my own sins and a family in turmoil and a mother's prayers.

It occurs to me that I've hardly talked to God the last few weeks. "Are You really up there?" would be the thing I'd want to ask. Somehow I can't bring myself to be that informal with God. If He's there at all, He's distant. Besides, why would He want to strike up a conversation with the likes of me?

When sleep won't come, I think of Mary Beth, and I wish she were in the next room. I've heard of people falling in love, but can it happen at my age? That's what it feels like. A head-over-heels tumble, landing me in a soft snowdrift. If grace can happen to a kid my age, certainly it came through that kiss, that stooping of a divine being to smack me where I least deserve it, on the lips.

Somehow, just before morning dawns, I fall asleep, maybe not an atheist like my friend Danny Brown. Thinking of Mary Beth has mellowed me to an agnostic.

—⁓—

I can count on my left hand the Sunday mornings I haven't spent in church, and today is the index finger. The thumb was my very first Sunday on the planet, and Mother was too tired to listen to sermons that day or to accept congratulations.

Before any of the Swansons are stirring, I lean a note against the Philips—thanking Michael for everything—and sneak out the front door, which is unlocked, like the front door of every other house in town. The wind is icy cold, and I pull the hood on my parka tight about my face. It's a five-minute hike to our white-stained house on Third Avenue, and though I've yet to visit a funeral parlor, the atmosphere within must come close.

Mom is up, pushing herself around the kitchen, not really accomplishing anything, just searching out distractions. Tony is as somber as I've seen him in my life, moving reverently too, looking for car keys. "We're going over to the hospital, Tare," announces Liz in a lower voice than the one I remember her having. "You're coming. Hurry up."

"Why? Anything happen?"

"No, we're just going. Mom says so."

I'd rather stay home on account of bad news being easier to swallow filtered through a third party. Mom has managed to get her coat on all by herself, though—a remarkable thing in itself—and there's no way she's going without me.

"Did you plug in the car heater yet?" Liz asks Tony.

"Nope." But he does it without being reminded again, the block heater warming the engine core.

Tony drives, Mom slumps against the door, and I lock it from behind her, just to be safe. Liz is beside me, minding thoughts of her own, perhaps wishing our heater blew hot air instead of icicles.

Anna is off duty, but the other nurses are kind, pointing the way, looking on in pity. "Make sure you're quiet," one of them says, looking directly at me and raising a finger to her lips. "We don't know what he can understand," says another. "Do keep the talk positive, he may be cognizant." There are four of them in white dresses and whiter hats, possibly the same angels who helped me into this world.

Tony finds a wheelchair for Mom, and I lag behind, scuffing my socks on the shiny linoleum, thinking I'd prefer to stay in the waiting room. "Come, Terry," Mom motions, and I press through the doorway into Dad's room haltingly, still barely able to look.

Room 105 points northeast, a bare poplar tree out its window, its sole inhabitant my father. A single bed faces the poplar and the morning sun, which is barely up, pink as anything you'll see. I wonder if Dad will ever wake to see either. I wonder if all of this is somehow my doing. If the latest catastrophe is God's judgment on my wickedness.

Mom leans forward from the wheelchair and touches his haggard face. I am having trouble watching. I look instead at the crank on the end of the bed and wonder if I should try it out. It smells like cleaning solution in here.

"Come, children…come say something to your father," Mom quietly directs us.

I have seen him before, of course, but Liz has not. She steps forward, awkwardly, as if she's in the Christmas program at school but has forgotten her lines. I know how she feels.

What do you say to the hollow shell that was your father? A man you'd always thought invincible, unstoppable, a true saint of God? His face is gaunt, his cheeks deathly white. They have hooked him up to some sort of blinking apparatus to aid in his breathing, something that wasn't there last night, and I can't help noticing he is strapped to the bed now, perhaps to keep him from falling out. I sit down on a chair and stare at the crank again, swinging my legs, which are propped up to rest on the backs of my hands.

Mom leans forward even further. Her voice is thin, crackly, like a bad connection.

"I'm here, Honey," she whispers. "I love you. The children are here too." She names the three of us one by one and tells him how much he is missed. "You've gotta fight, John," she says. "We need you."

She is rubbing his arm with one hand and touching his forehead with the other.

Dad doesn't respond. He just lies there like he is sleeping or pretending to. I remember when I was smaller how he'd play a game with us in the living room at night, just lying there like this, stretched out on the floor. We'd run around and around him, like gerbils on a wheel, whipping ourselves into a frenzy until he'd suddenly spring to life, grab the nearest one and toss us onto the sofa where we'd wait for the capturing of the others and hope he'd do it all again.

How I long for him to leap upward as he did on those glorious nights. To jump from the bed like it was all some big joke. To laugh his deep hearty laugh and hoist me on his shoulders and walk and run and sing like he does in church—I won't mind him being off-key.

But I cannot suppress the knowledge that those days are gone forever. That as surely as if a car had swerved into our lane, or our house had burnt to the ground, everything has changed in an instant. I cannot remember ever feeling so small, so inadequate, so helpless.

And I cannot hide the fact that I am crying.

—⁓—

I've been with Dad an hour now, and when several men from the church arrive to pray over him, I quietly duck from the room and find Tony here, slumped in a soft green chair in a pale green waiting room.

Already my father is like a priest listening to an endless procession of sinners, evangelicals who never had a priest of their own. Some want to be alone with him. They want to tell him things he cannot hear.

Tony is reading an old *Reader's Digest* from July of 1961, the year he was born. The cover picture is a mountain scene of three boys playing in a stream; their brother is on horseback. He is reading the Book Section, "Rasputin: The Mad Monk of Russia," which is an attractive distraction for him, reading of this rude-mannered peasant with a passion for wine and women yet possessing miraculous healing powers. But he abandons it when I arrive and reads me jokes I don't get from "Laughter, the Best Medicine," and quotes I don't understand from "Points to Ponder" on page 18. Tony finds the jokes hilarious. There's one about Marilyn Monroe and sweaters and a pastor who prays for a horse to win and a man who went into a secondhand store "to buy one for his watch." I don't get it. The points I don't find myself pondering either. But Tony does.

"Trouble is the next best thing to enjoyment; there is no fate in the world so horrible as to have no share in either its joy or its sorrows." The quote is from Henry Wadsworth Longfellow. "Trouble," Tony says, leaving the word hanging there, as if I'm supposed to do something perceptive with it.

"I was reading a story in one of these magazines last night," he says, "but I don't know where it went." He starts pushing periodicals aside, searching for something a little more frantically than you'd expect. "It was a story about Padre Pio, the Italian priest. They said he bore the five wounds of Christ and healed tons of people who asked for his prayers. Anyhoo, this boy was visiting Italy with his family, and he got sick pretty bad. In fact, he was in a coma for two months, I think."

He has my attention now.

"The coma was from typhoid fever, I guess. He got it eating cherries off the ground." Tony is still shuffling magazines, still coming up empty. "So his family started praying, and the boy's mother wrote letters to Padre Pio and finally got him on the phone. She says, 'Padre, my only son is in a coma and has a fever of a hundred and five.' Padre Pio says, 'Ah, my child, tomorrow he will waken with a temperature of ninety-eight point six. He will be cured, and when he awakes, he will speak fluent Italian.'"

"Did he?" I want to know.

"Well, he did get better. Not the next day, but a week or two later."

"And did he speak Italian?"

"Pretty close," says Tony. "He spoke Swedish, nothing else. Had to learn English all over again."

"Did you make that up?"

"Some of it. The part about the Swedish. I just don't remember it all. The boy got better though. That's the main thing."

"Um…Tony. I know this sounds dumb, but should we call a priest? Like for Dad, I mean."

"No, God hears our guys too."

"Have you been praying much?"

"Since Friday. I haven't stopped. How 'bout you?"

"Oh, me too." It is another lie. Another milestone that separates me from good people like Tony as I run down this highway that takes me far from home. The lies don't surprise me as much anymore. God and I haven't exactly been on speaking terms lately. It's like He speaks Italian, and I speak another language altogether. Swedish maybe.

—〰—

On Wednesday, an old photo of Dad is smiling at us from the front page of the *Grace Chronicle*. It's the same picture we have on our piano, which mother hasn't played in years.

"Beloved Mechanic In Coma," it reads, in the largest Letraset font since Bernie Vanderhoof burned down the Exxon service station while dreaming about insurance. The accompanying story neglects numerous details about the revival and Mr. Swanson's near confession, controversial details that might have provoked too many letters to the editor, whose philosophy of journalism is simple: "All the news that's safe to print."

The next day, cards and letters begin to plug our mailbox. Kind letters all of them, some containing money. I've never seen so many envelopes on the table, and only one is from me. The one with four hundred dollars.

It says,

> There's more where this came from. Please find out the best place to treat Mrs. Anderson's illness and the money will be on its way.

The other letters are genuine. They share one theme: The writer's deep love for a man who would rather do something about his faith than say something about it.

> Dear Anderson family,
>
> Please accept the $20 and spend where most needed (hospital bills are steep). You will never know how much your father blessed us, what with the visiting while our little Amy passed away and the prayers he offered. God will bless you and we believe God will bring him around soon.
>
> Praying for you, The Martindales

Others were a little less polished:

> Dear Mrs. Anderson,
>
> Your wonderful husband fixed my car just after my third husband ruined my life, the jerk. When Elmer took off with his revolting secretary (you may remember her,

dirty blond curls, puffy-faced, a real number), the little ones and me had nary a clue as to how we'd make ends meet. My idiot husband cleaned out the bank account and even had the nerve to siphon all the gas from our old Merc before he left, the twit. But it hadn't been running for a while anyways. Your man didn't just fill the tank, he made that car run like it hadn't maybe ever and tore up the invoice, or I guess there never was one. Then he invited me to church. I shoulda gone. I considered going for a spell because of his kindness, but for some reason didn't. I think I'll try to convince my new man to go this very Sunday.

Respectfully, Hilda Wiebe-Evans-Hasborough (soon to be Steinburger)

PS: You're welcome to attend our wedding over at the courthouse Friday.

At the end of the day, we are holding close to six hundred dollars and trying to remember which envelopes they've fallen out of so we can thank people properly. Mother is in tears, overwhelmed by kindness and dealing with one more struggle: how to accept folks' charity.

Some of the envelopes contain advice on potential cures, which doesn't surprise her, having been bombarded with every conceivable treatment when she was diagnosed with Huntington's. Some suggestions come in pamphlet form, others in a bottle, many on hand-scrawled notices. All are from those who genuinely care, if you count the ones from people who care primarily that we buy their product. We sit on Mom's bed, Tony reading them one by one, and some make us laugh. One advises playing alpha waves through a neurophone. Another claims that if you just yell loudly enough the patient will wake up (I'd already thought of this). "Tickling the comatose patient has worked at least twice that we know of," writes Mrs. Olson, who taught me Sunday school in second grade. "You should start with the feet." Still others employ terms like hyperbaric oxygenation, and the last one in the pile is a badly-reproduced brochure claiming that placing a television antenna on the bedside and wiring it to the patient's forehead will do the trick.

The food begins arriving too, as if a ship had just docked behind our house and sailors are stepping off the gangplank hoisting sacks of nutritional delights over their shoulders. We haven't eaten like this since last New Year's Day, when Uncle Roy took us to the Chinese Smorgasbord ("Two can dine for $1.99"). Soon we are knee-deep in casserole dishes, and it is sometimes my duty to redistribute them throughout town. Grown-ups tousle my head when I knock on their doors. Some offer me candy and I take it, though I'm almost sick of the stuff. Some pull me out of the cold and pray with me, and others tell me to hang in there, it will be okay. One lady just gives me a hug and tells me she's praying. Another lady reminds me of the story of Job. I don't want to hear it. Job got his answer in the end. He got his boils removed, his kids and his money back. Mom won't. Not ever. Don't talk to me of Job.

"God has a wonderful plan for your family," says a middle-aged man, whose name I do not know. "Even if your father doesn't pull through this. God is good all the time."

How quickly we throw words around.

I'd like to take two steps backward and drop his pie plate on the sidewalk—maybe on his toe—and then ask, "Is God still good? How about if I break every plate in your home and take you away from your family and cram you in a hospital bed and poke your arm with needles? Is He still good?"

Such are the thoughts that crowd my mind as I walk home, picking up speed all the while. I've almost forgotten the money in all of this, not that it is losing its appeal. But I'd give it all up in a heartbeat—the money, the casseroles, the attention—to pull Dad back from the brink of death. To bring Ben home. Life without either of them is like a black hole in space, an impossible prospect, one I keep pushing from my mind. I wonder where the Catholic priest lives. Or if I should just phone him and ask a favor. I wonder how much he'd charge for the healing. And what it would be like having a dad who speaks nothing but Swedish.

Another letter arrived today, one Tony tells me about as we are examining the spider plant, which is showing signs of not dying, despite a new tape he's playing by some guy by the name of Larry Norman. He has even more hair than the last guy. The letter is from jailbird Matt, and though Tony won't show it to me, he says Matt's been treating him like a friend and telling him some rather confidential matters. He says there have been some exciting developments and that we won't find out about them until Matt is released, which should be any day now.

I can hardly wait.

Eighteen

Letter

Conscience is a friend at first, but when ignored it changes roles and becomes a judge. I notice this mostly at night. But even in the daytime I'm discovering that living with a bad conscience is like driving your car with the emergency brake on. Something starts to stink back there, and you're not sure what it is.

Life goes on, however. You grapple with schoolwork, argue with friends, and talk about the snow and the Minnesota Vikings. Complaining about the weather is our favorite indoor sport here during the long winter months—at least when we're not playing Rook, the only card game we are allowed. The Chinook is long gone, and the temperature has dipped to zero. But though the cold is back, the clouds don't hang around here long. Instead, wide skies adorn our short days and the sun is a constant companion, streaming in our attic window from the south. I've been thankful for that light the past few days as I stand up there whenever the coast is clear, carefully tallying the damage on a loose leaf sheet, transferring little paperbacks around, nervous as a match in a dynamite factory.

I'm not quite sure why I need to know the grand total of the loot, but for some reason it is an increasing obsession. I whittle away at it until my nerves get jumpy, and then I put things back in order and lie on my bed downstairs, clumsily calculating the columns.

On the left, I have kept a running inventory of the one-dollar bills, scratching a tick mark every time I count a hundred of them. In the next column are the fives, then the tens and twenties, for which I have done the same. I have to use the back of the sheet for the ones. Today I have left school early to nurse a bad headache, but once the tally is complete the headache is gone. In fact, I am in a delightful state of astonishment. I add the columns four, then five times to make sure my final figure is accurate. It's the most mathematics I've done all year. Miss Hoover would be proud of me.

There are more than three hundred tick marks in the ones column, which according to my arithmetic means that I have just over thirty thousand inked portraits of George Washington concealed in the attic, unless I have misplaced a decimal point. A chill climbs my spine and pinches my shoulders into an involuntary shudder. The ones are just a start. It gets better. According to the next column, there are almost eight thousand fivers bearing Abraham Lincoln's regal likeness, close to one thousand tens with a barely grinning Alexander Hamilton on the cover and well over four hundred twenties, courtesy of Andrew Jackson himself, topping things out at $88,411 (more if you figure what's in the washroom), an unimaginable sum to a child my age.

I snatch an old tennis ball from the floor and lay on my back, bouncing it off the ceiling, grinning to myself, the questions swirling once again.

What can you do with this much money? Anything you want, I suppose. But more than this I wonder where Matthew Jennings would come up with the nerve to pull such a heist. It's bad enough when the work's been done for you. I can't imagine. And where would he find such money? Not in this town, surely. Suppose Matt isn't the culprit after all. This is a new thought. Suppose it was someone else. But who? Matt's father? Perhaps. But isn't he in jail somewhere or banished from town or maybe even dead? I've heard all three explanations for his whereabouts. And the *Grace Chronicle* has never run a story about missing money, not that I'm aware of. I'd know it if they had, wouldn't I? Suppose someone in town hit the jackpot at a casino in Great Falls. That's it. But why would they hide it? Why wouldn't they spend it, or put it in the bank? My brother Ben comes to mind, but that's impossible. Unthinkable. Then again, why not? The devil takes small steps, our old pastor once said. One day you're smoking cigarettes, the next you're pilfering cash registers.

I stop tossing the ball for a moment as a new thought dawns: What if it *was* someone on our side of the creek? Someone in our church?

The pastor maybe. Pastor Davis. I know it's tough to imagine him and Irene plugging quarters into a slot machine in some smoky room with no windows, but why not? Casinos are illegal in these parts, I'm pretty sure, but it could happen. Yes, Mr. Davis has preached against the ills of gambling, but maybe he had to research it first. I could picture him and Irene sneaking into some murky place with a name like Riverboat Roulette, her with a pink kerchief over her hair and dark sunglasses aboard her nose. Reverend Davis would don a wig of course, and one of those fake moustaches. Maybe an unlit cigar. Or a lit one, for that matter. If he's an anonymous gambler, why wouldn't he light it? He would probably walk with a slight limp just in case someone knew him, and maybe have a patch over one eye. The boss of the place would have a name like Tony Vanelli, and Timothy and Irene would be surrounded by conniving, back-stabbing cheats and thieves, none of them exchanging occupational information. I smile to think of their delight—or is it dismay—when all those quarters begin cascading from the machine and they are trying to catch it all.

When I was a boy of six or seven, we drove through the sticky heat of a Nevada August to visit an uncle who worked at an Air Force base near Fresno, California. I remember almost nothing of my uncle, but two distinct events from that trip stick to my mind.

I remember Mother releasing her hair from its perpetual bun the minute we left town, shaking it out over her shoulders and snapping clip-on earrings into place. I had never seen her decked out like this. She even had a tiny mirror for applying lipstick and moderate eye shadow, which made her look younger, even prettier than she already was.

The rest of the trip is a blank save for the night we spent in Las Vegas, of all places, on account of there being a cheap room and an even cheaper buffet. I'm sure there were plenty of warnings as we approached Vanity Fair, as Dad dubbed it. Warnings about alcohol, women, betting, and the lure of the world. Tony's questions on gambling began during the decadent breakfast, and they seemed to put Dad in mind of an idea. So when we'd eaten our fill, we ambled into one of the establishments—I do not remember which one—and stood in the grand entry, the six of us, watching people with blank faces stuff machines full of change. In Dad's mind, this was the best antidote to gambling—to show his own children the awfulness of sin firsthand. But the experiment did not halt Tony's questions, which seemed born of sincerity. When he asked Dad to explain the intricacies of the machines, my father took him by the hand, strode boldly over to an idle one-armed bandit, and inched a nickel into its greedy mouth, telling Tony all the while, I am sure, just what the odds were and how ridiculous it was, people spending their cash and time here.

They pulled the handle together, father and son, the first and last time my father would ever engage in such behavior. Dad said a few words to Tony that I did not hear, and as the two of them walked our way, lights began to blink and nickels began to swoosh from the machine. You should have seen us Christian kids, scrambling around the floor, stuffing coins into our pockets. Even mother joined in. Dad just stood there shaking his head, wondering how he could ever tell this story to anyone in our church.

The memory almost makes me smile.

Surely it's possible. But wait a minute. There are no nickels or quarters upstairs. No, Pastor and Mrs. Davis were embracing much bigger stakes. Maybe bingo over at the liberal church Saturday afternoons. Boy, I would like to see their disguises then. Or how about horse racing? Do they have them in Great Falls? What about blackjack in Billings? Billiards in Butte? I am holding the tennis ball and squeezing it hard.

But it all comes down to this: The mystery is not mine to solve so much as the money is mine to spend. And spend it I will.

Or will I?

Once again the doubts creep steadily forward. I wish that this nagging feeling would depart. That the guilt would make itself scarce, for it is the worst of things. I wake each morning and it's there on the pillow next to me, pointing its gnarly index finger, reminding me that the guilty person is his own executioner. I have been unable to voice a genuine prayer for two weeks. Or sleep soundly. The whole of my life has changed. Noises startle me. Suspicion haunts me. There are questions to be feared and subjects to be avoided. There are eyes whose glance I cannot hold like I once did and thoughts I'd rather not think. My recurring dream the last few nights takes place on the platform of our church, and it involves two huge hairy hands—I know not whose, for I cannot make out the face—grasping my throat and squeezing hard until the truth spills from my quivering lips, poisoning the sanctuary and killing the parishioners. I know this will have to end one day, but it cannot end now. Not today. Not when I have such delicious plans. But are the plans worth the agony? I haven't laughed out loud in how long? Nor played hockey with my friends. What would happen if I confessed to the police? Do they jail kids my age?

One thing for sure, I'd better not carry this wad of twenties I have in my pocket. There's a fine line between being clever and being really stupid, and I've crossed it enough lately. I can't stuff it in Tony's drawer. I've already destroyed one brother.

Hopping quickly from the bed, I sneak back into the attic, where the light is fading fast. I tiptoe to the bag and bend over, zipping the bills back in their rightful spot. Standing up, I bump my head against a rafter. "Darn!" Behind me is the cedar chest, and I steady myself against it with one hand, holding my sore head with the other. Curiosity bids me lift the lid, and the scent of cedar reaches out at me.

There isn't much inside, save for Mom's old wedding dress, the clipping I mentioned earlier, and Dad's army stuff. But what's this? A large brown envelope with "Will" rubber-stamped across the front. It is unsealed, so I cautiously dump out its contents. A few typed sheets with elegant crests at the top emerge. They don't interest me much. Deeper down I find four envelopes addressed to Ben, Liz, Tony, and me. These aren't sealed either, so I crack mine open.

It is a letter from Dad to me, handwritten on a single sheet. I hold it on angle so the fading light hits it just right.

My dearest Terry,

If you are reading this, then life has taken an unexpected turn for us all, and I trust God will give you the grace to persevere. Don't worry about me, I will be dancing with the angels, which will be something new for this old Baptist! The only sadness in all of this is leaving those I love. I cannot help but hope I have left nothing unsaid, but if I have, I want you to know that you have brought great joy into our lives and into the Anderson home. Never mind that some were chosen, all of you were loved. I have loved you since the moment I knew you'd be joining us. Perhaps one day you will understand a father's love, should God give you children of your own. If there remains anything between us, please forgive me and know that you are forgiven a thousand times. God's grace has been shown to me so often, Terry, how could I withhold it from the son I love?

My eyes fill with tears as I write this now because I cannot imagine life without your smile, your gentle laughter, your perceptive questions, and your presence by my side. Yet, I am in a far better place and I wait for you now, cheering you on. I will try not to make too much trouble, leaving that to you and your brothers when you get here! I have thought long about what to say to you. About practical advice like, "Never shop in stores with signs like 'You break it, you buy it,'" or "Don't do something just because someone dares you to." But instead I wish to leave you a few thoughts I think will shape your life if you let them.

In Matthew 5, Jesus says, "Blessed are those who hunger and thirst for righteousness, for they will be filled." My prayer for you all these years has been simple. It's written on a bookmark in my old Bible, and I have referred to it almost every day since you were five or six. It says, "Keep him hungry for the right things today." We are each of us hungry creatures, Terry. Only God, by His Spirit, has the kind of food that will satisfy, if we will but daily come to Him for it. I have watched God answer prayer through the years in ways you will never know. Turn to Him in trouble. Find in Him all you will need.

If you are reading this, you probably know about the inheritance by now. Don't get sidetracked. Work on who you are. And never forget Whose you are.

If Mother is still with you, I know you will care for her the best you can. I married her knowing that this disease was a possibility. When you're young, you think you're invincible, that nothing harmful will touch you. The years show you otherwise. But I have no regrets. A thankful heart changes everything.

Take care of your sister too. Don't let her walk the aisle with just any rascal! You are on this earth for a short while, Son. Your life is a vapor, a flower that fades. So live every day for that which will outlast you. And remember, I have no greater joy than to hear that my children walk in truth.

Eternally yours, Dad

A twelve-year-old boy is not accustomed to tears flowing this fast. Though it is cold up here, they are hot against my face. I wipe them with the shoulders of my T-shirt, tuck the letter back in the envelope and lower the lid of the cedar chest. More questions than ever descend upon me as I slink down to my bedroom and lie there on my back. What's this about an inheritance? What could it possibly mean? Could we be rich without knowing it? And what does he mean, "some were chosen"? I don't understand.

Suddenly it doesn't matter. I want to visit my father. I want to hug him hard and tell him everything. If only he could hear.

"Dear God," I can't believe I am praying, "what should I do?"

And the answer is as clear as if someone set off a foghorn three feet from my ear: *You know.* Ah, but that is not an easy task. Not when you've been chasing the things I've been chasing. Not when you've gone as far as I have. But sometimes the push to do the

right thing isn't so much a spiritual one as it is a practical one.
The fact is, the loot is killing me and everything it touches. Burying
me as surely as I am trying to bury it.

Forbidden fruit is sweet, but it spoils fast.

I will come clean. This time for sure.

A weight slips from my shoulders as surely as if the bony-kneed
person you're piggy-backing has jumped down. I can breathe
again. Without thinking, I am bouncing the ball off the ceiling
again, bump, bump, bump.

Nineteen

Matthew

Matt Jennings chooses the southernmost seat of the northbound Greyhound partly out of habit and partly out of necessity. He wants to be as close to the restroom as possible. It isn't that he has the urge to peel off his clothes as my brother Tony claimed prisoners were in the habit of doing upon their first taste of freedom. He simply has a nervous stomach. No wonder. This is his first day on the outside since the breaking and entering conviction eighteen months ago, after which he'd gone directly to jail without passing Go or collecting two hundred dollars.

Liberty County Jail was a nightmare he prayed he'd never have to repeat, with the time passing about as quickly as the Middle Ages. Apart from his cell mate, the company wasn't something you'd want to keep. Matt's body tells him to find a cigarette. "You've done real well, going two days without one," it says, fighting to be heard above the road noise. "You should be real proud of yourself. Now, we want tobacco. All of us. Your lungs, your arteries, your spleen. Give us nicotine." They say this in time to the clacking of the wheels on the old bus. "Your spleen wants nicotine, give us nicotine."

But the days of addiction are coming to an end for Matthew Jennings. He hasn't touched a coffin nail, as he calls them, for

213

almost forty-eight hours now. The front of his Bible tells the story. The one Tony sent him, that is. "November 14," it reads. "Accepted God thru faith in Jesus. Can't put this book down. Wish I understood more. This is the most freedom I've felt ever, man. Thanks, God, for a roommate who practiced what he preached and wasn't afraid to say stuff. And thanks for my pen pal, Tony."

The parole board was its skeptical self of course, as was his parole officer and any of the inmates who heard about it. They'd watched this movie before. A little repentance shortens the sentence, one of them said. There weren't many spotless leopards out there, he added.

On the empty seat next to him is a small knapsack filled with the clothing he'd worn the day they locked him up. Matt wonders if any of it fits. Fishing around, he finds his Bible. His roommate has written something in there...now where is it? Wasn't it in the front too? "Hey Matt! Seek the right treasure this time. It will make all the difference. Matthew 6:33. Vince."

"That's the New Testament, isn't it?" he asks himself out loud, above the clacking of the wheels.

He scans the silky pages of the Bible but finally has to look at the index. Two minutes later he is reading the verse, his index finger pointing the way. "But seek ye first the kingdom of God, and His righteousness; and all these things shall be added unto you."

In front of him some guy is blowing magnificent smoke rings into the air. Matt watches them filter lazily his way and inhales the air deeply. Who needs to buy your own cigarettes when you travel Greyhound?

The delightful aroma fills his lungs and reminds him that this new chapter of his life isn't going to be easy.

He opens a letter he received from Tony. A notorious letter I will learn about soon enough:

Dear Matt,

It's been fun exchanging letters with you the past little while. You don't have to worry about anything you've told me; your secret is safe with me. Folks here will be suspicious about your newfound faith at first, but that's okay. What really matters is that you've done the right thing and that you continue to pursue your new life. When you get here, I want you to talk with our youth pastor (I'll give you his number) and get an honest job. Remember, even a mosquito doesn't get a pat on the back until he starts to work! I'll help you search for you know what when you come home for good. There are things only the two of us need to know.

63,000 Blessings! Tony

Matt leans a little to his left and looks out the window. The sleepy town of Grace is coming into view. Matt wishes for a moment that he is heading for New York City with its skyscrapers and taxis and enviable anonymity. News travels fast through Grace. People know your sins before you commit them.

He thinks of his friends and the bar he loves. He thinks of his crooked father, of leopards, and of spots.

—⟨⟩—

Martin Chandler is the best principal I've ever had in my brief career as a student. The only one too. He sports the same crew cut and the same suit every school day all year long—a deep gray or maybe green with barely discernible pinstripes. Silver ones, I think. I'm sure you will forgive my lagging powers of observation when you realize that the only time I saw those pinstripes up close and personal was in his office, when I was thinking of other things, namely clutching my ankles and taking my medi-cine. Today while he has me in that position he has a sudden change of heart. I still don't know why. When I realize that the storm has passed with ample lightning but no hail, I slowly straighten up and find him standing there behind me with tear-stained cheeks. Things you learn later in life cause regret some-times, but how am I supposed to know that Mr. Chandler had lost a boy the year before in a farming accident? All grown-ups seem old to me. I can't imagine him having a small child.

He loops the huge leather strap back onto a nail on the wall before speaking of my sins of yesterday. "Don't you ever write those words on the bathroom wall again, Mr. Anderson. Or yell them in the playground."

"I won't, Sir." And I am certain I won't. Today is the day I will turn things around. Come four o'clock I will visit my dad and tell him everything. Then I'll visit the police.

The words the principal refers to I learned from an eighth grader named Byron Hanson, and I didn't know what a one of them meant. I only knew that they seemed to feel good in my mouth and that they brought some of the children to rapid atten-tion when I yelled them during recess. I will spare you the more graphic details, but allow me to say that much of my newfound vocabulary was even worse than what our pastor refers to as minced oaths during his annual sermon against them.

When I let loose with, "Hey, you guys, what the heck you doing? Dad gummit!" on the soccer field at Grace Elementary School, it had the effect of snapping fellow students' heads around like dogs who had come to the end of their ropes. Words like these are not used here, not even during church baseball games, and we all know why.

Our previous pastor had gone so far as to list minced oaths in the church bulletin for the purpose of clarification. If you'll pardon me, the list of second-cousin cuss words included doggone it, dag burn it, darn, gee, golly, good gravy, gosh, heck, my word, hocus pick, Jiminy Cricket, jumping Jehoshophat, Sam Hill, shucks, tarnation, and heavens to Betsy. I won't belabor the point. You get the picture.

During the sermon, Tony leaned over and asked me if I knew where heck was.

I didn't.

He said, "It's where people go who don't believe in Gosh."

I wasn't sure if I should laugh or not because I knew our former pastor had made a pretty good case when he read the words of the apostle James, who called the tongue a restless evil, full of deadly poison. "Therewith bless we God, even the Father; and therewith curse we men, which are made after the similitude of God. Out of the same mouth proceedeth blessing and cursing. My brethren, these things ought not so to be."

Who could argue with that? Not I. Nor am I about to argue with Mr. Chandler today as I stand upright and thank him for not letting me have it with the strap.

If I have painted Mr. Chandler as a tyrant, forgive me. It is not so. He is a kind sort and not the one you'd want to surprise as I ended up surprising him after he sent me back to the seventh-grade classroom.

Mr. Chandler strides down the hall, poking his head into a few classrooms on his way to the boys' washroom. There he chooses the last stall, the farthest one from the door. I imagine him sitting there humming to himself and perhaps noticing that the janitor has neglected to replenish the toilet paper, when suddenly and with no warning whatsoever, the ceiling gives way above him.

Now, when a man is in that position, sitting there minding his own business, and the roof caves in on him, pelting his vulnerable body with tightly-bound rolls of cash he does not begin to relax again anytime soon. In fact, he probably considers first off that it is a prank. Experience tells him it should have been. Perhaps they are rolls of TP intended for one of the teachers or himself. But as the loot descends, and as he begins to scoop up more money than he makes in three months, he realizes that this is no joke. And by the time he delivers the small fortune to the police later that afternoon, he is already lining up the suspects, including a number of children who have been a problem for him all year.

Corporal Benson makes the call to Matthew Jennings' parole officer, asking him to bring the boy in and to hurry up about it.

"What? Already? He's been out less than a day."

"Yup. Looks like we've found the dough lickity-split."

"Good thing I kept them letters. Damning evidence, those."

I couldn't have known any of these things, of course. But I would in short order.

—⁓—

The black cop car has been parked outside the school much of the afternoon. I can see it if I turn my head ninety terrifying degrees. I'm not dumb. I begin to imagine that they are looking for me. The restroom has been declared off limits, and already I can hear the hallways filling with excited whispers. Whispers of an awful crime having taken place in there, possibly a murder or a hanging. Afternoon recess finds scores of kids gathering around and just staring at the door as if it will yield some morose secret. I join them. What if they've found the money? It's the most likely explanation.

Tony doesn't have a clue what's happening until they haul him out of physics class in the midst of a test as if they were changing the guard at Buckingham Palace. Corporal Benson brings along rookie officer Hodges, who has combed his hair carefully in case a reporter from the *Chronicle* is there. He has handcuffs out and everything. Man oh man, I still can't believe it. Someone told me one of them had drawn a gun too, though I'm not convinced.

As I traipse home that terrifying afternoon, I am planning to drop my books off and make a beeline to the confessional. But when I turn the corner onto Third Avenue and see the same black police cruiser in front of our house, the only thing I can think to do is run. Turning quickly, I retrace my steps toward the school, my pace quickening noticeably. But where does a kid my age go in the midst of a harsh winter? Or anytime of the year, for that matter? Great Falls? Kansas? The Catskill mountains? Does he attempt it on foot? Or hitchhike? Does he steal his father's car and kidnap the girl he loves? It's not something I've thought much about before, to be honest. "This is ridiculous," I tell myself. "You don't run, you come clean. Remember your decision yesterday? This is the time. This is the place."

And so it is that I find myself pressing open our front door and stomping my boots. I stare at two strangers sitting at our kitchen table, sipping our coffee and talking with Tony. One wears a uniform, the other a suit. Neither is holding a gun. Mother is absent, most likely asleep in her room. Liz has yet to arrive home. How I wish Ben were here.

They turn to me with a brief nod, and Tony gives me a pleading glance.

I am trembling; my tiny body is unable to move.

They are holding a letter in front of him and poking at what appear to be underlined words. "Your secret is safe with me?" the cop says. "What's that supposed to mean, Ronny?"

"Tony," says the one in the suit.

"And this: 'I'll help you search for you know what when you come home for good'? 'You know what'? Tony, we're not stupid. Are you saying we're stupid?"

I haven't a clue what they're talking about, but my brother looks to be in trouble. It's time to play a card and hope it's trump.

"I…uh, I did it," I manage to say.

The two of them grin, seemingly amused. "Did what?" the uniformed one asks.

"Took it."

Tony's face registers confusion.

"Took what?"

"The money."

"The money?"

"Yep. I'll show you. It's upstairs."

"Sorry, kid. We've already found the money."

They turn to each other, then to me, then to Tony. "Any relation to you, Dim Bulb?" asks one. And they laugh as if they haven't heard anything remotely funny in years. I suppose they deem a twelve-year-old kid less capable of stealing the money than he is of protecting his older brother's secret.

—m—

Three regrets I carry with me to this day.

That I didn't show the authorities the cash the first day I found it.

That they didn't believe a word of my confession once I got around to spilling the truth.

And worst of all: them leading my sixteen-year-old brother, Tony, out the front door and into a waiting police car.

Twenty

Dreams

I am sitting in the morning church service with the hymnal open before me, and all I can think about is how many people are missing from our pew, the third one from the front. We used to take up the entire row, back when the Andersons were a family. Mom at the end. Dad beside her looking like Sylvester when he finally snared Tweety Bird. How I yearn for those days. Days when I would crane my neck and see them holding hands and sometimes Dad throwing an arm about Mom's shoulders, often leaving it there for the duration of the sermon. But today it is only Liz and me at the worship hour. Everything seems upside-down and backward and confusing. Even the air isn't right, and the sound system hurts my ears. The windows have been altered somehow. We didn't have stained glass before, I'm quite sure, and the service starts a few minutes early, which hasn't happened in my lifetime that I can recall.

"I'm wondering if the ushers would come up here now," says Pastor Davis with a trace of impatience, and it seems his eyes are on me. The ushers have never been summoned in this manner, and certainly not at five to eleven. In the past it has always been about eleven-thirty, and Pastor Davis is never this informal. He usually says, "Would the ushers please come forward as we bring our tithes and offerings to the Lord."

Pastor Davis is looking my way, about to make a pronouncement. I hang my head in shame. He knows my secret.

And then, in the midst of it, he is there.

My father. Handsome as ever. Dressed in a proper suit and tie for the first time I can remember.

He strides to the platform, smiles, and says, "Turn with me if you will to hymn number 327, that's 3-2-7 in your Glad Tidings Hymnals, 'O Worship the King.'" No one else seems to notice it is he. Not even Liz. She sits there, turning pages, looking for the three hundreds. "We'll sing the first and the second stanzas in unison," Dad is saying, his voice as clear as a winter sky, "the ladies will sing the third, and the men together on the fourth."

He doesn't sing of course, but I want to leap from the pew and holler. I want to tell the whole world, "What's wrong with you? That's my father up there! He was in the hospital, and now he's healed! It's amazing!"

But I can't move or speak.

My hands are cuffed, my waist strapped by a leather belt to the hard mahogany pew.

At least that's the way it happens in my dream.

—⁓—

I am not the only one dreaming these days. Tony awakens often in the middle of the night, probably from visions of the inside of a prison. It's been quite a day for him. Down to the police station. Playing twenty questions before a one-way mirror. Sweating. Sighing. Shaking his head. No, you don't understand. Please, you've gotta believe me. I'm telling the truth, honest to God.

He's only sixteen, so they're not about to lock him up and swallow the key, but the interrogation is punishment enough.

Tony and Liz and I have just sat down for supper so he can fill us in on the scary details. The light of day is long gone and darkness has descended, a darkness I find myself dreading more each day.

And then, the unthinkable happens.

The door opens and there stands Ben, large as life, a frazzled suitcase matching the look on his face.

I've never seen my brothers embrace before, but Tony is reduced to tears as he hugs his big brother hard. Liz is next in line. Then me. Then Mom, who comes from her bedroom faster than I've seen her in years. I am so glad I'm ready to kneel down and confess everything if someone would just give an altar call.

Mother's face is beaming. She parades about the kitchen, rearranging plates that don't need it, and I almost expect her to drag out the old skillet and begin smacking eggs against the side of it, so delighted is she with Ben's homecoming.

"How did you hear about Dad?" asks Tony, sitting down eagerly and pulling the lid from a hot cheese casserole. Ben's story is simple. He couldn't find a place to stay, so he returned to Uncle Mothball's house and then caught the first bus he could when he heard the news of Dad's condition.

I sit there wondering if the drugs and the money are in his suitcase. We are so excited we forget to thank God for the food.

When Ben finally fills his mouth, Tony tells him about his arrest, and we all listen wide-eared. "They questioned us separately, then together," he reports. "The big thing was this letter I'd written and this so-called secret that I mentioned. Do you really think I'd be dumb enough to write stuff like that in a letter to prison?"

I wasn't sure. I'd done some dumb things lately. It didn't seem out of the question for someone else.

"So what's the secret?" asks Liz, watching Mom swagger back to the bedroom, worn out from the excitement.

"I can't tell." Tony shakes his head. "You just have to trust me. It has nothing to do with the money in my drawer."

Ben heaps his plate with the creamy casserole but pauses mid-scoop. "By the way, I can't figure out where that hundred bucks came from. The money in my drawer."

"You didn't steal it?" asks Tony.

"No. I've done some bad stuff, but I'm sure I didn't leave money there," says Ben.

Liz either doesn't believe him or she's more concerned with Tony's story. "So the secret has nothing to do with money? Is that what you told the cops?"

"At first I did," says Tony. "Then I knew I had to tell them everything. The secret just had to do with Matt's life before he got in this mess, that's all."

"Did they believe you?"

"Nope. Not at first. Then they made some phone calls."

"Did Matt kill someone?" Liz asks this, serious as can be.

"No," Tony snickers. "It's just...it doesn't matter. Anyhoo, they seemed satisfied and they let me go. But they said they'd watch me."

Tony glances my way. "Can't believe you'd try to lie like that to protect me," he jokes. "Did you think I'd run while you took them upstairs?"

"I guess so," is all I can think to say.

"So they find all this money in the washroom the same week Matt is released from prison?" Liz won't let the matter die. "Sounds suspicious to me."

I am saying nothing because I have nothing to add and because I've been wondering if now is the time to come clean or if I should keep playing charades. What ever will I do now that I've got all of us in this jam?

The last two nights I've been lying awake scratching my head and wondering what to do with the money. The only solution I can think of is to make it disappear, and the only way I can accomplish this is to set fire to our house. I know it sounds crazy, but what other options am I left? I'll have to warn what's left of the family somehow. And get mother out. The place won't go up as rapidly as Bernie Vanderhoof's service station, I don't think, but at least the money will be gone. I wonder if Dad has insurance like Bernie did. I can't think of a tactful way to find out, but surely he does.

What kind of stuff should I rescue before I strike the match? Shirts and pants? Food? Probably not. Surely the authorities would be suspicious if we had the boxes labeled and lined up on the neighbor's lawn and me sitting out there in our big green rocker, watching the place burn when the fire truck arrives. But what about rescuing some clothing or coats or photo albums? No one would notice if a few of these survived the blaze.

I haven't even reached for the casserole yet, and it does not go unnoticed. "Eat up, boy," says Liz. "We've got three more just like it in the freezer."

She shovels it onto my plate like we are staying at the Ritz.

It's not easy concentrating on macaroni when you're considering a career change from thief to arsonist, but already I am thinking about the tools of the trade and the modus operandi. I would wait until everyone is asleep and use firecrackers to get things hopping. Should I light them in the attic? The sawdust insulation would be a good start. But what if Tony awakens from his bad dreams and hears me first? What if he walks into the hall and finds me up there? Or worse, what if he thinks I'm up there and back in bed all at the same time, like little Marty or Bart, and he wakes the whole house screaming?

No, it will be easier to light the wicker laundry hamper on fire while playing with matches.

—ᴡᴡ—

Saturday night, and it's colder than a polar bear's air conditioner. The temperature plunges to minus twenty, and it begins to snow—a hard snow that covers sidewalks once again. And the seats on our swingset. And my banana-seat bicycle, which I should have rescued back in October. From my bed I can see frost growing thick on an electrical outlet just inches away (I won't lick it like I did when I was six), and I hunker down, longing for one more blanket. Tony has moved the spider plant further from the window, and I'm happy to report it is doing well.

Tomorrow is Sunday, but I haven't the heart for church. Dreaming about it last night was enough. Either I stop putting this off and come clean, or the misery will continue. I've got to find a way.

Last year at this time I could scarcely wait for Christmas. The anticipation was almost too much for me. If I could not sleep then, it was for thoughts of the school party, where we would watch Laurel and Hardy movies and eat sugar by the spoonful and chips with both hands. This year is another matter. Suddenly I realize that even the church program and Uncle Roy's gifts have lost their charm. For the first time in my life I am viewing the season with dread. What would Christmas be without Dad? I push the thought far from me, but not for long. All of this is God's punishment for my sins. Even a fourth grader can figure this out.

Having Ben back helps. Tonight he is on the air once again, and there is no particular topic on "Evenings with Ben." It's open line, says our radio host, who is four feet above me in the coal-cellar black. I am so glad to hear the springs squeaking again. The calls Tony places range from talk of funny-sounding names in our town (Warren Battle, Ida Butz, Mona Lott) to more palindromes ("Ana, nab a banana" and "No sir! Away! A papaya war is on").

When things revert to dead air, I try to snag some sleep. But it won't come. Finally I place a call to suggest talking about prac-tical jokes, mostly because I've been thinking about firecrackers and whether or not I should blow the place up or burn it down. Most good practical jokers employ fireworks at some point.

"What kind of jokes have you been involved in, ladies and gentleman?" says our host, who is trying out an East Indian accent tonight and succeeding quite well. "Oh please do be telling me. Call in tonight and you could win a free trip for two to Delhi. Second prize is a trip for four." When there is silence from both Tony and me, he decides to rephrase the question. "Have you heard about others who have played practical jokes in this town, or have you ever been (here he inserts a drum roll) the victim?"

"Remember when we glued a quarter to the sidewalk in front of the Golden Years Lodge and watched Miss Fanny McCourt whack it with her cane for a full ten minutes?" says Tony.

I don't remember this, but he and Ben do. They have a good laugh together.

"She used some words that surprised me," says Tony. "Didn't she teach us Sunday school?"

"Substitute teacher," clarifies Ben.

"Or the time we told the usher we wanted a seat at the front of the church and then let him go on ahead while we ditched him?"

"It was like telling the gullible kid on the football field to go for a long bomb."

Tony is the king of practical jokers, and he loves to tell about it. I am more cautious than he and less talkative, partly because I have watched such jokes fizzle. One summer night we set Black Cat firecrackers on the Rosbergs' windowsill as they were having family devotions, but they turned out to be duds (the firecrackers, that is).

On another occasion, during lunch hour we strung fishing line from the back of Mrs. Hoover's desk drawer upward to a wide fluorescent light fixture directly over her head. To the other end of the line I had attached a mousetrap, and standing on tiptoe, I placed it atop the light. In theory, the opening of the drawer was to trigger a delightful chain reaction, snapping the mousetrap *bang!* and releasing a handful of gold stars we had discovered in Mrs. Hoover's desk, stars she gave us for good behavior. All morning I had visions of her sitting there, turning her head to look at us with wrinkled brow. Then she would open her desk to fish for breath mints to disguise her coffee breath and hear the muffled snapping sound overhead. The whole class would witness the slow, glittery descent of a golden cloud of stars that would settle over her head and shoulders as she assumed an expression of appreciative resignation.

But when she opened the drawer, nothing happened.

The line did not move.

The trap did not snap.

Minutes later, Cheryl Wiens, a petite blond, who until that point had always been kind to me, went forward to sharpen her pencil and ran nose-first into the line. The trap came careening downward, narrowly missing her head and whamming the blackboard behind Mrs. Hoover. I hunched my shoulders and ground my teeth and closed my eyes. It was tough to watch. Even tougher when Cheryl squealed on us and we were asked to wait in the office remembering those gold stars and knowing it was the last time we would see them that year.

Tony's cackle snaps me back from reverie. "One night I put Cherry Kool-Aid in our showerhead just before Liz went in there," he admits. "She screamed pretty good and tracked me down. Dad was smiling, I'm pretty sure, but I can remember his warning: Practical jokes are anything but."

"Yes, friends, he was right," says Ben, who loves to wax philosophical on the radio. "They are hard to resist though. A sword of this magnitude is tough to cease wielding in favor of obedience. One tends to view things like a can of shaving cream or a bottle of detergent not so much as objects but as opportunities."

I haven't thought so much of playing jokes lately as I have of making sure I'm not the brunt of one. Besides, I cannot be nearly as resourceful as my brother Tony, who has crammed more fun into sixteen years than anyone I know. His jokes are more elaborate and sometimes require actual money. I don't think he will mind if I tell you that he is the one who poured the entire bottle of liquid detergent into the toilet tank of the downstairs washroom at church. He has also played numerous phone pranks, including the time he and a friend dialed the number of the Giddy Ridge Funeral Chapel to inform them that the fourth-grade teacher, Mr. Rasmuson, was dead. He even furnished the address where they could pick him up, though I'm not sure they went for it.

He has phoned random numbers informing folks that he is with the phone company and that there is trouble with their line.

"Please do not answer any calls for the next five minutes, or the person on the other end may be electrocuted. Thank you," he says in a cheerful but businesslike voice. Then he hangs up, waits two minutes, and calls back. If they answer, he begins screaming, "Aaaah!" and hangs up again.

Tony tells a few of these old standards tonight, and we laugh like we're hearing them for the first time. Then, with ample dramatics, he tells us one he hasn't told before. One that almost causes me to forget the corner I've painted myself into.

Seems this very last summer, Tony and his friend Gary came up with a devious plan as they worked for Mr. Guenther, nailing shingles to the roof of Mrs. Brewer's new bungalow. They waited for Sunday night, and when ten-thirty rolled around, Tony was listening for Ben and I to fall asleep. Benjamin was rolling around on pins and needles (he always does this, perhaps from nicotine withdrawal), and my soft snores sounded like a five-watt buzz saw. Easing the covers away from his body, Tony eyed the window. Nah. Too hard. Too noisy. He pushed his legs through his jeans and tugged on a sweater. He slunk down the hall then, pulled a carton of eggs from the fridge, a box of matches from a cupboard, and quietly stepped outside. The air was chilly for a summer night, so he briefly reconsidered, but Gary was there. Waiting. Grinning too. They knelt in the backyard and in hushed tones compared what they'd brought.

"Look at this, Tone." Gary said breathlessly, extracting from his jacket a battered roll of masking tape, a plastic bread bag of unpopped corn, and from his pocket a few firecrackers. "Just in case," he said.

Eight or nine copies of the *Grace Chronicle* awaited them on the back step, and though they made themselves busy taping sheets of newspaper together, Tony said he was yawning into the back of his arm and wondering what would possess him to leave his warm bed. "Let's try this tomorrow night," he suggested. Gary, who must have napped soundly that afternoon, paid him no attention. He chattered away in anticipation, naming the potential recipient of their creativity. On this night they had decided to go for the granddaddy of them all:

The pastor's house.

—☽—

I am sure you will agree that they did not pick the best moment. A preacher of the gospel is not at his most accommodating late on a Sunday evening, nor should we expect him to be. He has lugged more than a few people's burdens—some of them pretty heavy ones, listened to a number of complaints about sermon length and content, and been chided for not visiting enough shut-ins, so I will grant you that the lads' timing was not impeccable. But since Tony had sat listening to the message on forgiveness that morning, the prank had been stirring within him—to the point where he had been unable to nap. And though we have often heard our minister say that his wife practices what he preaches, both boys were curious to discover how he himself would do if afforded the opportunity.

Pastor Davis's message had been a good one. "The Forgiveness Factor," Tony says it was entitled. And he padded it with four points: God forgives Fully, Freely, Favorably, and Finally. He discussed the miracle of forgiveness, the mandate of forgiveness, and the model of forgiveness. Then he demonstrated through the use of illustrations how forgiveness releases the bonds of bitterness, reveals love to the skeptic, restores unity among believers, and reopens channels of blessing. The conclusion was a pretty good one too.

A story from the Gospel of Matthew about a king who is owed millions of dollars by a man whom he forgives, only to find out that the slug promptly left the palace, looked up a guy who owed him a few thousand dollars, choked him real good, and threw him into prison. "Mercy imitates God and disappoints the devil," said Reverend Davis in conclusion. "So let's practice it this week. And remember," (I knew what was coming next because he always closed this way) "Don't put a question mark where God put a period." Tony knew all of this because he had written the closing sentence below the outline on his note pad, knowing that Dad often questioned us at dinner and those who had the answers sometimes ate dessert first (if there was any) while the others watched.

Their plan was simple. Boldly approach the front of the house (the light is off and everyone is in bed) and apply the newspaper they'd been taping together so it covered the doorframe nearly to the top. Then, hoist some things through the slat up there, allowing them to lodge between the newspaper and the outside of the door. First will come a few hundred tight wads of newspaper. Then the unpopped corn. And finally, when there's very little room left, a cat or two.

I sit up in bed. "What? Cats?"

"Just kidding," says Tony.

The cats were Gary's idea, but since the ones he caught were hard to hang onto, they had to settle for the eggs. A dozen of them, cradled gently on the newspaper. If the plan goes without a hitch, they would seal the top, ring the doorbell, and watch from a secluded spot as Reverend Davis opens the door just as you would a Cracker Jack box to claim your surprise.

The plan went flawlessly, though Gary was trembling so badly he could hardly hold the newspaper as Tony taped it to the doorframe. At last they were successful. Returning a lawn chair they had used for height, they crouched behind a low hedge. Gary lit the firecrackers, rang the doorbell and ran, leaping into the foliage beside Tony, banging his head on a low-hanging branch and muttering to himself.

Their eyes were wide, watching in nervous expectancy.

A thought struck Tony. What if the door opens outward? There was no time to change things now.

The porch light flickered on.

The firecrackers exploded.

Then a crash.

Tony is silent, and I can't wait.

"What then? What happened?" I demand.

"Well, our pastor came busting through the newspaper with his slippers covered in eggs and at least one of them oozing down his pajama bottoms, and he looked around and then started to laugh. In fact, he started laughing so hard that he had to sit down on the lawn chair. That's where he sat on the egg carton I'd forgotten there. Mom always put our name on the cartons, remember? I don't know why. Anyhoo, he just sat there laughing. We didn't know what to do. Finally we slunk away, hunched over so he wouldn't see us.

"'Thanks for the popcorn, Tony Anderson!' he yelled. 'And was that you, Gary? Goodnight, guys.'"

—⁓—

As I drift off, it strikes me that I too have left my share of egg cartons behind. My secret will come out in the end. Ben's too. And when it does, is forgiveness too great a thing to ask? Is it really possible that this same man could offer it to me as surely as he did to Tony and Gary? What about Matt? Suspicious people would like him back behind bars. Will he ever forgive me? What about all the people I've lied to? Or a family whose house I've just decided against burning to the ground?

Larry Norman is singing nearby:

> One way, one way to heaven
> Hold up high your hand
> Follow, free and forgiven
> Children of the Lamb

Mercy sounds good in sermons and on tape, but when you're most in need of it, it is a slippery concept indeed. But still I go to sleep this night dreaming it could be mine.

Ah, I've had some great dreams in my day.

Twenty-One

Visitor

Just before the worship service on the third Sunday of Advent, two things happen within one minute of each other. First of all, Pastor Davis approaches me as I amble toward our pew, and he bends to ask a favor. "Would you mind lighting the Advent candles, Larry? The gold one first, then the white, then the green?" He seems preoccupied, exhausted, rumpled even.

"*Terry,*" I correct him, using my respectful voice.

"I'm sorry, Terry. Would you? I'll give you the match, Terry, and you can just come up front when I call you right before my message. Okay, Terry?"

I've since been told this is a good way to remember names.

The second happening is stranger still. A man enters the church wearing a jacket that's much too light for our climate, dog-eared leather boots that could use a shine or two, and an expression reminiscent of a five-year-old who's just swallowed pickle juice believing it was apple. The visitor could be twenty or a hundred for all I know. Reminds me of the time a bum wandered into our church, all tattered and smelly. It turned out he was the visiting speaker, who commenced to preach quite a message on judgmentalism, using personal illustrations from the way he'd been treated that very morning. Apparently the message hadn't gotten through. Not knowing what to say or do, people hurry to clear a path for the stranger as he ambles forward, his eyes darting about the room guardedly. I hold my breath as he considers choosing our pew but then settles right in the front row, next to the pastor and his wife, who pat him on the shoulder and shake his hand as if everything is normal, as if the stranger is dressed in a three-piece suit complete with corsage.

I'm barely to my seat when Mary Beth Swanson's family files down the aisle past their normal row and tries squeezing into the pew behind us. But things are tight back there, so Mary Beth moves forward and sits next to me, leaving her little brother Michael wedged between his parents once again. Gladly I make room for her, smiling at my good fortune, pleased that coming to church today has already yielded such a blessing.

"I'm sorry about your dad," she whispers sweetly, and her breath smells like a spring breeze that has soared across fields of clover and a bubbling brook. You could package it and hang it from your rearview mirror.

"That's nice," I say. "You're welcome."

This is surprisingly dumb, but what did I expect? She leans close enough for me to feel the puff of her lacy sleeve against my bare arm. Goose bumps rise and my face feels like it's catching fire. Will Liz or Tony, who is seated to the left of me, notice? I needn't wonder long. Tony leans ever so slightly and says in a whisper that's not quite enough of one: "First comes love, then comes marriage, then comes Bubba in a baby carriage." Mary Beth has good ears. I dare not look to see if she is using them.

As the service commences, my imagination carries me away again, and I find myself walking her to the altar and lifting her veil and kissing her right there within inches of the big King James Bible opened on the communion table. Kneeling, I recite the words

I've heard my Dad use a dozen times when flattering my mother, "Let me not to the marriage of true minds admit impediments," and I try to think of some elegant Shakespearean prose of my own. Perhaps:

> Last night I wrote thy name upon the sand,
> Then came the waves and washed it all away.
> And so I wrote it this time on my heart,
> That evermore thy name shall with me stay.

If food is the key to a man's heart, then surely poetry will unlock a woman's. Mary Beth takes my head in both her hands and pulls me to her, ruffling my hair and kissing my lips, not seeming to care that the entire congregation is behind us, standing to its feet now, applauding.

"I do," she says. "Do I ever."

"I now pronounce you man and wife," says Pastor Davis, smiling over his wire rims. "If anyone objects, let him speak now or forever hush up." Miss Hoover, my sinewy teacher, stands, her hands on her hips, her lips puckered, her mouth wide from the shock of it all.

But rather than take Mary Beth to the altar, I speak to her in a soft voice, trying a lower octave for effect: "So, I've gotta light it," I tell her, as if it's not a big deal being selected for such an honor, as if she knows what I'm talking about.

"Light what?" she asks.

"Uh...the um—" my mind goes blank and finally registers. "Uh...candles."

The stubby one looks more gray than green to me, and I keep my eyes on it until the Scripture reading from Isaiah 9, wherein the people in darkness see a great light. "Angels from the Realms of Glory" is the first duet Mary Beth and I have sung together, and I can't help being impressed. We share the hymnal, me grasping it right in the middle and hoping she doesn't notice that my wrist is pitifully thin. When we reach "Seek the great Desire of nations, ye have seen His natal star," I am experimenting with lofty harmonies and tilting her way, listening to the brook and inhaling the clover.

Perhaps we will minister one day as husband and wife, singing and traveling the country, me on the guitar, her telling weepy stories. Ah, how I love these songs of Christmas. But I must follow the next hymn carefully or I get the words mixed up: "Peace on earth and mercy mild, Gold and silver make me smile." And now comes a slow and sad rendition of "I Heard the Bells on Christmas Day," and I must leave the clover fields and the bubbling brook and the concert halls and descend to the church to consider my duties here this morning.

Getting up before people gives me what Dad calls the heebie-jeebies. Always has. What if I can't remember the order of the candles? Was it gold first, or white? What if the match doesn't work? What if I can't move, like in a dream? What if they ask me to say something? Maybe share a word of personal testimony? Worse yet, what if my hands begin to shake and I cannot connect with the wicks? Mary Beth will see it, and that will be the end of my plans for our traveling ministry. "I kinda liked him, but he was unsteady," she will say at our twentieth high school reunion. I will be single, lonely, and devastated. I once heard of a Catholic altar boy who passed out while holding a candle and fell over, thereby setting his hair on fire. That would be the peak of irony and justice for the connivings of a reformed arsonist like myself.

Tony is doodling religious palindromes on the bulletin, having been unable to find any bloopers therein (like "sin and share" or

"Evening massage—7 P.M."). He passes them my way and I try to work them out: "Cain: A maniac!" "Eve damned Eden, mad Eve," and "Satan, oscillate my metallic sonatas." To support his doodling, Tony is using a thick stack consisting of the most mail in the history of our foyer mailbox. Most are sympathy cards. One is a letter he passes to me. It is a seventh-generation copy on dark green paper, sent by Michael's dad, whose ministry it is to keep members of our fellowship aware of pressing issues like long hair and short skirts and what the Bible has to say about earrings. I read it as Pastor Davis shares the announcements:

Santa is an imposter!
The letters of his name also spell Satan!
Note these counterfeits!

1. God is the giver of every good gift. Santa brings gifts!

2. God rides in a chariot. Santa rides in a sleigh!

3. God dwells in the north. Santa dwells in the north!

4. God has a book of remembrance. Santa keeps a record!

5. God is all-seeing, all-knowing. Santa knows if you've been naughty or nice!

6. God rewards good deeds. Santa rewards good deeds!

7. Jesus' blood cleanses "white as snow." Santa wears a red and white suit!

8. Jesus will return unexpectedly from the clouds. Santa does the same!

9. Jesus lets you rest in his arms. Santa lets you sit on his lap!

I wonder what Pastor Davis will think when he pulls this from his mailbox. He is climbing the steps to the podium now, wearing the second-best suit he has—the blue one—and gazing out upon his little flock. He nods his head when he gets to me, a twelve-year-old kid, his evangelical altar boy. "I've asked Larry Anderson to come and light our Advent candles," he says ceremoniously. Tony snickers at my name, and I drop the Santa sheet. Brushing past Mary Beth, I wonder if I should face her or turn away. Surprisingly, the candle lighting goes off without me falling or igniting myself, and though a blizzard begins to rage outside, the sermon subject is so unusual as to be the focus of my entire attention.

"I've been with you a year now," Pastor Davis begins, shuffling a few notes, but not really looking at them. "I think it's time you heard my story. Advent is a special time for celebrating Christ's birth, but for Irene and me it's also a painful reminder…well, let me tell you about it."

Snow is pelting the window so hard it sounds like rain, and all that's missing are a cozy blanket and a flickering fire and maybe some marshmallows. Those with plans to read a passage of Scripture during the message reconsider, and a few teens who had slipped paperbacks inside their Bibles look up as if someone has just said, "Hey, look at this. I want to show you something."

"Two Christmases ago I had given up on church," says the pastor, startling me with his frankness. "We celebrated ten years in ministry that summer, quite an accomplishment these days." He sighs and smiles, then moves beside the pulpit and leans an elbow on it. "But it looked to be our last. Decisions made in youth are companions for life, I guess, and I made some bad ones."

I've been inching closer to Mary Beth throughout the introduction, until there is nowhere left to go without crossing the point of obvious. Mary Beth is listening intently, seemingly unaware of my advances. Our school handbook pointedly requires boys and girls to remain at least a Bible width apart, but is that a family Bible or one of these thin ones you can put in your shirt pocket, the ones with the small type? Should you lay it flat or turn it on edge?

"I grew up in a fine Christian home," Mr. Davis interrupts my foolish thoughts. "Mom and Dad modeled the kind of life I knew I wanted. I enrolled in Bible college the minute high school ran out, and though my parents prayed for me and cheered me on, it soon became apparent that the truths I was learning were not sifting down as far as my heart. One professor often referred to the verse, 'Except a corn of wheat fall into the ground and die, it abideth alone: but if it die, it bringeth forth much fruit.' But after one semester, I left school angry at the rules and the legalism and ready to sow some seeds of my own.

"A fine-paying job in the city allowed me anything I wanted, and I made no pretense to live for God. I'd seen too many Pharisees, so church went out the window. I became the consummate prodigal, rejecting everything I'd ever been taught, living for myself, for parties and fun and cornhusks. I don't need to recount it all here, but I will say that my parents never ceased loving me and writing letters and praying. Soon I found myself in the company of bad friends, including a young woman. When I came to my senses, she was...well, very much pregnant."

I haven't heard the word used right here in the church before, and it's like someone set off a cherry bomb. Mr. Solynka, our Ukrainian broadcaster, has his head snap back involuntarily, leaving him looking in need of a chiropractor. But the story continues as if the teller hasn't noticed a thing.

"God pays us the compliment of allowing us to choose His way or reject it, I suppose. I rejected it. And my bad choices started a chain reaction." He hangs his head. "I'm ashamed to tell you that I ran. I ran from my responsibilities, knowing all the while I was running down the wrong road. I ran from the truth like a house on fire. And when finally I met it head on and repented, I returned home, broken and contrite, to the waiting arms of my parents. Soon they convinced me to contact the young lady who would bear my child, but I was unable to locate her. To complicate matters, she had lied about her name. Said it was Annie Lischer. There was no record of an Annie Lischer in that area. Believe me, we searched."

Mary Beth is definitely into it now. I am sitting close enough to tell. Her body stiffens then relaxes at all the right parts and I wonder if she needs me to swing an arm about her shoulder for comfort. Or place a hand on her knee—maybe whisper soothing words.

"No one knew my secret save for my parents, and after a time I decided to head back to Bible college and then on to seminary," the pastor is saying. "From there I went straight into the ministry. The years pass so quickly, don't they? Some of you know that Irene and I would love to have children, but we've been unable to. There was a time when I viewed it as God's judgment on me, though Irene assured me God doesn't operate that way. She has been so supportive through all of this." He looks at her and has to pause a moment. "Often I thought of my child out there somewhere, never knowing a father."

I am old enough to know the scandal of it, and I wonder what the others are thinking. Couldn't this cost him his job, such an admission? I've been through enough sermons to know we won't forget this one. I can't imagine our previous pastor being this honest, this vulnerable. He seemed more concerned with remaining aloof, more interested that people were taking notes, giving him bonus marks for alliteration.

"Several years ago on the afternoon of the first Sunday of Advent, a phone call changed everything," our minister is saying.

"I thought it was my mother, who calls often during the Christmas season, but the caller was abrupt, angry. 'Mr. Davis,' a stern female voice demanded, 'is this Timothy Davis who lived and worked in Minneapolis, oh, along about fourteen years ago?' I told her it was. 'I have a woman here who says she has something that's yours.' As she said this, a knot welled up in my stomach. The next thing I knew, I heard a voice from my past, a voice I hadn't heard since I ran from the truth so many years ago.

"'Annie, is that you?'"

"'Abby,' she said, 'Abby Fisher.'"

"I told her how long I had waited for her call and asked her forgiveness. 'It's a little late for that,' she said. 'I'm dying.'"

Well, even I am into it now. Pastor Davis' voice falters on these words, and he starts biting his bottom lip and looking at the floor. When finally he gets the story back on track, he tells how she wasn't expected to live long after the cancer diagnosis and that she'd been searching for him for months. "Would you take care of our Jonathan?" she wanted to know. "Give him a good home?"

"We spent the first two weeks of December in Minneapolis, Irene and me. For fourteen years I'd longed for this day, then dreaded it, then dreamed of it. I remember introducing myself clumsily to my son, and how tough it was to get him to look me in the eye. But finally, as we began to compare physical features and talents, we discovered that we laughed alike and that, best of all," here his voice falters again, "he knew God.

"We led Abby to Christ together, Irene and me, two days before she passed on. I even preached at the tiny funeral service. The three of us arrived home, the paperwork completed, all nervous and excited. But as you might suspect, some people don't take too kindly to skeletons falling out of closets, and Jonathan's presence brought so many questions that the answers got jumbled. Soon rumors started swirling. When I got up in church to tell my story, it was the last sermon I preached to that little congregation. They were dear people, many of them. I hope I do not sound bitter, but it's been a long road. My son was so angry with the gossip and the whispers that he took to running like his father had done all those years ago, vowing he'd never enter a church again. I've been writing him the past while, telling him about the wonderful congregation here, that churches are hospitals for the sick, not resorts for the healthy. Telling him I think it's time for him to come home.

"I wrote something in my Bible last night just before I fell asleep. I'd like to hang it outside our church one day. On a big banner. 'Sinners only, please.'"

The minister pauses to wipe his eyes before continuing.

"I am sorry if you thought your pastor was anything but a sinner. I have failed. I have fallen short. I am comforted to know that the greatest saints have also been the greatest sinners. That a saint is simply one who lets God's light shine through him. A few years ago I determined that it would not be my name I would spend my life defending, but the name of my Lord and Savior. I have sought God's pardon, and I have found it. In finding it, I've discovered that He loves me and accepts me and that He will never let go of me even if He's not all that impressed with what He has to work with."

Pastor Davis smiles. "I have to tell you that when I received the call to come and preach here, I was intrigued by the name of the town. You see, I turned my back on the church for a time. God's grace brought me back. The Bible tells us in Romans 3 that God sent Jesus to take the punishment for our sins and to satisfy God's anger against us. We are made right with Him when we believe that Jesus shed His blood, sacrificing His life for us. God has always given His best gifts to those who didn't deserve them. He forgives and forgets when we come to Him.

"One of you asked me recently why I refer to the Psalms so often. During the dark nights of my soul, I have lapped them up like a thirsty creature, finding hope and assurance and mercy. But I suppose the most tearstained pages in my Bible bear these words from Jeremiah 31 in a paraphrase called *The Living Bible:* 'The Lord…will gather them together and watch over them as a shepherd does his flock…I will turn their mourning into joy, and I will comfort them and make them rejoice, for their captivity with all its sorrows will be behind them.' I have turned these words into a prayer for my wandering son.

"I believe this is the message of Christmas. That God sent His only Son not to condemn us but to reconcile us to Him. There are only two kinds of people in this world, my friend Mr. Anderson told me once," and here he looks at what remains of our family, "those who are forgiven, and those who are in trouble. I stand before you today one of the forgiven."

Hearing him use my father's words only adds to the amazement I'm already feeling. Surely I'm not the only one to notice that this is the first admission of failure to come from this pulpit. But Pastor Davis hasn't quite reached the punch line.

"Last night when I was working on the sermon I would give this morning, Irene answered a knock at the door. The man who stepped through our threshold was covered in snow and ill-dressed for it. Like me, he'd spent a lot of years running, and like me, he had come home to find comfort in a parent's arms. It was our Jonathan. You'll forgive me if I'm a little tired this morning. We've been up much of the night crying and laughing and studying old photographs. You'll also understand if you see me hugging a tall dark teenager after the service. He's the best gift I'll receive this Christmas. And I'd like you to meet him this morning."

He points to the front row.

Well, you could knock me over with a bulletin, I am that shocked. The stranger sitting beside the pastor's wife stands to his feet and turns to wave shyly to the congregation. His smile is an exact replication of the one grinning at us from behind the pulpit.

A smile all of us are coming to love.

—⚏—

The first Advent candle is almost out when Pastor Davis closes in prayer. I have not asked Tony for the time even once during the sermon—a record for me. The prayer is finished, yet no one is moving.

Slowly I am aware of a sound I've not heard before. It is the soft sound of people weeping. Mary Beth is one of them. A few of the men are crying too.

Outside the wind is howling and the snow has reached the windowsills. Eugene Miller, one of the bachelors, pulls a coat and hat on and tries to open the door to leave. It won't budge. The drift is too high. The hat comes off first, then the coat, and then Mr. Miller sits down, somehow knowing that lunch can wait. It is evident that most aren't thinking of the roast back home.

They have other things on their minds.

Things they need to confess.

Twenty-Two

Revelation

Andrew Weigum is first.

I can't believe a man as skinny as him can still muster the courage to leave his house in the morning, but here he is, taking long strides to the front of the church, standing before us terrified, swallowing hard, his Adam's apple bobbing up and down, like a swimmer coming up for air.

"You're not alone, Pastor," says Andrew in a voice that still hasn't quite reached puberty. "I'm one of those sinners you say is welcome here. Every day of the week I fight the urge to lie and lie good. I once made a living as a traveling salesman, selling my wares from town to town back in the old days. If you'll pardon me, I used to yell, 'Skinny men and women! Gain five, ten, fifteen pounds! Bony limbs fill out. Neck no longer scrawny. Body loses half-starved, sickly bean-pole look. Thousands are now proud of shapely, healthy-looking bodies. They thank the special vigor-building, flesh-constructing tonic, Creatox, because it improves appetite and digestion. Don't fear getting too fat. Stop when you've gained the weight you wanted. Only sixty cents a bottle.'"

People laugh heartily at the comic relief. I can't help but smile too.

"Didn't sell much of it because I was so skinny myself. Guess I still am. So guess what I tried to sell next? That's right. Hair tonic."

We laugh much harder on this one, for Andrew has been chrome bald for as long as we've known him. When people mention it, he always has a witty comeback: "Grass won't grow on a busy street." "Marble tops don't go on cheap furniture."

"I'd arrive in town balder than an eight ball and set up my stand, hoping to sell the latest hair growth tonic. People were skeptical for the first few days, but they'd see me drinking it and by the third or fourth day my hair was growing fast and thick and blond, so they couldn't resist. They'd buy it by the caseload. Then I'd move on to the next town. Of course, no one knew that I just shaved my head bald between each town. I'm not proud of this of course. Just thought you should know. Thought I should get it off my chest. I've told God that I want to be a man of truth. Hearing you say what you said this morning gave me the courage, Reverend."

Pastor Davis steps forward and puts an arm around Andrew's shoulders, assuring him of God's forgiveness. I wonder if his baldness is God's judgment, or if he still shaves it out of habit. But what did the pastor say? God isn't all that impressed? But still He loves us?

Smiles greet Mr. Weigum as he humbly steps from the platform and sits down. There is an uncomfortable silence, so the pastor approaches the podium to once again close in prayer.

Then a rustling sound. First one person stands, then another. Something is happening, something an unfinished revival meeting unleashed a few short weeks ago. Something our pastor just steps back and lets happen.

Some of the confessions border on the ridiculous. Like Carol Clegg's admission that she once took a pen by accident after signing a check at the Five and Dime and neglected to return it, or Morris Munkholm's divulgence that he loves windy days because of what they do to the lady's dresses, which leaves Pastor Davis looking like a deer caught in the headlights, wondering if the vehicle bearing down on him has brakes.

"God's Word commands us to confess our faults to one another," he says, trying to be short on words and long on tact, "but let us make sure these things are helpful to the building up and edifying of one another. Those who would like to pray with someone can meet with an elder in the prayer room. Everything need not be confessed to this group."

It is a disappointing announcement to me, but I suppose he is right. All around me are people whose stories most of us know. You'd have to be deaf not to hear them in a town like ours.

There's Jamie Friesen, for instance, an eleventh-grade boarding student, who last year had the entire church praying for her as she duked it out with cancer. It's not every year you get to celebrate "Christmas" in June, but there we were shoveling presents onto Jamie's desk, politely, knowing that this would be her last "Christmas" and that she wouldn't live to see the real one in December. I remember how no one got too close to her or asked the questions we really wanted to ask: What was it like to hear the news that she has cancer? Is she mad at God? Or the doctors? Is there anything she'd really like to do before she dies?

Each Thursday Jamie had a friend drive her to the city for treatments, and she wouldn't return until Monday. She began to wear a hat to hide the hair loss, and several in her class shaved their heads to show their support. But as it turned out, the only cancer she had was a lack of attention, and this was her way of curing it, to lie about a terrible disease, filling the town with rumors and the entire high school with skeptics.

Others are confessing now, but I am thinking of Jamie's sins, and thinking of them has me thinking of my own. Could I ever confess my sins in such a place? Before Pastor Davis arrived, this was a place of judgment. I have seen folks verbally stoned or socially ostracized in the wake of such confessions. You can go a long way in this town by just toeing the line, by keeping quiet, by looking pious. But today has seen a noticeable shift.

Without knowing it, I am staring at the candles again. Especially the white one. Once sturdy and strong, the flame has reduced it to nothing. It is tapered, truncated, and flattened. I feel strangely sad for it—as if it were a living thing—for it was I who did the damage. I lit the thing. I started it. It took less than an hour to rob its beauty, to splay the candle, to lay it flat. It has taken longer for me to be laid out, but I feel like the candle. What has it been? A month? It seems an eternity to carry a burden I was not meant to bear on shoulders as narrow as these.

What on earth would I say if I stood on stage? Where would I possibly start? Would these people stone me with their words as they had others? What will be the cost of releasing this burden? One thing is sure, this girl seated next to me would never look at me again. But surely if the dear people of Grace Community were honest with themselves, how could they judge someone like me? What did Pastor Davis say? "Sinners only, please." It's just that some of us sin a little more publicly, I guess. Not to excuse myself, but I have come to realize that there is a rather thin margin separating the sinners from those who appear to have it together. It is opportunity. And there is less than you think that separates the pious from the righteous. It is the simple admission of wrong.

Tony elbows me hard. "It's Matt," he says. "Listen."

Matthew Jennings is in tears before he speaks—they seem to be in ample supply today. I can't imagine what it will be like once he starts. But his voice is steady, strong.

"I had to come up here," he is saying. "Pastor Davis' story is my story. Only I'm where he was years ago. I'm getting ready to run.

Started packing my bags last night. You see, I got my freedom this week, only to be called to account for someone else's sin. I know many of you won't believe that I'm innocent," Matt ventures, "that I didn't steal the money they found, but that doesn't matter. What matters is that I take the blame for the things I have done in the past. I have sinned often, and were it not for the faithful witness of Tony Anderson, I'd be locked up back at Liberty County today. Or dead. Like our pastor, I must confess that in my wanderings I fathered a child too. Two of them actually. I'm here to tell you that the running is over and I'll be doing the right thing. I hope you're willing to marry us," he says, turning to our smiling pastor. "I'm not the only one who needs a fresh start."

So this is the secret that almost slammed my brother in jail. *Your secret is safe with me.*

I slide lower in the pew. If Matt finds out I'm the one who took the money, he'll kill me.

I'd really like to leave now, but how? I'm trapped between Saint Tony and the girl I love.

The clock is honing in on one P.M. when finally Mr. Swanson stands to his feet. Every eye follows him as he limps to the front to confess what he was about to confess that tragic night. Mary Beth squirms uneasily beside me.

He glances at the baptismal first. "Don't worry," he says, "I won't stand on it." People smile. I am not one of them. Looking down, he squeezes his nose between his thumb and index finger. His shoulders begin to shake. Reverend Davis just leaves him there. Finally he speaks. "This is the most difficult thing I've ever had to do in my life," he says. "On the night of the revival service I was about to tell the story of my failure, but I guess God had other plans. The guilt and shame I have felt since that night are unspeakable. Mr. Anderson was...*is* a good man, and were it not for me and my sins, well, he would be here this morning rejoicing with us to see how God is working."

I glance at Tony. His head is down, his eyes leveled at his shoes.

"I…I have lived a double life. I have stood here to preach, knowing all the while that I should be struck by lightning. That I should get things right, but I put it off until it seemed impossible. I have been a hypocrite in so many areas of my life, and I am truly sorry."

Mr. Swanson hauls from his suit jacket pocket a huge handkerchief the size of a beach towel and commences to blow several notes into it before folding it neatly and continuing.

"I have been your head usher and treasurer of this church for many years. Eighteen, I think. I have taught your sons and daughters in Sunday School. And during all those years I have been—" Here he stops as if looking for a door or a window, any possible escape route. Finding none, he resumes his story. "During those years I have…I have taken something that isn't mine… money from the treasury. Yes, from the offering—*your* offering. The Lord's offering."

There is an audible gasp from behind me, but I dare not turn to see who issued it. It has been a morning of surprises, but none comes close to this. The murmurs and whispers are impossible to hide. "No, it cannot be! Not him!" Mary Beth is wooden, like a statue.

"It started with small stuff at first, but then I realized I could take larger bills, and so I did," Mr. Swanson acknowledges between sniffles. "I stole from you, my brothers and sisters. I found that if I took about a hundred dollars a week, no one would notice and I would have enough to be comfortable by the time I retire. My family knew nothing of this. I acted alone. I am here to ask your forgiveness and tell you that I will make it right—down to the last penny. With interest."

No one can move. The pastor is stunned. His jaw has dropped and he doesn't know it. This man has been pilfering his salary, his book allowance, stealing from the building fund, from the work of missionaries, from the work of the Lord. I fully expect a fist-fight. It will be a fitting conclusion to the most unusual service in our history. A brawl on the platform. Maybe the pastor will hurl him down the baptismal chute.

He looks to the pastor, like a man searching for a lifeboat. But there is none to be found, and his story is unfinished.

"I thought of lying to you, it got that bad." He coughs a time or two before continuing. "Of telling you that an uncle had sent me a lottery ticket or that some distant relative had left an inheritance, but the more lies I concocted, the more complex it became, and I knew my time was up. I want you to know that the other ushers are innocent, that I merely folded the bills into my pocket before we got to counting it. I assure you that I have spent nothing. I have kept the money hidden, moving it from place to place. It is somewhere around ninety thousand dollars."

More gasping. But the worst is yet to come. "Yesterday when the Spirit had completed His work in me and I determined to confess, I went to retrieve the money so I could return it to the church."

People are wide-eyed, as if they are watching the conclusion of an epic movie.

"It was gone. Stolen, I suspect."

Well, if ever you thought church was boring and you showed up on this particular morning, you'd change your tune in a flash. It was like *Radio Mystery Theater* on a Saturday night. I am shaking my head with the rest of them, wondering how a man can be so wicked, how he can stand up and preach after stooping so low, when the truth comes crashing in on me like the stone David wielded against Goliath.

The money?

Ninety thousand dollars?

Hidden?

Stashed away?

Gone?

I am not a straight-A student, nor the son of one, but I can connect these dots.

Well, if ever there was a time in my life when I longed for the Rapture my brother once threatened me with, it is now. Wouldn't that be something? Everyone sucked through the ceiling, naked as the day they came into this world, and me rescued from this awful predicament?

Everyone but me, that is. Liars and thieves don't fly so well, Tony says. But what else can I hope for now? I have exhausted every lie in my vocabulary, every devious scheme in my book.

I never wanted to be the climax to any story, but what options am I left with? My mind is a mess. My body, too. These secrets are too much for it to hold.

The still small voice I have managed to muzzle for a while is gaining volume once again. I cannot bring myself to look at Tony. Or Liz. Or Ben. Or my mother. I haven't really been able to for weeks. Ah, the wages of sin are death down here too.

I keep my eyes on the candle as I stand to my feet. There is still time to change my mind. I can pretend I am visiting the restroom. All I have to do is take a left toward Argentina. But what then? You can't bury things like this forever, can you? For all of us there comes a time when we must face the truth. This is the time. And this is the truth: I am a sinner. God will not exchange my sorrow for rejoicing until I come clean. Guilt has nudged me up against repentance, and the desire to repent has me taking a right toward Canada, toward the platform. I am terrified of the stares, fully aware that I haven't a clue what to say. This is not something they prepare you for. Not in the classes at our school.

I am standing on the platform now, forgetting that the baptismal trapdoor is directly below me, the door from which my father lost consciousness. The pastor gently tugs me from it.

I sneak a glance at my family, all of them with looks of surprise and shock on their faces. Mom's eyes are blinking wildly and I dare not keep my eyes on her. I dare not think of my father either.

"I…um…just think that I hope you will listen to me…and forgive me too, as well…okay?" If Mary Beth weren't here, this would be easier. "I bought a snowmobile with the money Mr. Swanson was talking about, two hundred dollars of it, and I bought candies—loads of them. I took it, you know. I found it and I took it. It was the wrong thing and I knew it, even though I didn't know where it came from. Um…just…but I know where the rest of it is, and I will give it back. Today. I have kept track of how much I spent, and I'll get Mr. Swanson's money back to you. Somehow. All of it. I promise. I'm so sorry to God and to you."

I cannot move. It's as if I've been running the Boston marathon and I can't go another step without collapsing.

Tony is looking at me with his mouth open and a piece of gum just lying there on his lip, frozen in time.

No one expects what's coming next, least of all me.

A strong arm comes to rest gently on my shoulder.

The arm of our shepherd, Reverend Davis.

He stoops and pulls me to him, issuing what is possibly the first platform hug ever issued in a church of non-huggers. The tears scramble down my cheeks, and I am not alone. Reverend Davis is crying. So is my mother. And Ben and Liz and Tony. Crying with relief, I suppose. And maybe from a lack of roast beef and a joy too deep to show itself any other way.

Mary Beth's head is down, and I think she's crying too.

The pastor pulls the microphone from its cradle and doesn't even notice the momentary feedback.

"I was reading just a few days ago about the Seven Wonders of the ancient world. Did you know that only one exists today? It's the Egyptian Pyramids at Giza. Fires and floods and earthquakes have destroyed the others. I'm sure we'll try to replace them, but none of the monuments we erect and none of the wonders we discover will come close to the greatest wonder of them all: God's grace. We've seen that grace today, and I pray it will continue."

That comforting arm is still about my shoulder.

"Terry," he says, getting my name right for the first time in history, "you are in the company of sinners."

Wiping his eyes, he turns to the congregation. "Dear ones," he says, "I will personally see that safeguards are put in place to ensure this cannot happen again. And Terry here will be cutting some grass around here come summertime. Lots of it."

He smiles down at me, squeezing my skinny shoulder and closing his eyes to pray.

"Almighty God, Your grace has been amazing in all of our lives. Please accompany us as we work through these things. As we walk with You, as we follow in Your steps. And would You take this young man and use him? Would You raise his father up, if that suits Your purposes? And may all of us take the grace You've given us this day and pass it around this community."

And here I stand. Deserving condemnation. But finding compassion. Deserving judgment. Discovering grace.

I open my eyes.

This is no dream.

This is much better.

Twenty-Three

Resurrection

Another dream. This time for real.

I am sitting in my father's hospital room alone, having been dropped here for the supper shift. The hallways are decorated for Christmas. Bright lights adorn the banisters, tinsel too. It is Monday night, twelve days from Christmas, and the last few days are a splendid blur. The money was removed at lunchtime by Pastor Davis and two kind men whose names I can't recall. I'll admit to a twinge of sadness as I watched it being ushered out to their Volvo. The magnet that first drew me to it still has some pull, and I feel guilt whenever I regret doing the right thing.

There have been meetings and more meetings, prayer meetings and reconciliation meetings. Tony and Matt and I talked. Then we talked again. Looks like the two of them are becoming friends.

Late last night I sat on the edge of Mom's bed and watched her sleep. The wind was howling, and the snow had piled up huge drifts we'll be able to jump into from the rooftops. For the first time I noticed a plaque hanging by the closet: "Oh, what joy for those whose disobedience is forgiven, whose sins are put out of sight." For the first time in a long while, I said, "Amen to that."

And that's when Mom awoke. She took my hands in her shaky ones and her eyes filled with tears. "I love you, Son," was all she said.

At lunch today, Ben and I met with Pastor Davis to discuss my future. Still finding it difficult to grasp the concept of grace, I prepared myself for a terrifying event worthy of future editions of *Foxe's Book of Martyrs*. Instead Mr. Davis told me that my math was relatively accurate, that there was almost eighty-nine thousand dollars in the hockey bag, minus a snowmobile, some anonymous donations to my family, and a few miscellaneous expenses I had accrued. Six hundred and fifty dollars, by my estimate.

"You can do it, Terry Anderson," said the pastor, and I was happy he'd got my name right again. "I'm going to ask you to come up with the fifty dollars yourself, the rest you can work off." I was then informed I had volunteered for a part-time job, shoveling snow until summer, at which time I would have the privilege of building my biceps by mowing a few acres of grass each week. I might even get to help them build the new addition to the church—a small price to pay for the sense of happiness and relief that accompanies a fresh start.

I've brought along some homework tonight, and when I took it with me, Ben and Tony knew I'd turned over a new leaf for sure. I have four packages of gum in my pocket, the last remnants of my stash, gum I tried to take back to the Dairy King, whose proprietors refused to exchange it for real money. It was a blow to a kid who is wondering how to chip away at that fifty dollars. The store wouldn't take Liz's silver ring back either, the one with E.A. on it. So she gave it to Eunice Archibald, who held her hands aloft and blessed my sister over and over.

Did you know that you can squeeze four packages of Wrigley's Juicy Fruit into your mouth at one time if you remove the wrappers first? It takes some doing, but it's true. Chewing it does not make your homework any easier though.

Funny how the grown-ups have me trudging to school as if everything is normal, learning about atoms and molecules as if the world is right and my father is fine.

Strange how I find myself tiptoeing shamefully about his room, whispering whenever someone is near, as if I am afraid of the very thing I want most in all the world: to wake Dad up. He is the one person on earth who knows nothing of my sin. I find myself longing to keep it that way.

I am sitting quietly now, school binder on my knees, pen poised for the solving of some fuzzy math equation.

Suddenly my peripheral vision screams at me, jarring me alert. Dad has moved.

Maybe just a toe or a foot, but something has happened, that's for sure.

It's like a thousand spiders are climbing my spine all at once. I shake the spiders and quickly stand to my feet. I move next to Dad, a hand outstretched, wanting to touch him. Afraid of missing something, I hold my breath. And slowly, with my left hand, remove the wad of gum from my mouth.

"Oh God, please."

With my free hand, I massage his leg, the one I thought I saw move. Perhaps it was wishful thinking, or a twitch, some involuntary movement that means nothing.

"Dad," I whisper, leaning toward him, as if the old days could really come back. As if my hopes are about to land faceup for a change. I put a hand on his shoulder and gently shake him. "Dad. It's me. Terry. Terry Paul."

Nothing.

All imagined.

Or was it?

I reach for the buzzer. Should I ring for a nurse? Surely I'd look like a fool: "Um…I think I saw him move. Maybe. Almost. I think it was his toe. Or…or maybe…something else. I…uh…don't know. I'm sorry. I'll just sit here. Do my homework."

Dad is rigid, the sheet on his chest rising and then sinking almost indiscernibly. I watch hopefully, sit back down, and slowly shake my head side to side. But the glimmer of hope will not leave me. I pull the chair closer, trying not to scrape against the patterned linoleum. The binder is on the floor, forgotten.

"Dad, I…I…I'm sorry." I hear myself saying. "I've done some stuff I shouldn't have done. I…really need to tell you. I found some money…a huge bundle of it…and I wanted it to be mine…to fix everything, to make our family better, to make Mom better." The things I've done are sounding positively heroic. "I…I wanted to… I'm sorry…I was wrong."

My shoulders sag. I look down. "God, I'm sorry. Please don't make Dad pay for my sins. I'm really—"

It amazes me to this day how many ways a second can split, how many things can happen before the second hand moves again.

As surely as I am writing this, Dad's eyes flicker open, halting my prayers in their stammering tracks, leaving my mouth wide. And those eyes, those kind eyes that had smiled down on me through a thousand goodnights; those eyes that had glared indignation and shed tears too, they focus on me once again. And he says these words, past parched lips, but clear as the truth softly spoken: "Egg salad sandwich."

I kid you not.

I almost collapse as my legs go weak. I almost start to scream. It's one of those moments when the impossible happens and you don't know what to do with it. Like the day Brent Austring, the kindest kid in the entire school, whacked me with a three-iron right in my own backyard, and several moments elapsed before I could convince myself that he would ever do such a thing.

I drop my pen and hit the call buzzer and lunge at my dad, grabbing his hand, getting Juicy Fruit all over it. He is making incomprehensible noises, his left leg twitching in an uncoordinated, repetitive manner.

The nurses come scurrying—Anna is first. "He…he moved," is all I can manage. "He said something. I think he's hungry. I think maybe he…" My voice trails off into babbling. The nurses can see these things for themselves, but still I jabber away. "He was just there and I was here and it just happened, I wasn't, I can't, I didn't…" Anna puts a hand on my shoulder and tells me it's okay. She seems as excited as I am though, cleaning up the gum, darting about the room without purpose, flustered, shocked, like she got an A without studying.

In a matter of minutes Ben bursts through the door, with Liz goading him from behind and telling Tony to hurry up with Mom and the wheelchair. None of them could believe the phone call when it came, and all of them stand beside Dad in various stages of shock and denial and jubilation. Dad closes his eyes and opens them, slowly, on and off, and though his tuning dial still seems stuck on another frequency, he is smiling that same smile I have missed so badly.

Mom is trembling as badly as ever I've seen her.

"Honey," she says, leaning over and embracing him, "Thank God you're home."

—∿—

I wish I could report to you that Dad *was* home. That he stood up and walked into our church the very next Sunday to lead the singing and cause me to wonder at the premonitions of my dreams. The truth is, his recovery will take some time. He seems groggy at times, his movements unpredictable, his speech slurred, as if he's been into the suds at the tavern across town.

Dr. Mason cautions us about expecting a full recovery, but how can we hope for any less? The truth is, they are whispering terms like *miracle,* and phrases like *I've never seen anything like it.*

My hopes for a full recovery are pinned on Christmas, knowing it would be complete with him there. "Dear God, bring him home," I pray. "I won't ask for any other presents this year."

A neurologist comes from Great Falls to analyze him and even takes time to ask me questions. I am proud to tell him I'd been rubbing Dad's leg just before he awoke. And I find myself fighting the urge to offer him some magic formula I had used, like... well, like something involving chewing gum—a big wad of it. I'd get my name in the papers, that's for sure.

Boy Cures Father With Unconventional Medicine

[Associated Press] GRACE—A twelve-year-old boy from this small town discovered a most unusual cure yesterday when he wakened his own father from a deep 11-day coma by rubbing chewing gum on the back of his hand, sources say. "It was Juicy Fruit," the boy disclosed at a press conference earlier today, "lots of it." According to the *American Journal of Medicine,* the gum contains Hereboinia, a sticky herbal substance that can, in some instances, open the very pores it covers. A spokesman for Wrigley, the gum's manufacturer, said that discussions are underway to enlist the boy as company mascot, and he will likely appear on each package of their gum in the future. "Perhaps," said the spokesman, "toothpaste will no longer be necessary. People will just chew gum."

Instead, I tell him the unvarnished truth. I can't believe it. It feels much better than ever I thought it could.

—◊◊◊—

On Saturday afternoon, Ben takes me to the Garlic Grill so I can savor an Orange Crush. He is back waiting tables here, while Tony has been banished to the kitchen, where he scrapes pots and pans. We sit there together, Ben joking with the management, me not saying much. I haven't enjoyed a soda pop since yesterday when Anna gave me one, and it's thirsty work, all this waiting.

"Ben, um, those twenties in your drawer—um, they came from me. I stuck 'em there."

"I know," he says, grinning. "I figured it out Sunday."

"I'm so sorry."

"I know," he says again.

"Ben," I am trying to suck the last drop of soda from a striped straw. "Um, do you know much about it...the disease?"

He squares his shoulders and leans forward. "You mean Huntington's? Like Mom has?"

"Yeah. Dad hasn't said much. I was just wondering."

He shrugs. "I just know that it's serious, that you're at risk."

"What do you mean?"

"The doctor says you have a fifty-fifty chance of getting it."

"But doesn't that worry you? That you might get it, I mean?"

For a minute Ben's eyes won't meet mine. They follow a fork he is toying with. At last he says, "I want you to know something, Terry. Mom and Dad weren't looking for more children when you came along. The doctor advised them against having kids because of the risk. He said it was the only way of stopping this terrible disease. You see, it's only passed on genetically, through the children. So…Mom and Dad adopted Liz and me. I'm sorry, I shouldn't have said—" Ben clearly wasn't planning on this. "I can't believe you weren't told."

I am stunned. "But what—how do—what?" I fumble with this new truth, trying hard to grasp hold of it. "You mean—" I cannot finish.

The truth explains some things. My hair color being so different from theirs. Dad's letter. "Some of you were chosen, all of you were loved."

"Do you remember when they took your blood? They were hopeful you'd be a match. And you were. You've got the same blood type as Dad."

The straw is clenched hard in my teeth now and my mind is whirling. "What about Tony? Was he adopted too?"

My question is momentarily forgotten as the fork Ben has been toying with stabs through a package of ketchup, splattering the front of my hand-me-down jeans with the sticky substance.

Snickering erupts from the tables around us, and Ben throws some change on the table. "Let's go," he says, as we duck for the door, "There's something I think you'll like."

—⚬—

At the Ricochet Clothing Store, I try on a pair of black pants I badly need for the Christmas program. Ben insists on it. The mothballed establishment, which specializes in "like-new clothing," is located on Main Street, on property that often changes ownership. He has been raking in tips over at the café, has Ben, and he seems to take great pleasure in treating his youngest brother. "Try 'em on," he says, pointing at a pair of blue jeans, the nicest pair I've ever seen in my life. "See how they fit."

They are a little loose in the waist, which is good, and Ben says he'll wrap them up to place under the tree. I can't believe the price: two whole dollars. "Can I wear 'em home?" I ask, not wanting to let them out of my sight. He says I can. We'll wrap them up later.

On the way home, I stick my hands deep in the pockets, pulling out some lint. My left one rubs up against a slip of paper.

I tug it out. And stare in amazement at a fifty-dollar bill.

The store manager says he has no way to trace the original owner.

"Finders, keepers," he pronounces.

"Should I take it to the police?"

The manager laughs. "No, they couldn't do anything. But I love a conscientious kid."

"That's amazing," smiles Ben. "They paid us forty-eight bucks to take those jeans off their hands." I wonder if we should try on some more, maybe look through some shirt pockets too.

The miracles are not over, however.

Back home, Tony's plant is thriving, stretching forth its tender limbs to find the light and the water and the music it has come to love.

And as the calendar moves toward Christmas, our excitement increases. Each day Dad shows improvement; each day is a step closer to home.

With one week to go before the annual celebration, Dad says goodbye to the room that has held him since that awful night. I carry his suitcase, Liz has his pillow, and Tony lugs a pillowcase full of stuff.

I can't believe it. My prayer has been answered. Will wonders never cease?

Twenty-Four

Brown Christmas

C hristmases of my childhood were marked by two certain events: the coming of Uncle Roy and the Sunday school program. I'm not sure which excited me more this year. My mom's older brother promised to bring the only extravagance we Andersons knew. A tree buoyed by presents. A table laden with delectable treasures. But the program I loved too, for it slammed the door on three months of school and opened another on two weeks of holidays.

Grown-ups are an interesting study at Christmastime. The season seems to bring out the best in them, causing them to giggle for no apparent reason at all and to do things they normally would not do were they in their right minds. Tonight I overhear my parents laughing the kind of laugh adults employ when children aren't supposed to get the joke. The kind of laugh that stifling only makes funnier. I want to share in it, to revel in it, for laughter is not something we've heard enough of lately, so I sneak up behind them on the couch where Dad sits massaging Mother's shoulders.

Lying quietly there, I listen to their punctuated whispers. It's surprising how much you can learn this way.

Seems that Mr. and Mrs. Swanson were playing Scrabble the previous night, and Mr. Swanson lost badly. The two had never played table games before last Sunday, and now they have a standing agreement: The loser will be subjected to some form of punishment selected by the winner, punishment which includes doing the dishes, bathing Harry the dog, or bringing breakfast in bed. But this night, Mrs. Swanson, being in a particularly festive mood, decided that she would like it very much if her husband of twenty some years ran around their car, clad only in his boxer shorts—a juvenile thing for sure but something that seemed funnier to her during the yuletide season.

It is not exactly a mild winter, you'll remember, but the pudgy Mr. Swanson has always been unable to resist a dare. So, assuring himself of the fact that it was pitch black out there, that everyone was asleep, and that he was a pretty fast runner back in high school, he peeled off his shirt and pants and socks and shoes and made a dash for it wearing only a wince and a pair of flowered boxers. As he started to waddle around the rear of the Chevy in six inches of snow he heard two distinct clicks.

One was the door of his own home being locked.

The other was the porch light being switched on.

Dancing nimbly from foot to foot and banging wildly on the door, he pleaded with his eyes: "Dog biscuits, Agnes! Come on! Let me in!" But his beloved wife just stood inside, smiling through the frosted windowpane and holding the phone to her ear. "I'm calling the police," she said loudly enough for him to wonder if she was really capable of such a thing. All of this was amusing to one of them, and it certainly was not Mr. Swanson.

I couldn't help but let out a snicker from my hiding spot behind the couch at the part about the police. "Then what happened?" I blurt out.

Knowing I heard the story only makes it funnier to my parents, and they are using hankies now, lost in a steady stream of laughter that comes from more than the story they have just told.

"He's still out there," says Dad.

"No. She let him in," says Mom.

I catch myself smiling, knowing that this will be the best Christmas yet, for my father is home, and I am too. Perhaps this is an adequate excuse for the mischief that is to follow.

—⁓—

Danny Brown has been looking at Christmas from the outside all his life, and it's not been easy for him out there. His father, the atheist, is the reason.

This year as we practice for the Christmas program, Danny sits in the balcony of our church, only once with his father but always with a frown. Christmas is not Mr. Brown's favorite time of year, and yanking his son from the program is his last act of protest to a season gone mad with shopping and carols and mention of the Almighty. A few short weeks ago, I looked on Danny with scorn, this sinner boy destined for hell. All that has changed. From my perch on the platform I feel sorry for him and all he is missing. The fun of practice each Friday afternoon. Memorizing our lines and tormenting girls and dreaming of candy bags. "Performance is its own reward," say our teachers, but those paper bags are a delightful bonus for the performers, a bonus Danny cannot have.

The teachers don't find the practices quite as much fun as we do, judging from the looks they dart our way. Miss Thomas, the choir director, is a massive woman who has never married, and I'm not sure why. She is so cheerful and would make the perfect match for any of a number of the bachelors about town. She likes to cook too. I love to watch her lead the singing. Her arms weigh more than two of me, and she gets quite a workout bringing them up to speed, which is four-four time. They wobble side to side like bathtubs of marmalade jam, and I wouldn't be honest if I didn't admit to you that they were a distraction and that some of us have given them names (never mind what they are). Miss Thomas stayed up late Thursday night stapling holly boughs to the wall behind us, and the fatigue shows on her normally sunny countenance. The boughs frame the edges of a huge white banner ("What Child Is This?"), a backdrop for the choir.

I never knew that holly had such sharp points until this Friday afternoon and that if I take a small piece of it and place it on the seat in front of me interesting things happen. We stand to sing "While Shepherds Watch Their Flocks by Night," and I ease a thorny clipping onto Shelley Morrison's chair. When we finally stop singing and sit down, she lets out a holler nine times her size and stands up faster than even she can believe.

"Why you little—" she turns and shakes her tiny fist at me, using the other one to subtract the holly, "—jerk!" Miss Thomas, who had already noticed me midway through the first rehearsal back in November, composes herself and asks me to go sit in the balcony with Danny Brown. "NOWWW!" she bellows, scrunching her teeth together, her chins trembling.

Danny is alone and has removed his shoes to massage his little toes. "Hey," he says, but doesn't finish. We don't say a lot when we're together. I'd like to tell him about Christmas and about Jesus and about the forgiveness I've seen in this place. Instead, I sit down and begin making monkey faces at my friends in the choir, pulling on my ears and puffing out my cheeks. Danny's toes are skinny and they smell, or maybe it's his socks.

"What's it like?" he wants to know.

"What's *what* like?"

"Bein' in the program?"

"It's okay. But I wonder if she'll let me back in." I am suddenly remorseful, thinking about my candy bag without me rooting through it. I'm also aware of a sense of sadness as I think about Danny.

He scratches the big toe on his left foot. "You can sit here if they don't."

The privileged ones are singing beautifully now about angels and shepherds and the glory that shone around, and for reasons I'll never know I tell Danny the alternate words, which my mother won't let me use: "While shepherds washed their socks by night all seated on the ground, the angel of the Lord came down and passed the soap around." He finds this funnier than I thought he would, so I use my opera voice to sing him both stanzas of another one Tony taught me:

> We three kings of Orient are
> Smoking on a rubber cigar
> It was loaded, it exploded
> Now we're on yonder star.

> We three kings of Butternut square,
> Try to sell some cheap underwear,
> They're fantastic, no elastic,
> Why don't you buy a pair?

This is too much for Danny. A volcanic laugh begins to build within him, so he stuffs a sock in his mouth hoping to stifle things, an act which causes me to do the same with my fist. Everything is funnier when it's not supposed to be—every child knows this—and we have to bury our faces in our knees to keep from being heard, like my parents on the couch.

Early in life I discovered that there are only two kinds of laughter suitable for church. There is the low guffaw, which sounds like a frog croaking underwater. It is a polite and useful laugh when a visiting minister has opened with the same joke the last visiting minister used. Sort of a mild *ha ha,* almost an apology. Then there is the songbird's laugh, sweet and higher pitched and perfect when the pastor you have loved for years relays to the congregation something his toddler said at the breakfast table that morning, something like, "If God is my Heavenly Father, are you my Homely Father?" But too often while I am laughing sweetly at such jokes, my mind takes me somewhere I had not anticipated and I let out a pig snort (the third stage), which triggers the fourth and final stage—the chimpanzee laugh, which quickly soars out of control and submits the bearer to turned heads and harsh threats of severe punishment. If someone says something remotely humorous during the fourth stage, if they snort or giggle, or just look funny—or try not to, you laugh so hard you can't find your breath and you think you will die and worry that you won't. It is a tap you cannot shut off, going around and around in your hands.

Danny and I are in the second stage when he turns to me and burps the vowels A-E-I-O-U, something that wouldn't hit me so hard were it performed over by the swing set during recess but which is positively hilarious here in the balcony of the church. It ushers me rapidly to the fourth stage, and raucous laughter fills the sanctuary compliments of me. Miss Thomas brings her arms to a wobbly halt in the middle of "and glory shone ar—," turns from her music stand as quickly as her huge body will enable her, and yells, "I've had about enough, Terry Anderson!"

I stop momentarily, knowing she'll tell my parents.

Danny says loudly enough for just the two of us to hear, "Then quit eating fudge."

I double over and bury my head in my lap, wishing I could crawl under a rock and knowing that this year there will be no Christmas program for so foolish a child and that my parents will undoubtedly agree with the decision.

———٭٭٭———

But by Sunday night, the night of the program, no one has informed me that I am not to participate. So I stand before a mirror practicing my lines, a condemned boy deserving the guillotine but extended a pardon or at least a temporary reprieve because my executioners have other things to do. Those who cheat death should at least look good, so I slick my hair back with just the right amount of Vaseline, which I always thought rhymed with baseline. Will my father spring it on me at the last moment? "You cannot take part, Son." Apparently not. It is another unexplainable gift in a long line of grace.

I am so excited about the program that colors are brighter and my sister's jokes are even funny. "Why did the elephant wear his red shoes?" she asks me as we munch fresh-baked waffles topped with margarine and genuine maple syrup Ben has bought, a step up from our previous tradition of toast. "Because his blue ones were in the wash." I don't do cartwheels, but I do offer her a stage-one laugh, "Ha, ha."

I have locked myself in our bathroom to gaze at my face from various angles, hoping, among other things, for signs of whiskers. I allow myself the illusion that I have been asked to sing duets with Olivia Newton John, whose records my brother Tony regrets burning. I imagine myself receiving a phone call from her wherein she mentions in her breathy tone that she has heard of the loveliness of my voice when I use it in church and is wondering if I would be interested in singing with her at the Radio City Christmas Spectacular on Christmas Eve. I don't have to pray long for the answer, and soon I am waking up at the Plaza Hotel (in the same room from which the Beatles stole four hangers the month I was born) to breakfast (croissant, caviar, and Coca-Cola) in a king-sized bed I can't quite find the edges of. I am just sucking the last of the Coke through a straw when a call from the spacious lobby bids me ride the limo to Radio City Music Hall where Miss John and I rehearse "White Christmas" and something new she is working on called "Please, Mr., Please." She sometimes cocks her head and turns to me with a painful look of unrequited love and once reaches over and puts a hand on my shoulder, so caught up is she in our duets. I am older, of course, and wearing red plaid pants and a green turtleneck, and she compliments me on them both. It's a long way from where I live to New York and singing with the most beautiful girl in Australia, but I hope you won't think less of me for having such aspirations.

In the midst of my fantasy, there is yelling and I must open the door to my sister. "When you gotta go, you gotta go," I say as I dodge past her. Still she manages to punch me hard on the arm where one day I will have muscles.

"Nice hair," she says.

Ah, how I love my sister.

The night is cold. So cold that the Vaseline adorning my head freezes solid in the time it takes me to dash through the crunchy snow to our rusty old Diplomat. I pat my frozen hair as the big car lurches forward, bearing three of us and Uncle Roy in the back, Liz and me jam-packed with anticipation of candy bags.

Ben is driving. Mom snuggles up to Dad in the front and Tony leads us in a baritone "Silent Night," which he starts too low and finds that none of us can reach. There is laughter and we start again. "'Tis in a DeSoto sedan I sit," sings Tony to the tune of "O

Little Town of Bethlehem." But the palindrome goes unnoticed by the others.

The atmosphere is charged with magic, and I can scarce contain my excitement. I busy myself with scraping Mary Beth's name in frost on the inside of the window and thinking of candy bags and the Saturday I have just spent at Danny Brown's house.

Why does the world I look out on seem so much brighter than Danny's world? His dad is rarely around, out job hunting he says, but who hires an atheist in a town like this one? Danny can have the bathroom any old time he likes—there's no one to fight him for it, but there's no tree adorning his living room either, no lights or presents, no relatives set to arrive, and no promise of treats of any kind.

"Fairy tales," Danny says, when talking of Christmas. "A buncha clowns looking for an excuse to make more money. I wouldn't give a wooden nickel for it." Sunday nights during church he watches "Wonderful World of Disney," but not in December. "Even old Walt can't pass up the money Christmas has to offer," says Danny's dad, "so leave it off or I'll cuff your ears."

The only Christmas song he knows is one his father made up: "O Come Let Us *Ignore* Him." I wonder if Danny will be there tonight or if he'll ignore my invitation too. I wish there was some way I could change his mind about Christmas.

—⁂—

The church is electric with squealing children and frantic parents bearing combs and brushes and barrettes. Ned Norris arrives with two Chiquita banana boxes bursting with candy bags, and we turn as if in worship, raising ourselves on tiptoe to measure the bags for thickness. Last year they were primarily peanuts, a few Brazil nuts, a walnut or two. In the midst of the nuts, a small brown sack holds delightful treasures, hard candy and a few sugary ones, the mint green being my favorite. Mr. Norris holds the boxes higher to keep us from peeking. "Product of Brazil," is all we can see. The teenagers spent Saturday stuffing the bags, and I can't wait until I'm old enough to hold such an envious job. I'll have to fight the urge to stuff more than the bags, that's for sure.

Miss Thomas is decked out in a jet black dress that somehow makes her seem smaller, pretty even. Music flows from the organ—heavenly music. I expect an angel to be playing by ear, but it is Larry Harper, who last October informed my parents that I was sticking rotten apples to the side of his house with my pitching arm (true), which landed me a Saturday job I had not been hunting for. Tonight for the first time, October doesn't much matter. The more I know of myself, the more I forgive in others.

The children are assembled in jagged rows now, having dropped our White Gift envelopes in a golden box, money that will buy a motorcycle for the Wells family in India, something they need to reach remote tribes with the gospel. I am near the back, one of the big kids, so I try not to show my excitement. Parents smile nervously. Youngsters wave, and the slightest faux pas infects the audience with giggles. As the kindergartners sing "Away in a Manger," I am searching the auditorium, but there's no Danny Brown.

"And there were in the same country shepherds abiding in the field, keeping watch over their flock by night." Shelley Morrison stands center stage. The words are memorized, her enunciation flawless. She inserts a pause without meaning to, so Miss Thomas coaxes her along, mouthing the words widely. Shelley straightens her spine and continues: "And, lo, the angel of the Lord came upon them, and the glory of the Lord shone round about them: and they were sore afraid." Shelley has a gold-ribboned corsage pinned to her lapel. The holly seems forgotten.

I am scanning the audience. Still no Danny.

"And the angel said unto them, 'Fear not: for, behold, I bring you good tidings of great joy, which shall be to all people. For unto you is born this day in the city of David a Savior, which is Christ the Lord. And this shall be a sign unto you; Ye shall find the Babe wrapped in swaddling clothes, lying in a manger.'"

There he is. Danny. Making faces at me from the balcony, a few rows behind his usual seat. I don't know why I am so happy to see him. Perhaps I just want him to sample a small taste of Christmas, or to hear my part in the program, for I am up next.

"Unto us a child is born," I am saying, as if in a dream. "Unto us a Son is given: and the government shall be upon his shoulder: and his name shall be called Wonderful, Counselor, The Mighty God, the everlasting Father, the Prince of Peace." The words have brought a quiet reverence to the audience and even to me. I pause, hoping I won't forget my poem:

> The best Christmas gift I ever got,
> Was not a gift my Mother bought.
> It was a gift from up above,
> A Father's gift of Christmas love.

There is one more verse to the poem, but suddenly I am looking at Pastor Davis sitting there with his wife, Irene, and his prodigal son, all of them fighting tears, and I think of the past two weeks and how much I've been forgiven and how much trouble may still lie ahead. Ben is there too, sitting proudly beside the parents who loved him enough to adopt him, and Tony is trying to get my attention, making faces. Hot tears spill onto my cheeks, and I sit down, thankful the lights are low. No one seems to notice except for Miss Thomas who is smiling at me for the first time in her life.

Mary Beth is seated behind her. She is smiling too.

—∽—

Only the performers are allowed the sacred candy bags, of course. But following the final prayer, older brothers and visiting cousins stand at the front, ready to help with leftovers. There will be none. Ned Norris's mathematics are impeccable. Calling us backstage, he dispenses the bags one by one, looking carefully at each face, memorizing them in case we are repeat customers. "Well done," he smiles. We squeeze the contents greedily, peeking in other kid's bags, measuring for fairness. "Don't eat them until you're outside the church," Ned warns.

Never in all my years of performing in the Christmas program do I recall seeing one extra bag, though I checked carefully each time. But this year there are two, and Ned Norris stands with one in each hand, a little confused, wondering what to do with them and wondering about his math. For reasons I'm still not sure of, I clear my throat and say out loud, "Hey, what about Danny Brown?"

Mr. Norris smiles and nods his head. He places the bags in the big brown box, but I am not through. "I think I'll give him some of mine too," I say, walking over to where Mr. Norris stands, and pulling a handful of treasure from my sack, I drop it, *thunk,* into the box. One by one, the other kids follow. A few sneak out, but most of us give quickly, before changing our minds.

—∽—

In all these years, I've never understood how Danny Brown could leave that night with twenty pounds of peanuts, two oranges (one of them mine), and a handful of soft candies in an overflowing Chiquita banana box, while none of the rest of us seemed to miss a single thing in our own bags. Call it a miracle if you like, because when I opened my little paper treasure chest in the back-seat of our DeSoto, I found another mandarin orange there and five soft candies, all of them mint green.

I never did get to sing that duet with Olivia Newton John or stay at the Plaza Hotel in New York City. And God never gave me a million bucks or healed my mother, though I asked Him so many times. And I didn't find out yet about the inheritance. But I did get to see an atheist boy's eyes light up and a few other things I still can't explain. Like the fact that Mr. Brown came to Christmas dinner. I couldn't believe he said yes.

He bows his head politely as my father prays in a halting voice, thanking God for Liz's golden turkey and the special dressing, for the buttered yams and the mashed potatoes, for the world's best gravy and its heaviest fruitcake. The laying on of Christmas, my mother calls it. Mr. Brown doesn't close his eyes or anything—he has a ways to go—but it is more than any of us could have hoped for.

Later that night, after Liz has herded the whole bunch of us past the Christmas tree with its meager gifts and into the living room, one more miracle awaits us.

Mother sits up against Dad, him grasping both her shaky hands in his big strong ones, and she closes her eyes and starts to sing a song I've associated with Christmas ever since:

> Amazing grace, how sweet the sound
> That saved a wretch like me!
> I once was lost but now am found—
> Was blind, but now I see.

And then a remarkable thing happens: My father joins her in a soft tenor voice, wobbly at first, then entirely on key.

I am the first to notice, but I can't interrupt the singing.

> When we've been there ten thousand years,
> Bright shining as the sun,
> We've no less days to sing God's praise
> Than when we'd first begun.

I can't help myself now. "Dad, you're singing on tune!" I exclaim.

He is the only one who isn't amazed. "What do you mean? I thought I had a fine singing voice all along."

I suppose I wouldn't have seen it if I hadn't believed.

My father starts to laugh that deep laugh of his that I have missed for so long. The slur is still there, but it beats him speaking Swedish, that's for sure.

And what is a twelve-year-old child to make of all of this? I only know that for a few weeks one winter, what I deserved and what I got were two entirely different things. That those weeks changed forever the way I view the sins of others. For now I see them through the lens of my own shortcomings, thankful that each of my sins is rinsed in Jesus' blood, confident theirs can be too.

Perhaps you're not much good until you find out how bad you are.

I cannot know what lies ahead. I only know that tonight my family is together. That my brother Tony is telling Liz a Christmas palindrome, "Leon Noel," and my mother's head is resting against my father's strong arm. Her eyes are closed, and a grin is tugging upward at the corners of her mouth.

"Thank you, God, for Christmas," I whisper.

I guess my father was right after all: Wonders never cease.

Acknowledgements

For five years, my favorite editor, Terry Glaspey, gently pestered me to embark on this maiden voyage. Thanks, Terry, for pushing me out from shore and pelting me with life jackets! I was accompanied by so many on this journey. My brother Tim, a wiser man than I, offered invaluable insight as I steered. My children, Stephen, Rachael, and Jeffrey, spent many a summer evening aboard—listening to this story, making suggestions, and also snacking. Their love and friendship make me smile often, causing people to wonder what type of medication I'm on. When the horizon was lost and the wind was low, my wife, Ramona, hoisted the sails of encouragement and sometimes the ice cream and ginger ale. Thanks also to my faithful assistant, Pat Massey, my loving parents, and a fabulous editor, Gene Skinner.

If I got things right, it is a credit to them. If I blew it, it is my brother Tim's fault.

Like the Andersons, our family has experienced the pain of Huntington's disease. Miriam and Jim, Bill and Cynthia, Annette and Dennis are lighthouses of faithfulness in the midst of the very worst. This book was inspired by their lives, and they are daily in our prayers.

I'm so thankful for the hundreds of letters I receive each year, assuring me that wonderful people like you have invested time in reading what I write. I apologize to the one whose wife was reading to him as he drove, causing him to hit a tree from all the laughing. If I have kept you awake reading this, I apologize as well. Do write and tell me about it.

Lastly, I thank God for His amazing grace. Like Terry Anderson, I have stepped far out of line and found His love waiting there. I am the boy who wrestled with God and lost. But unlike Jacob, I walked away with renewed energy and scarcely a limp. I am the boy who ran from God. But like Jonah, I discovered that the farther and faster I ran, the closer I got to the very arms I was running from. Strong arms those. Long ones, too. My prayer is that you've found that grace, and if you haven't, I hope you will write.

A final word: I was planning on lowering the sails and heading for port, but Terry Glaspey informs me that I am about to embark on book two of the Anderson story. And so, I hope we'll meet again.

—〰—

Phil would love to hear from you. Write him at

Laugh and Learn, Inc.
PO Box 4576
Three Hills, Alberta Canada
T0M 2N0

About the Author

Phil Callaway is editor of Prairie Bible Institute's *Servant* magazine and author of fifteen books, including *I Used to Have Answers, Now I Have Kids; Making Life Rich Without Any Money; With God on the Golf Course;* and *Who Put My Life on Fast Forward?* Most weekends find him taking a message of laughter, hope, and joy to conferences, churches, marriage retreats, and events like Promise Keepers. A frequent guest on national radio and television, Phil partners with Compassion, an international Christian child-development agency. His writings have won more than a dozen international awards and have been translated into Spanish, Chinese, Portuguese, Dutch, Polish, and English (one of which he speaks fluently). His five-part video series "The Big Picture" is being viewed in 80,000 churches worldwide. To find out about Phil's other books or tapes, check out his website at www.philcallaway.com. To request a complimentary one-year subscription to *Servant,* write

Servant Magazine
PO Box 4000
Three Hills, Alberta Canada
T0M 2N0

Wonders Never Cease

Eighteen-year-old Terry Anderson never expected to find a body. Not a dead one, that's for sure. After all, the sleepy town of Grace, Montana, is not Miami or Washington. It's a town of churchgoers, where people don't lock their doors at night, where you can't get lost if your brother tells you to, where you know who wears which pair of pants when you see them hanging from the clothesline.

Terry had no idea that the grisly body would turn his world upside down and shake it so hard. Nor did he realize that the gnarled fingers would point toward his family, prying open secrets long buried. He never would have suspected that every ounce of faith he ever had would be tested, that all his answers would be questioned.

For Terry, finding a murderer is one thing. Finding his faith again is another.

—w—

"Reading Phil Callaway is one of life's purest pleasures."
—Ellen Vaughn, coauthor
(with Chuck Colson) of *The Body*